The
Dead
Queen's
Garden

The Dead Queen's Garden

Nicola Slade

ROBERT HALE · LONDON

© Nicola Slade 2013
First published in Great Britain 2013

ISBN 978-0-7198-1038-1

Robert Hale Limited
Clerkenwell House
Clerkenwell Green
London EC1R 0HT

www.halebooks.com

2 4 6 8 10 9 7 5 3

Typeset in 10.5/14pt Palatino
Printed in the UK by the Berforts Information Press Ltd

ACKNOWLEDGEMENTS

Although the places and people in *The Dead Queen's Garden* are figments of my imagination, the inspiration for the novel came from the real 'Queen Eleanor's Garden' which adjoins Winchester's Great Hall. This is a must-see recreation of a mediaeval garden, designed by Dr Sylvia Landsberg and opened in 1986 by the Queen Mother. My Victorian version is nothing like the original, however, and any errors in planting are entirely mine.

Florence Nightingale, who makes a brief appearance in this novel, lived at Embley Park, about twelve miles from the Hampshire village of Otterbourne, on which Charlotte's home at Finchbourne is based, so it's perfectly plausible that the Nightingale and Richmond families would be acquainted.

Thanks as always to my brilliant readers, Olivia Barnes and Linda Gruchy, who can spot a plot hole at a hundred paces.

Particular thanks are due to Granville Winship and Oz Forster whose names I've 'borrowed' for this book.

DRAMATIS PERSONAE

Charlotte Richmond	A young widow who approves of a quiet life
Barnard Richmond	An Olde English Squire who approves of hospitality
Lily Richmond	The Squire's lady who approves of a lordly title
Lady Frampton	A grandmother who approves of a good square meal
Lady Granville	A dramatic gardener who approves of the Middle Ages
Lord Granville	A genial old party who approves of pretty women
Oz Granville	A cosseted child who strongly disapproves of his name
Kit Knightley	A godfather with sorrow on his mind
Elaine Knightley	The reason for his sorrow
Sibella Armstrong	An unemployed governess
Verena Chant	Her sister, who is married to:
Dr Montagu Chant	Doctor to Prince Albert, and makes sure everyone knows it
Florence Nightingale	The Lady with the Lamp
Melicent Penbury	The Lady with the Limp
Capt Horatio Penbury	A bluff sailor with a greedy appetite
Miss Ethelreda Cole	A poor relation
Bessie Railton	May cause an earthquake in Charlotte's peaceful life

A vicar, a vicar's wife, a doctor, a baby, a butler, a blacksmith and other villagers, a cat with kittens, and a fat pony with a grievance.

The Dead Queen's Garden

'**M**URDER! THERE'S ACTUALLY *been a murder, isn't it delicious?'*
'*What? What's that you say?'*

The great west door slammed open letting in a blast of icy sleet and the speaker, a young, fair-haired lady, hurried into the shadowy darkness of the cathedral. Ignoring the verger who was struggling to close the door again, she shook out her umbrella and addressed the other young woman who had risen to greet her.

'Dear Lord, what a dreary tomb,' she exclaimed, in a light, mocking, voice. 'How can everyone be so deluded as to praise antiquity so fulsomely, when as far as I can see all it is fit for is to cast us into the deepest gloom.' Her tinkling laugh echoed in the ancient stillness of the great church. 'That, and to make us all contract galloping pneumonia.'

'But what is this about a murder? I can scarcely believe you,' was the response in a low, protesting tone. She hesitated then continued, 'And you should not mock so in a place of worship, it is not fitting. As you are perfectly well aware, Winchester Cathedral is famed throughout the world as a magnificent example of religious architecture.'

'Dear me, you are always so instructive and so solemn! Oh, very well then, my dear,' there was a laughing apology. 'I shall not mock. Instead, I shall gratify your curiosity. I heard the shocking news just now as I hurried to meet you. Apparently some old woman has been battered to death, and the countryside is in uproar, crying rape and ravishment, with the murderer not yet apprehended.' She laughed again as they took a turn down the venerable aisle. 'But here is the cream, my dear – oh, very well,' she pouted as her companion showed a shocked countenance.

'A life has been lost; you should not be so unfeeling.' The quieter lady sank down onto a chair, looking shaken while her companion glanced at her unabashed.

'I apologize if you must be so pious. However, this dastardly event took place only a few days ago in the very place where we are to attend tomorrow's christening! In Finchbourne village, no less.' She shivered, 'Come, we must walk, or we shall freeze.'

There was a swish of bright silks and velvets from the laughing lady, together with a more modest murmur of serviceable grey merino from her companion, as the two women strolled along towards the altar, neither of them paying any attention to the two other occupants of the nave.

At the word 'Murder', another woman, perhaps in her fifties, who was seated half way down the aisle, had jumped perceptibly as her round, pink, face lost colour and she clutched a hand to her plump bosom. She looked over her shoulder, apparently seeking the perpetrators of this outrage, her brow creased further in a petulant frown at the frivolous peal of laughter. The two young women had disappeared towards the grand new organ, so she applied a handkerchief to her eyes and returned to her devotions. The episode had clearly distressed her however, as her shoulders heaved and the handkerchief flapped continually.

The other onlooker, a decade or so older and a stone or two stouter, had patently sought the cathedral as a place of rest and shelter from the freezing rain, and was unashamedly taking the weight off her elderly feet.

The tinkling laugh rang out again, regardless of the sacred nature of the surroundings.

'Well? Shall we be daunted by a sudden outbreak of murder or shall we attend this tiresome party, do you think? Young Mrs Richmond was quite insistent, was she not? And I must admit that this town is so dull that even the prospect of something like a provincial christening will help to relieve the tedium. No, my dear,' she laughed once more, 'I know you do not wish to be sociable but I must insist. I am bored to tears and after all, there is to be a wassail bowl! Apparently that is some kind of hot punch with spices and fruit or some such. Did you not hear Mrs Richmond waxing lyrical upon the subject? How can we resist such entertainment?'

Their tour of the cathedral complete, the two ladies enquired of the verger as to the state of the weather. On being informed that the rain had ceased, they left the great building without a backward glance, the laughing lady remarking, 'Did I tell you that there is a further treat in store at the manor? Some Australian relative who was lately in India was apparently caught up in the Mutiny and escaped to England with only the clothes she stood up in. Her husband was reported killed in an ambush, but later he miraculously turned up in Hampshire, only to die almost at once. I do trust she is not too dreary, you know how much a widow can cast a pall on the proceedings!'

The seated worshippers remained in continued silence but not one of the four women present in the cathedral that day had the slightest inkling that death would soon once more stalk the quiet Hampshire countryside.

Chapter One

Hampshire, December 1858

'DEAR LORD, BUT that baby squeals louder than any pigling I ever 'ad the pleasure of meeting.' The stout old lady's cockney whisper was mercifully drowned by the wails of the infant in question, who was being presented at the font by his harassed godparents. She added, 'I declare it would surely be a kindness if Percy dropped the little beggar and put us all out of our misery.'

Charlotte Richmond felt some sympathy for this radical point of view but she shook her head with a smile at the old lady, her late husband's grandmother.

'Percy wouldn't dream of being so clumsy and Agnes is on tiptoe waiting to step in if the need arises,' she murmured in response, glancing towards the vicar's wife, Charlotte's elder sister-in-law, who was anxiously watching the proceedings. 'Besides, he knows full well that Lily would rise up and slaughter him if he did.' The baby's proud mother, Lily Richmond, Charlotte's other, younger, sister-in-law, was glaring at the vicar obviously daring him to put a foot wrong.

'Well,' snorted old Lady Frampton, 'at least the devil's well out of the child, to judge by the racket 'e's making.'

A slight snort of amusement came from behind to her left, and Charlotte half turned, to meet a pair of twinkling blue eyes as a young boy sitting at the end of the pew grinned at her. He looked about ten or eleven and his shock of flaxen fair hair shone even under the meagre light given by the candle sconce above him. The hand which had flown to his mouth to conceal his laughter at the

old lady's remark was scratched and slightly grubby but his presence in the pews, and his good clothes, indicated that he was
clearly an official guest at the christening. Charlotte shot him a
sympathetic smile as she wondered who he could be.

The noise the baby was making was deafening, so Charlotte
merely nodded to her elderly companion with a smile as she
bowed her head in a final prayer for the future health, happiness
and prosperity of Master Fairfax Algernon Granville Richmond,
heir to the manor of Finchbourne in the county of Hampshire. The
bearer of this great responsibility was her late husband's nephew
and there had been a brief moment of anxiety a week or so earlier,
when Charlotte had feared she might be required to take on the
duties of godmother to Algy, as he was to be known in the family.
Her reluctance, and relief at not being thus invited, had nothing to
do with lack of affection or interest, but all to do with the imperious
nature of the baby's mother.

'You 'ad a lucky escape there, me dear.' The old lady's whisper
competed with the baby's howls as she nodded towards the font
and Charlotte's eyes creased in amusement.

Lily had been frank with her. 'Barnard wanted you as godmother,
Charlotte,' she had said. 'But I know you can have no objection
when I tell you I've asked Lord and Lady Granville to stand as
sponsors instead. They're near neighbours and very highly-
regarded locally, and it turns out that they have now decided to
leave London and come home to Hampshire permanently.'

What her sister-in-law had not needed to mention was that the
Granvilles were extremely wealthy, but Charlotte knew that was a
consideration with Lily. Relieved of the responsibility that had
hung, all unknown, over her head, she graciously assured both
parents that she was happy to hand over the task to more illustrious godparents who would ensure that little Algy was raised as
a Christian. She was also quite certain that Lily would refrain from
meddling and pointing out the duties of a godparent to the
Granvilles, as she would not, alas, have failed to do so, had
Charlotte been so appointed. She concealed a quiet smile, picturing
Lily's face had she known of Charlotte's antecedents: her late
mother, unjustly accused of theft and transported to Australia, and

Will, her beloved stepfather who had died in India. He had been an escaped convict who posed convincingly as a clergyman, raising funds for churches that would never be built. Lily might have been more impressed by Charlotte's godmother, but her approval would have vanished upon learning that Lady Meg's noble brother had paid her to go to Australia where her overgenerous ways with men would no longer embarrass him.

A glance upwards made her shiver. The ornate memorial plaque placed there by his distraught mother, proclaimed the alleged virtues of her own, mercifully dead, husband. Charlotte's mother-in-law had been at first in raptures when Frampton, thought to be dead in an Indian ambush, had been restored to her at the manor, but his subsequent death had shaken the family to the core, resulting in the elder Mrs Richmond's departure to take the cure on the Continent. Charlotte still woke in shuddering fear when she dreamed of Frampton Richmond's vicious tongue, and she tried to suppress all reminders of him.

Most Sundays she managed not to sit anywhere near the memorial, but today the old lady had wheezed so alarmingly that Charlotte was grateful for any resting place. She shivered and cast about for a less unhappy train of thought, hailing with gratitude a solution to her earlier puzzlement which occurred to her now, as she slid another surreptitious glance at the fair-haired boy.

'Gran?' she nudged her companion. 'Is that the Granville boy?'

Lady Frampton heaved herself round and stared, responding with a smile to the boy's friendly grin. 'That's 'im,' she replied, turning back. 'The precious son and heir, nice-looking lad, ain't he?

Charlotte felt a moment's surprise; the child looked intelligent and was clearly possessed of a sense of humour, traits she had so far failed to observe in her slight acquaintance with his parents, though to be sure his father seemed a jolly enough old fellow. Her glance fell on the other godfather, Kit Knightley, from nearby Knightley Hall, an old schoolfellow of the baby's proud father, Barnard Richmond, and husband to Charlotte's closest friend. The final godparent represented an even greater coup for Lily, and Charlotte shot a second covert glance towards the silently brooding woman beside Kit Knightley.

Seated, as a nod to her continued ill-health, Miss Nightingale's face exhibited such disapproval and severity that Charlotte thought she resembled the Bad Fairy at Sleeping Beauty's christening. Shaking herself out of such a fancy, she wondered yet again what on earth could have persuaded the Heroine of the Crimea to agree to take on this responsibility. True, the Nightingale and Richmond families were well known to each other and moved in much the same social circles since childhood, living as they did a mere twelve miles or so apart, but according to local gossip Miss Nightingale was at present mainly confined to her own room by some lingering though unspecified ailment. Indeed, it was clear that even her own mother had been startled by this sudden acceptance of the honour, coupled as it was with a brief emergence from seclusion. To judge by Mrs Nightingale's fretful expression, as she darted anxious glances towards her famous daughter, she was afraid of some kind of relapse.

She need not worry, opined Charlotte, weighing up the strength of character in the famous lady's drawn but handsome face. Miss Nightingale, who must be in her late thirties, had for some unknown reason clearly made up her mind that she should interrupt her ailing solitude and until that purpose was fulfilled, Charlotte was quite sure that there would be no relapse and no withdrawal from the christening party. She abandoned her discreet observation of the famous lady and turned her curious glance across the church towards the Granvilles, who had left their son in the pew and now stood at the font. Although she had now lived in Finchbourne for nearly eight months since her escape from the Mutiny, she had not previously encountered these particular neighbours as they spent most of their time in London and abroad.

'They are persons of the greatest nobility,' Lily had told her with unconcealed satisfaction. 'They are accustomed to move in the highest circles of Society, so it is excessively condescending of them to honour our little Algy in such a way.'

Well now, Charlotte looked at them with some curiosity. Nobility and wealth along with great positions might be desirable, but to her critical eye Lady Granville had less natural elegance than the landlady of 'The Three Pigeons' just across the village green. Lady

Granville, shrouded in opulent brocades and cashmere in an unbecoming shade of brown, and covered overall by a bulky sealskin mantle, was nonetheless badly-dressed. She had an air of abstraction, as if clothes had no interest at all for her, so that she looked to have thrown on whatever garments had been put out for her, without regard to style or whether they suited her, merely as covering to preserve the decencies and to keep her warm. She was a tall, large-boned woman, possibly in her late 40s, even a little older, mid-50s perhaps, her dark hair frosted with silver, although it was mostly hidden under an unbecoming bonnet.

Evidently thinking along the same lines, Lady Frampton gave Charlotte a sharp poke in the arm as she whispered loudly, 'That bonnet looks like a bloomin' coal scuttle; whatever was she thinkin' of when she bought it?'

Stifling a giggle, Charlotte had to agree. Despite her taste in clothes, the distinguished guest still bore the vestiges of a ravaged beauty, although her discontented mouth and air of chilly abstraction seemed at odds with the un-English darkness of her complexion; but there was no sign of the agitation one might expect of someone whose personal maid had so lately been found murdered almost on the lady's own doorstep.

The shocking news had run like wildfire through the village some days earlier and Charlotte, on her way to the manor whence she had been summoned by Lily, had come upon several huddles of women, shocked and excited by the terrible event. A babble of voices had assailed her,

'Oh, Miss,' squealed the wheelwright's wife. 'There's been murder done!'

Shocked, Charlotte had demanded to know all about it and the women vied to tell her what they knew.

'It was Lady Granville's maid, Miss. That old Maria Dunster who've been with her ladyship for ever. Set upon in the very drive to Brambrook Abbey, she was.'

'She used to be her ladyship's nurse,' an officious newcomer informed Charlotte, and the others chimed in. 'Dunster was a good enough soul in days gone by, though she did hold her nose up at anyone what her ladyship disapproved of,' said one.

'Sadly gone off, though,' added two more in unison. 'Poor old soul's mind was beginning to fail.'

At the manor, Lily was in despair and Charlotte was required to comfort and advise her on the propriety of holding a christening party so hard on the heels of such a crime. A note from Lady Granville had decided the matter: Mr and Mrs Richmond were please to carry out their original intention, if they would, and her ladyship had every expectation of attending the ceremony and the celebration to follow. The inquest had taken place, as had the funeral of the unfortunate victim, and the whole sorry business was concluded.

Charlotte found such *sang-froid* chilly but practical. The village constable had been called to the scene of the crime and taken a statement from the only witness to the effect that a burly man had been seen making away over the fields. The coroner had found for murder by person or persons unknown and now, in church, Charlotte glanced at the poor victim's employer and marvelled at her composure.

Bellowing his responses, Lord Granville also seemed unperturbed by the shocking occurrence on his own drive. At least a decade older than his wife, he resembled nothing so much as a robust countryman, with a shock of wiry, grizzled hair, ruddy complexion and whiskery countenance; he was above middling height and almost as broad as he was tall. He looked to be hail-fellow-well-met as he peered at everyone, his small, round blue eyes disappearing into slits in his fleshy face as he nodded genially on his progress back to his own pew.

'Give me an 'and to get up, girl,' demanded the old lady beside her, and Charlotte helped her to heave her considerable bulk up off the stout oak pew. The congregation straggled to its feet for the final hymn which was sung with gusto and with anticipation of the christening feast to come.

As she sang, Charlotte returned to her earlier thoughts, then sighed and gave a philosophical shrug. Lord Granville had an eye for the ladies, of that there could be no doubt. She had the bruising to prove it where he had squeezed her hand in a fervent greeting, along with the recollection of his hot breath on her face where he had come far too close on being introduced. She supposed he was accustomed to take liberties unless – a thought struck her – was he perhaps a little short-sighted? It had not been until he was right beside her that his eyes had brightened, with a sudden gleam in his eye as he appraised her tall slender figure clad against the December chill in her best winter outfit: a green cashmere dress with a velvet jacket. The plain bodice of the dress was buttoned high to the neck, relieved only by a lace collar which was pinned with her godmother's gold acanthus leaf brooch. She wore a narrow sable tippet that matched an edging of fur on her saucy little green velvet-hat, the whole ensemble finished off with the muff, also of sable, that she carried primly in her hand.

Oh well, after today I need not run across his lordship again, she consoled herself. He looks like a spent force so I expect he's harmless enough and besides, I've met his like before; at his age they are usually content with little pats and the occasional surreptitious pinch, but seldom anything more encroaching.

With the closing notes of the last hymn, it was time to make the short journey from the chilly, ancient stone church across the village green to the old Tudor manor house, Charlotte's home for the first few months of her widowhood in England. In no particular hurry, she waited while Lady Frampton gathered up her shawls and muff, as well as her prayer book and capacious reticule. As they made their slow promenade down the aisle, Lady Frampton decided she needed to take a further rest, and subsided with a groan of relief on to a chair near the porch.

'You go and see if that idle groom is 'andy,' she instructed Charlotte with a peremptory wave of her hand. 'Then, when I've 'ad a bit of a breather, you can give me an 'and up and 'elp me down to the road.'

Obediently, Charlotte headed into the porch but was held up at the door while Lady Granville's companion, fussing all the time, made her way towards the exit. People stared and gave way to her, whispering all the while that this was the poor soul who had found the body of Lady Granville's maid. Deep curiosity, tempered with respect, caused the congregation to allow her to join her employer who, however, remained inside the church, talking to a neighbour

18

and waved the companion on ahead. Charlotte made her way into the crowded porch, but suddenly there was a commotion just ahead of her; cries of alarm, voices raised in concern and a general flurry of questions, comments and complaints. Several people cried, *'Murder!'* and even, *'Fire!'* and were hastily hushed.

Someone beside Charlotte knocked against her, setting her off balance, and she found herself tottering as the crowd of about a dozen people surged forward. Luckily, she was at the side of the group and managed to clutch at the iron ring protruding from the porch wall. Unable to see who was pushing, or why, she fought for breath and was about to relinquish her hold on the ring, when she realized that there had been an accident. Someone had actually fallen into an open grave close to the door.

'Good heavens,' she exclaimed aloud, edging curiously towards the crowd milling about outside the porch. After looking round to check that Gran was safely out of harm's way, she stood on tiptoe and tried to see what was happening, while keeping away from the excitable spectators. All she could see was a balding pate that looked familiar. 'Why, that's the vicar! What on earth is he doing kneeling over that grave? And who is down there?'

'You may well ask.' The response came from an unexpected source. Lady Granville had turned back towards the church looking so flushed and angry that Charlotte took her arm.

'Do come and sit in the porch for a moment,' she suggested in a soothing voice as the lady fussed about arranging her cloak tidily. 'You are quite shaken, I'm sure you should take a few minutes to catch your breath. Are you hurt, ma'am?'

'Did you see who pushed me?' Lady Granville did as she was bidden but her voice bore a throbbing undertone of something like hysteria that surprised Charlotte.

'Pushed you?' Charlotte could only parrot the question. 'No, I saw nothing, I'm afraid. I was right at the back of the crowd, to the side, and knew nothing until I was caught up in the rush to look. Are you injured in any way, ma'am? No? You didn't fall, did you? But what in the world happened, pray?'

'I was pushed,' came the startling pronouncement. 'I felt a sharp jab in my back and was knocked a little off balance so that I had to reach out and grab at whatever was handy. Fortunately, my son had only seconds earlier skipped away to the side of the porch or he would certainly have been sent flying into the open grave as, I believe, has happened to the curate.'

Lady Granville had by now resumed her colour and she straightened up, looking composed once more.

'A most disgraceful episode,' she said sternly. 'I did not see the instigator of this outrage but I am most disturbed. I shall not however, say anything to Mrs Richmond. I do not wish her to feel mortification at the behaviour of some of her guests.'

'Most magnanimous of you, ma'am, she will appreciate such consideration.' Charlotte kept a straight face and was rewarded with a slight nod of approval as the lady made her stately way out of the church to join her husband. At her approach, the gabbling group beside the grave seemed to melt away, no doubt recalling urgent business as they did so. Lady Granville, Charlotte reflected, wore a most forbidding expression.

Her husband, ignorant of the near-calamity, was engaged in jovial banter with assorted other gentlemen at the lych-gate. Lady Granville's plump but dowdy companion, heroine of the recent crime, was fussing and fluttering about, flapping her handkerchief in a distracted fashion as she waited to assist her employer down the two shallow steps. Charlotte had spotted her sitting at the back of the church, as befitted her lowly situation, though with a scornful look about her down-turned mouth that belied her humble posture. She looked gratified at the number of people who stopped to offer their condolences and congratulations at her narrow escape, but resumed her humble demeanour as she approached her employer once more.

Charlotte made to move towards the kneeling vicar, then stopped. The fuss was dying down and, as there seemed no real cause for alarm, no need for her to rush to anyone's assistance and add to the confusion, she tugged at the heavy door handle and joined her elderly relative. It might be advisable, she thought, to wait inside the church for several minutes until peace reigned outside so she wandered around the ancient building that she loved so dearly, admiring the seasonal arrangements of Christmas roses and holly, adorned with sprigs of mistletoe and wreathed round with trails of ivy.

'Give me an 'and up again, gal.' The order came from the old lady who had been reposing bolt upright with her hands folded on her ample bosom, and with her eyes tightly shut. 'It don't seem as if there's any call for us to commence to worry. Whatever it was that 'appened seems to have sorted itself out.' She nodded philosophically at Charlotte. 'Most fings do, I find,' she said. 'Did I 'ear some daft soul calling out "Murder"?' she added. 'He's long gone, that fellow, days ago, if 'e 'as any sense, and there'd be no sense at all hanging about in a churchyard.'

Indeed, there was certainly no remaining sign of accident or distress outside, still less of a lurking ruffian, and the congregation could be seen straggling across the village green towards the manor, leaving only the vicar's wife who was fussing over several long streaks of mud that disfigured her husband's surplice.

'Oh really, Percy,' she was complaining as she darted ineffectual little dabs at his flowing robes. 'I do think you could have left it to someone else to get dirty. You simply must remember the dignity of your position nowadays.' She looked up at the newcomers' approach and left off her attempts. 'Grandmama? And Charlotte? Did you see what happened? Such a commotion and just look at Percy.'

'What in the world has happened, Agnes?' Charlotte addressed her sister-in-law as they headed towards the lych-gate, while the vicar escaped thankfully across the churchyard to the sanctuary of his vicarage. Charlotte watched him go with a smile; he had been the meek curate of the parish, secretly engaged to the daughter of the manor, but if he had believed his promotion would make him less downtrodden, he was mistaken. Since her marriage, Agnes had blossomed into a most determined wife and she managed her husband for his own good. 'Lady Granville told me someone pushed her and that the curate fell into the grave. I saw Percy kneeling beside him, but how does he come to look now as if he has just climbed out of the grave himself?'

'He has,' was the startling reply. Agnes still looked put out and was clearly glad of an audience for her complaints. 'I'm not perfectly sure what happened, but in the press of people coming out of the church, someone must have pushed against Lady Granville for she cried out: "Stop that at once, stop pushing me!" Imagine, how rude; to push a lady so, and one of her years and standing too. Anyway, she stumbled against the person in front of her who happened to be Miss Armstrong. You remember Lily and I met her and her sister at a Deanery tea party? Poor Miss Armstrong in her turn staggered and almost fell against her sister, Mrs Chant.'

'It sounds like a game of human dominoes,' commented Charlotte. 'I was right at the back and didn't observe anyone pushing, though I was caught up in the general teetering as someone started to fall. I do hope nobody was hurt in the crush?'

'Thankfully not,' Agnes shook her head. 'Though when Mrs Chant was tilted off balance she did bump into the new curate and he, silly creature, fell into the grave that has been opened up for the blacksmith's old aunt. If you recall, that was her family grave and the old lady insisted she'd haunt them unless she was buried there, even though it's almost full to bursting. That's how Percy managed to get covered in mud, pulling the curate out of the grave.' She shook her head, with a frown of annoyance. 'And what must the silly young man do, but pull so hard at poor Percy's hand, that they both ended up in the mud, and there's been so much rain lately.'

'Did Lady Granville say who had pushed her?' In spite of her better judgement, Charlotte gazed round anxiously, infected by the recent violent death in the village and by today's general clamour at the graveside. 'She didn't tell me. It seems remarkably clumsy of whoever it was.'

'She couldn't tell,' Agnes replied. 'But she did give short shrift to whoever was shouting about murder. Oh dear, I'd better go and make sure Percy is all right, he's so helpless about things like clean surplices. I'll see you both in a few minutes.'

'We seem to have missed all the excitement,' Charlotte complained with a grin, as she helped the waiting groom to hoist Lady Frampton into her pony chaise for the short journey from church to manor. She and the old lady had been carried in this conveyance on the outward journey from her own home, but now

Charlotte decided to walk along beside the equipage, keeping pace comfortably with the fat cob that had, in any case, no notion of travelling quickly.

'I'd like to have seen the curate fall into a grave. He's such a pompous youth it must have done considerable damage to his self-importance.'

It was noticeable that those guests who were walking the short distance to the manor kept close together, several of them casting anxious glances round and shivering as the shadows lengthened. Charlotte sympathised. The news had shocked them all to the core and nobody was likely to venture out alone tonight.

But wait, wasn't that the Granville boy sidling alongside the wall of the churchyard? Charlotte opened her mouth to call out, then closed it as she saw him shoot a glare of considerable dislike at his mother's companion who was hallooing and waving to him. Oh well, he can't come to any harm, Charlotte decided. He was in company with some of the village lads and was probably heading down Church Lane towards the shop, so she decided not to give him away. The sky was still showing one or two streaks of daylight and there were plenty of people milling about to keep an eye on him. He'd no doubt join his parents at the manor shortly.

As they passed Rowan Lodge, a compact brick-built house next to the vicarage, Charlotte sighed with undiluted pleasure. This was her home now, where she and old Lady Frampton had lately taken up residence, leaving Lily resplendent as chatelaine of the manor. The relief was unspeakable and Charlotte looked up at the old lady with a slight smile.

'Best thing we ever did, eh girl?' Lady Frampton clearly knew where Charlotte's thoughts lay. Their loving friendship might have seemed unlikely to a casual observer – a girl from Australia who kept very quiet about her shady background, and the cockney whose vast inheritance from her husband, a London merchant, had made it possible for her now deceased son to marry into the aristocratic Richmond family and assume their surname. The link between Charlotte and Lady Frampton was their shared connection to the old lady's grandson, Charlotte's late and decidedly unlamented husband. 'Peace and quiet away from Lily's tantrums and

Barnard's bellowings,' Lady Frampton nodded complacently. 'And room to spread ourselves; good thing too, now the little piglet rules the roost over there.' She frowned, reaching forward to rap the groom on his shoulder. 'Get a move on, will you, my lad, I'm sharp-set and wanting my victuals.'

There was another chuckle at Charlotte's shoulder as the groom bullied the pony into breaking into a reluctant trot, and she glanced round to see the Granville boy, slightly breathless from running along behind her. There was a stickiness about his mouth so she had guessed correctly. The owner of the village shop was known to keep elastic opening hours and usually had a supply of home-made toffee on sale there. Still, she frowned slightly, relieved to see him; he ought not to be out alone at such an anxious time.

'I beg your pardon, ma'am,' he spoke diffidently as he fell into step beside her. 'But would you be so good as to tell me who that old lady is? She seems a regular good'un. Is she a relation of yours?'

'That's Lady Frampton,' she told him. 'Mr Richmond's grand-mother and my own grandmother by marriage. I'm Charlotte Richmond, the Squire's sister-in-law. And yes, you're perfectly right; she *is* a good'un and I love her dearly.' She looked round but could see no sign of his illustrious parents. 'You must be home for the Christmas holidays,' she suggested. 'Where do you go to school?'

A scowl disfigured the boy's face. 'I'm not allowed to go to school,' he muttered. 'My mama thinks I'm too delicate so I have a tutor, and my papa never bothers to argue with her.' He caught her speculative glance at his slight, but wiry frame. 'I know, it's nonsense. I'm perfectly tough and healthy but she will insist on coddling me. It wouldn't be quite so bad if only I had a brother or sister,' he added in a disconsolate tone. 'It would give Mama some-body else to worry over.' And keep her off my back, was the unspoken message Charlotte received.

'It must be lonely,' Charlotte sympathised and was surprised when he broke in on her speech, a glimmer of pleading in the blue eyes, his tone diffident.

'Oh, I do beg your pardon,' he apologised. 'But – I – don't suppose you and the old lady would like to come to tea tomorrow, would you? It would be so good and I'm sure Mama would be pleased.' He clearly expected a refusal and Charlotte could not bring herself to hurt him. Besides she felt a good deal of sympathy for a boy of his age, lonely and hedged around by anxious adults. He gave her no chance to refuse but went on urgently. 'I'll tell you what, ma'am, if I say to my mother that you and Lady Frampton are interested in gardening and in history, and would dearly love to see her mediaeval garden, I can ask her to invite you. She would be delighted to show off the garden and it would all go swimmingly. I'm sure you really would be interested anyway.'

'A mediaeval garden?' Charlotte was intrigued, her hazel eyes sparkling. 'I only know about growing vegetables and very little about flowers; our old gardener at Rowan Lodge is set in his ways and doesn't allow us to interfere, but a mediaeval garden? Yes, Lady Frampton and I might well be most intrigued.' She thought for a moment. 'As it happens, I believe we are both free tomorrow and I promise I'll come even if Lady Frampton doesn't feel equal to it. Provided of course, your mama really will wish to invite me?'

'Oh thank you, Mrs Richmond.' The boy was delighted beyond what seemed reasonable. 'My father makes jokes about it, saying that Mama is foolish to spend so much time and money on what he calls a "dead queen's garden" but lots of people do seem to find it interesting.' He kicked up a pebble and hunched his shoulders. 'Do come if you can, ma'am. Mama won't even let me out into the grounds on my own, not since Dunster – that was her maid – um, you know....'

There was a quiver in his voice and Charlotte was dismayed to see that his cheeks were pale. They had reached the porch of Finchbourne Manor now and she only had time for a quick question before they were swept into the house.

'It's understandable that your mama should be anxious.' Charlotte's warm sympathy did its work and the boy's colour was returning, but Charlotte still felt uneasy. 'Is there something worrying you?' she asked quietly. She thought he was about to confide in her, but although he slid a considering glance in her direction and hesitated, the moment was lost and he shook his head.

Never mind, she thought, another time perhaps, so she asked with a smile, 'Now, I know that you are Master Granville, but I don't believe I know your first name?'

'I'm Oz, ma'am,' he said, adding in a tone that brooked no further comment, a mulish expression at odds with his pleasant, lightly-freckled face. 'Just call me Oz,' and he was gone, slipping skilfully out of sight – clearly the result of much practice – as his anxious mother peered round the hall from the drawing-room door leaving Charlotte to wonder who was the 'dead queen' and how she had come to have a garden in Hampshire.

Chapter 2

THE DAY HAD begun with a severe frost and now in the early dusk, Charlotte, who still missed the sunshine of her Australian youth and the heat of last winter's Indian sojourn, gave a shiver, only too glad to make her way from the porch into the Tudor entrance hall at the manor. There, the customary gloom was lightened for once by an enormous Christmas tree radiant with wax candles. The tree's spreading branches happily concealed the depressing display of ancestral martial cutlery (relic of a bygone and more bellicose era) that was splayed in tarnished glory across the oak panelling. This arrangement had an unfortunate drawback by way of allowing the tree, with its long, pine-scented branches festooned with sharp needles, to attack the unwary.

A small ground-floor room just beyond the stairs had been set aside so that visiting ladies might take off their cloaks and refresh themselves, while any attendant maids and companions, such as Lady Granville's, had to make do with the servants' quarters. Charlotte however, made her way up the second staircase and turned left into the new wing (built in Queen Anne's time) to her own old room, now always kept in readiness for her occasional overnight visits. On her way downstairs once more, she exclaimed in annoyance, 'How annoying,' as she realized that a flounce from her petticoat was dangling a little below her skirt. 'Oh well, there is no-one about so I'll mend it here.' After a cautious look around to make sure she was unobserved, she sat in the gloom on the top stair of the final, shallow flight to pin it up. She was half-conscious of a movement on the landing above her, but a glance revealed only emptiness there and as she bent to her task she heard voices immediately below her in the shadows at the back of the hall, just outside the half-closed cloakroom door.

'Well?' The female voice was light and bore a faintly malicious note. 'How are you supporting the strain of this occasion? I had supposed today's gathering among the dull worthies of Hampshire would be tedious in the extreme but it is not at all what I expected. There has been the constant whispering about the recent frightful crime and I declare my blood has almost run cold, particularly when there was that nonsensical accident at the church door. Did you hear people crying out that it must be the murderer? Such foolishness! Besides that, it has certainly been a surprise to encounter one or two old… how shall I say? Acquaintances? Familiar faces, at any rate even though we have been *roundly* snubbed, but I must say it is proving rather invigorating, though I had not bargained for there to be quite so strenuous an exit from the church.'

The voice was unfamiliar to Charlotte and she could not make out the low-toned reply. She patted her hair to make sure her glossy brown plaits were still neatly in place, and was about to rise from her station at the turn of the landing when the unknown lady spoke again.

'I am finding it most amusing, you know,' she laughed. 'When you are in possession, as I am, of a secret – and *such* a surprising secret – and no, my dear, you need not raise your scolding finger, nor caution me; the very last thing I would dream of doing is to disclose that secret, not to a single soul. No indeed, what do you think I am? How can you possibly think such a thing? Nobody need go in fear of *my* knowledge, all is safe with me.'

The hall was temporarily deserted and Charlotte was frankly eavesdropping now, her hazel eyes bright with curiosity. What were these secrets and who on earth could the well-informed lady be? And who was her companion? The low murmuring voice was indistinguishable and might even, at a pinch, be that of a gentleman, though if that were indeed the case, what could a member of the stronger sex be doing outside the room set aside for the ladies at this time?

Maddeningly, to someone blessed with a lively curiosity, there was the sound of doors opening and shutting and a sudden influx of merry-makers into the hall. She deemed it politic to emerge from her seat on the stairs, so she made haste to return to the party. Here, her beefy, black-haired brother-in-law surged out of the drawing-room to greet her with a hearty kiss and a smile of real pleasure on his large rubicund face.

'Well, well, Charlotte, m'dear,' he addressed her. 'You're looking very handsome today in that green rig-out, but why have you taken off that fetching little hat, eh? It suited you, my dear, even Lily remarked upon it.'

'Dear Barnard,' Charlotte returned his kiss of greeting with great affection. 'My best hat is upstairs, of course, but I'm glad you approve. I almost jibbed at the price but it was so extremely becoming I threw caution to the winds.' She grinned at him and patted his arm. 'I think it all went very well, don't you? Your young Algy is such a large promising baby, I'm sure everyone admired him.'

'I should think myself that they were all in awe of his healthy lung capacity.' Kit Knightley, near neighbour and Algy's least illustrious godparent had come over to greet her and to shake Barnard heartily by the hand. 'Congratulations, old fellow, a job well done.'

He nodded to his old school friend and took Charlotte's hand between both his own. 'And how are you?' he asked, leading her towards the warmth and light of the drawing-room, which was to be found in the later addition to the old Tudor house. Here by the hearth stood a group of stout citizens, armed with song sheets and a lantern, singing their hearts out in carol after carol. Kit paused for a moment, merely thought Charlotte, to give an impression of listening with polite interest, before he steered her skilfully away from them to the other side of the room. 'I've seen very little of you for the last couple of months, Char, what with your removal to Rowan Lodge and my own....'

'What, what? What's that?' It was Lord Granville, breaking in on their conversation with a cheerful lack of ceremony and manners. 'Knightley, is that you? What was that you called this young lady? What, what? Was it "Char" for *Charming*, eh? Come now, my dear Mrs Richmond, I'll wager that's it. What do you say?'

His hand had sought and grasped Charlotte's own once more,

NICOLA SLADE

and he bent towards her, evidently admiring her tall slim figure and attractively angular features. As she struggled to disengage herself without offence she shook her head with a smile.

'It is merely a nickname, my lord,' she said. 'My baptismal name is Charlotte but I have sometimes been known as Char.'

'Just as I said,' he looked pleased with his own wit. 'Char short for *Char*ming; after all, it sounds the same. I shall call you so, what do you say? What?'

'Thank you, my lord,' she managed to conceal her transports of delight at this honour. 'But I had rather you did not, it's just a foolish family name. My present acquaintances call me by my given name, Charlotte, and I should feel honoured indeed, if you would do so.' She felt slightly hypocritical at this lofty pronouncement, bearing in mind that she was known as Miss Char to the entire village, but she reflected that Lord Granville needed no encouragement.

He looked momentarily abashed but recovered his composure quickly and was about to speak once more when he stopped short, staring after a group of ladies, his hand cupped to his ear. One of them, she could not tell which, had spoken as they promenaded round the large room now thronged with guests and at the sound of her voice, Lord Granville's face lost a shade of its ruddy hue. He now wore an expression of extreme surprise which was, she noted with interest, replaced by something like a furtive panic. Charlotte followed his gaze but saw nothing of moment in the cluster of guests round Lily. Lord Granville harrumphed, nodded amiably, and sauntered over to speak to some of the gentlemen present, though Charlotte observed that he continued to peer anxiously after the knot of ladies.

Someone else was watching them too, she realized, noticing that Lady Granville's companion was staring at the group of women. Lily had mentioned that a spinster lady, some kind of poor relation, was employed as a lady-in-waiting and that it was this Miss Cole who had unwittingly stumbled upon the body of her employer's maid. While Charlotte had the utmost sympathy for any woman who must be constantly at another's beck and call, and even more for one who had found herself confronted by a corpse and a villain too, she was repelled by the companion's turned-down mouth. A short, self-important looking woman, plumply pink and of uncertain years and clad in a plain grey dress, she had followed Charlotte downstairs and was now, after a nod and dismissive wave of the hand from Lady Granville, sitting on a hard, upright, chair, looking sour. Besides, the fussiness the woman displayed in constantly flapping a lace handkerchief to and fro in front of her face would probably drive one mad.

Charlotte, circling the room, greeting old friends and new, felt an idle curiosity as she glanced across at the companion. Miss Cole, having stared round at the assembled company, jumped up now and insistently hemmed her employer into a corner. Lady Granville, who appeared to have recovered from the upset at the church, listened with an impassive face as her companion whispered urgently into her lady's ear. Charlotte, watching discreetly as she had no wish to be caught staring, was fascinated by the plump woman's hairstyle, with its intricately plaited pepper-and-salt loops and twists that bobbed busily to and fro as she spoke. Like the ears on a King Charles spaniel, thought Charlotte, remembering a dog of her acquaintance in Sydney.

With another peremptory wave of dismissal, Lady Granville turned away from her companion and Charlotte saw that the lady – who had earlier looked down her nose with an air of chilly resignation while Lord Granville attempted to flirt with Charlotte – was now, after a brief glance at her husband, staring severely through her eyelashes at three particular women who were making desultory small talk where they had been left by their hostess.

There seemed nothing remarkable about the lady's disapproval. Charlotte had observed that whenever Lord Granville approached another woman, whether seventeen or seventy, his lady's brow had furrowed even more severely and she moved to distract him. I'm not surprised, Char sympathised in silence; his lordship looks to have been quite a handful in his younger days but he must be getting on now, so he is surely less of a worry? She glanced at the ladies currently under scrutiny; Lady Granville had clearly spotted her husband's passing interest and was taking a closer look at them on her own behalf as she positioned herself in such a way as to obscure her husband's view.

Two were ladies of recent acquaintance whom Lily Richmond and Agnes had met at the Deanery in Winchester, and surely introductions came with no higher recommendation of respectability, mused Charlotte. These were the individuals involved in the 'falling dominoes' incident Agnes had described at the church door but, like Lady Granville, they appeared to have suffered no lasting damage. They were sisters, Charlotte understood, though she had not come across them until today. There was no longer any requirement, thank heaven, to sit through Lily's interminable daily stories of what she and her cronies had discussed over tea when out visiting.

Under her lashes, she watched with amusement as Lord Granville sidled away from his monumental wife and tried to edge his way to be near the visiting women. He was soon thwarted by his lady who, apparently all unconscious of his intention, moved to take his arm and turn him into another direction. She must be accustomed to his habits, Charlotte thought, admiring the guest's strategy.

There must be forty or more guests, she thought, counting heads, and although the drawing-room was large enough, the heat was rising, what with the roaring fire, and she spotted several red faces. She had decided on a strategic retreat to find somewhere less crowded, when she heard her name hissed in conspiratorial tones.

'Char,' Lily had whisked into the room with a gracious smile pinned to her round pink face but with disaster written there unmistakably when she ran Charlotte to earth.

'You must help me, Char,' she whispered, making sure none of the guests were within hearing. 'I'm at my wits' end. The kitchen cat has brought in a dead rat and planted it right on top of Little Algy's christening cake. What in heaven's name are we to do?'

'Oh my goodness,' Charlotte stifled an urge to giggle; this was far too serious for laughter – Lily would never forgive her. 'I hope someone has taken it off? Good, that's the first thing, then….'

'But, Char,' Lily whispered again, even more urgently. 'The wretched cat has left footprints on the cake too.'

'Don't worry, Lily. I remember that my stepfather met with something like this in one of his parishes in South Australia. The thing to do is to conceal the damage and act as if nothing had happened. I know....' Her gaze fell on one of the bowls of pot-pourri dotted around the room, evidence of her own efforts as a result of her delight in last summer's flowers. No, not flowers, of course, but... 'Are there any of those candied fruits left over? Cherries? Excellent, tell Cook to give the top of the cake a quick wipe over with a clean damp cloth to get rid of any dirt and she should press the cherries down all over the cake top.'

It was a makeshift solution but Lily's gratitude was heartfelt as she vanished towards the kitchen. Charlotte recalled her stepfather's mirth: *'Luckily I had stepped into the parlour shortly before the company made its way there and I found the lady of the house in hysterics. Her precious cat had chosen that day of all days to move her kittens from a dark cupboard somewhere, but she must have been startled somehow and leaped on to the table, only to drop one poor little thing into the punch bowl.'* Will had laughed anew at the calamity. *'What with the cat going frantic to rescue its child and the lady even more in a state, with her illustrious visitors almost upon us, I did the only thing possible. I rescued the kitten and got it and its careless parent out of the way, then I seized a knife and cut up some fruit to throw in the punchbowl, along with half a bottle of brandy.'* He had winked at his stepdaughter. *'I thought it best to forego the punch myself – the kitten had had quite a fright, after all – though as it turned out, nobody suffered any ill effects, not even the kitten.'*

Fortunately, nobody seemed to have noticed their hostess's agitation, so Charlotte returned to her covert observation of the ladies in whom both Lord and Lady Granville had taken an interest. No, nothing to mark them out, she decided. Both ladies were short rather than tall, slightly built rather than sturdy. The elder sister was unmarried, a Miss Armstrong, Charlotte understood, and with her quiet demeanour, her blue eyes modestly lowered and her light brown hair plainly plaited, pleasant-looking rather than pretty, possibly in her late twenties or even into her thirties. She was neatly turned out in a dove grey merino with black mourning ribbons, soberly dressed with an eye to economy as Charlotte's practised eye revealed to her. Charlotte thought she looked as though she had been ill. The other woman, Mrs Chant, looked somewhat younger, perhaps in her mid-twenties or so, though Charlotte looked at her thoughtfully; those very fair complexions could, she was aware, be deceptive sometimes. Unlike her spinster sister, she was clad in the silks and velvets appropriate to an affluent young matron, her rose pinks and silver lace trimmings admirably suiting her fair, blue-eyed prettiness. There had been time only for a brief introduction before the ceremony but now Charlotte was seized by a sense that the younger sister was in some way familiar. She shook her head; it was quite impossible that they could have met, of that she was convinced.

The third woman in the group was only too familiar to Charlotte, who had first encountered her some months earlier, and had few fond memories of their meeting. As Miss Melicent Dunwoody, she had once been governess to dear Agnes. Triumphantly married only a matter of months ago, Melicent was now the wife of a retired naval man, Captain Penbury, and to Charlotte's chagrin they had arrived in Hampshire only a day earlier, on a visit to spend the Christmas season at the manor. Already Melicent, the new Mrs Penbury, had managed to grate upon everyone's nerves with her constant complaints and the frequency with which her feelings were hurt, so that Charlotte thanked heaven that she was no longer obliged to live in the same house as the damply depressing visitor.

'I declare, Gran,' she had announced only that morning, 'I could give you chapter and verse of every ailment Melicent has bravely suffered in the months since her wedding, all of them life-threatening and all…' she grinned, '*all* entailing extraordinarily revolting symptoms. I'll spare you, never fear, though dear Melicent certainly had no such care for *my* delicate sensibilities.'

Short and thin, Melicent's lank dark hair was strained back and caught up into a net, and she drooped now beside the other two women trying to look as if she was participating in their conversation. Charlotte, seized by her usual reluctant and exasperated pity, watched the former governess who, for a wonder, was defeated by the other ladies' polite indifference as she trailed over towards

Lily's prize visitor. Lord Granville's shoulders slumped and he abandoned his surreptitious attempts to scrutinize the ladies. He too headed across the room and Lady Granville now directed her disapproving gaze elsewhere, her brows meeting once more as her irrepressible lord attempted to lionize the guest of honour.

'Well now, Miss Nightingale,' he beamed, attempting to engage her in conversation, apparently undisturbed by the repulsion clearly expressed on her face as he edged towards her. 'This is a great occasion, is it not? A new little fellow ready to take his place in a good old local family?' His face softened for a moment and he poked his head forward to peer hopefully from beneath his rampant eyebrows. 'I must present my own young stripling to you, ma'am, a very promising lad.' However he failed to discover his own son, though Charlotte bit back a smile as she caught a glimpse of that very fair head going purposefully towards the dining-room. As though he felt her gaze upon him, the boy looked round and saw her, his blue eyes alight with mischief as he grinned and made good his escape. Frustrated in his search, Lord Granville disconsolately turned back to the lady he had expertly penned in the bay window. 'Tchah, he is not to be seen; well, well, lads will be lads, will they not? Now, my dear ma'am, you must allow me to be of service to you. What can I procure for you?'

'You may procure for me a large sum of money,' came the startling response as Miss Nightingale's weary features lightened for a moment and a fleeting colour warmed her pale, sickly-looking complexion. At Lord Granville's sudden, astonished silence, the famous lady waxed eloquent and her eyes gleamed with a zealous fervour. Charlotte, listening unashamedly, thought that here must lie the clue as to why Miss Nightingale had abandoned the seclusion of her sick room to mingle with so many people who were at most mere acquaintances, and, in the main, total strangers.

'I am collecting funds towards setting up a new nursing order and I shall be most happy to accept your banker's draft for five thousand pounds.' She held his stricken gaze with a basilisk stare and added, 'See, I have written your name at the very top of this list of today's guests, some of whom have already been delighted to subscribe. I took the precaution some days ago,' she explained, 'of discovering from our hostess, the names of those who were invited to attend today and as you, my lord, are the gentleman of highest rank present, to you must be the honour of setting a generous example by heading the page. To that end, I have left a large space for you to write in the amount.' Her tone brooked no refusal and she added, 'Here, my lord, on this desk I have laid out both pen and ink. It only remains for you to set the amount and sign your name. My bankers will do the rest. You see? We are agreed, are we not, upon five thousand pounds? Now, I will save you some trouble by inscribing that amount. You have only to append your signature – here.'

As Lord Granville, mesmerised by the famous lady's insistent gaze, set his signature obediently upon the paper, Barnard's voice rang out in a cheerful bellow as he stood foursquare on the staircase visible to all, through the wide open doors to both the drawing-room and the dining-room.

'Well, well, here we all are,' he began, stubbornly ignoring his wife's pained expression and little whispered hints. Charlotte distinctly heard her peevish complaint, 'You should have begun with, 'My Lords, Ladies and Gentlemen....'

'I'm glad to welcome one and all on this happy occasion, by God so I am, and I know I speak for Lily too, hey, m'dear?' He beamed down at his proud little wife who was clad sumptuously for the great day in a silk taffeta dress in a cheerful but unlikely tartan of purple and yellow trimmed with gold fringing which, Charlotte observed suddenly, emphasised Lily's growing resemblance to portraits of Her Gracious Majesty when young.

'I pride myself on a master stroke,' Barnard preened. 'That is, when I realized young Algy's christening would be so near to Christmas, it seemed only fitting to celebrate the day along with all the trappings of a grand Olde Englishe Yuletide.' Charlotte smiled fondly at the large young squire who had proved such a good brother to her. He was getting into his stride now, she grinned, and looking more and more jolly and festive by the minute.

'Well now, before we drink a toast to the hero of the hour, let us raise a glass to Absent Friends.' Barnard frowned in an attempt to make his genial features look solemn as he continued, 'Lily's father is sadly unable to be here as Lily's stepmother presented him with a bouncing pair of twin boys, not an hour before he was due to set out.'

Charlotte slid a glance at her sister-in-law who was failing to look delighted. She already had one infant half-brother, who had displaced her from her position as heir to her father's estate, and now here were two more. Barnard, serenely unaware of his wife's seething resentment, proposed another toast. 'As many of you know, my mama and my uncle are at present taking the cure on the Continent, so here's to them too, and let us hope we can soon celebrate their return home.'

Across the room, Kit Knightley caught Charlotte's eye and briefly lowered his left eyelid in a fleeting wink. He and she had both been instrumental in expediting the redoubtable elder Mrs Richmond's exile abroad after the death of Charlotte's husband, and they were united in their fervent prayer that she should certainly never reappear at Finchbourne Manor.

Barnard was making another speech. 'You have already heard the Waits who are here to entertain us with their carols, and they'll be in full voice again once I've said my piece. Sad to say though, the Mummers, who were to perform their play for us, have been obliged to stay away, as three of their number have gone down with the measles. Never mind that though, the wassail bowl is ready and waiting in the dining-room along with Olde English delicacies such as frumenty and … and other such,' he finished hastily as his memory clearly failed him. He mopped his flushed forehead with a large spotted silk handkerchief and wound up his welcome address by inviting his guests to hasten to the dining-room so they might enjoy the feast and join him in raising a cup of the wassail brew to little Algy's future happiness.

Charlotte waited till last to allow the guests first onslaught on the mountain of food piled on the vast mahogany table. She cast an anxious glance round the room, exchanged a covert smile with the young Granville lad, and met Kit Knightley's quizzical smile as her brows knitted in a slight anxiety.

'Why are you looking so worried, Char?' He came over to her, a broad-shouldered man, brown-haired and blue-eyed, his pleasant face shadowed by signs of anxiety that were not entirely eclipsed by his present amusement.

'I'm just hoping Gran doesn't eat too much of that rich food,' she explained, waving a hand towards the table. 'She has the constitution of an ox indeed, but I've never seen so many pies and pastries in my life and I know what she's like where food is concerned.'

'I shouldn't worry,' Kit laughed, as they observed Lady Frampton industriously shovelling spoonfuls of frumenty – which looked to Charlotte like a rather stodgy porridge – into her greedy mouth, at the same time as she selected sugar plums, candied fruit and other delicacies to pile high on her plate. She added a large slice of rich cake, generously topped with candied fruit, an innovation that was, Charlotte was relieved to notice, eliciting loud praise from the guests. Captain Penbury was vying with the old lady beside him as to the speed with which he crammed mince pies one after the other into his own mouth.

'Oh dear, they look as though they're having a race,' sighed Charlotte turning away in despair. 'The captain certainly shouldn't be eating so much of this food, he's very lax. He is supposed to be on an invalid diet to accommodate what he always calls his "trouble amidships" where he still carries a musket ball dating from an ancient naval engagement.'

With her pouting attendant a dutiful three paces behind her, Lady Granville sailed across the room, with a nod to Charlotte and Mr Knightley. She brushed aside all eager questions from the other guests regarding the murder of her poor maid, and inclined her large stately head towards Miss Nightingale. That lady, with his lordship's signature firmly on her list of promised donations, was now sitting with a group of potential benefactors.

'Ah, thank you Sir, you are most generous,'

Charlotte heard her being gracious to a hapless neighbour, as he bowed to her stronger will and signed his name to her list. 'And you, madam? I'm sure you will not hang back for such a worthy cause?'

Lord Granville, who had been looking shocked at the predatory manner in which she proceeded to milk her hapless fellow guests, now assumed an even more miserable expression as his lady hooked a proprietorial hand into his arm.

'Ah, Lady Granville.' There was a beadily-ingratiating smile on the face of the Lady with the Lamp as she raised her head from her notes and observed the newcomer. 'I am sure you will wish to match your husband's generosity by making a donation on your own behalf to my proposed training school for nurses?'

A chilly stare was the initial response she received followed by a decided shake of the head. 'I think not.' Lady Granville's response was cold, abrupt and, it had to be admitted, rude. 'If you have ensnared my husband and trespassed upon his well-known good-will – and, as I have observed, the goodwill of many of the other guests already – then that must suffice you, along with those remaining parties whom you no doubt intend to approach. Come, my lord, I cannot see our son, Osbert, anywhere and I am becoming anxious about him.'

Charlotte had to conceal a gasp of admiration at this fearless refusal.

'How brave,' she whispered to Kit Knightley. 'To give a set-down to Miss Nightingale, who is the most intimidating female I've ever encountered. She's even more daunting than a fearsome landlady of an outback lodging house where we once stayed. She was rumoured to have summarily disposed of seven husbands.'

Kit's blue eyes creased in a smile and Charlotte remembered Will Glover's comment, *'Ate 'em all on the wedding night, probably.'*

The heroine of the Crimean War, plainly gowned but tall and imposing, half rose in her seat, while her gathering frown struck fear into the guests in her immediate neighbourhood; but her quarry was gone. Lady Granville had dragged her lord away and was now bearing down on the groaning table where her son, trapped by his greed, was unable to escape. Charlotte watched with sympathy as the anxious mother loomed over the boy and began to pick out delicacies from the table and pile them on to his plate, frowning heavily as Captain Penbury whisked one particu-larly choice morsel away moments before her ladyship's hand descended to it.

Suddenly there was an outcry. Charlotte, who had shrugged and turned away, recognised her own name called out in Lady Frampton's stentorian tones and she craned round the heads in front of her, anxiety uppermost in her thoughts. A cry of 'Murder!' rang out from a couple of the guests and she felt her heart contract. What she saw made her elbow her way through the throng.

Captain Penbury had crashed to the floor with his hand clutched to his chest, the weather-beaten colouring fading rapidly from his broad, square face.

Chapter 3

LADY FRAMPTON STOPPED in mid-bellow as Charlotte rushed to her side.

'Sit down, Gran,' she urged once she had ascertained that the old lady was unhurt; all her shouting had been for her granddaughter to come to the aid of the captain. 'At once, do you hear? I'll see to this.'

There was still a clamour of voices shouting '*Help, murder!*' as she knelt beside the stricken sailor to loosen his collar. 'Cease that nonsense this instant,' she commanded and raised her head to seek assistance. 'Someone clear the room at once, if you please, ah, Mr Knightley? Thank you. And someone else please enquire whether Dr Perry has arrived, I know he is expected. Ask him to attend the captain directly.'

She bent to her task. Captain Penbury was breathing, although he looked distressed and his colour was still poor; she prayed that he was not having a heart attack. Charlotte slipped an arm beneath his head and looked up in gratitude as someone handed her a cushion.

'Thank you,' she said, and glanced round again, looking anxious. 'Is there another cushion, please? I believe he will be more comfortable if we can raise him a little higher.'

A second cushion was passed to her and presently a warm rug offered, which was placed over the patient, while a glass of brandy appeared to hand as if by magic.

'Thank you once more.' She looked up and was startled to see the heroine of the Crimea bending beside her. Charlotte nodded gratefully and helped the captain to take a restorative sip. 'I think he'll recover now, do not you, Miss Nightingale?' Her words were more hopeful than she felt but she saw to her relief that the naval man was showing some sign of improvement and making an attempt to sit up.

'Come, Captain,' she soothed, gesticulating hastily for a basin lest the captain's queasy-looking countenance should indicate actual vomiting. 'There,' she murmured as her patient regained some colour in his cheeks. 'Lean back against the wall for a few more minutes then we'll find some strong arms to help you to the morning-room where you may lie upon a sofa in peace until you are more composed.'

She rose and looked around the room for help and indicated to the hovering butler that a footman was needed. The captain's colour continued to improve so she moved a little to one side, to give him air, but ready to assist if need be.

'I am impressed, Mrs Richmond.' Standing near her, Miss Nightingale astonished Charlotte with a nugget of praise. 'Most impressed. I like to see a woman of resolution, particularly when the rest of the room is filled with squawking geese and silly sheep, all milling around to no purpose. I suppose you would not consider....' A slight commotion outside in the hall caused her to break off in mid-question and raise her eyes, while a sardonic smile lightened her expression for a moment. 'Oh dear me, our troubles are all at an end,' she murmured, a sarcastic note in her voice, 'now that I see Dr Chant is upon us. I spotted his giddy young wife here. At present he is said to be the Capital's most celebrated physician, even rumoured to be in occasional attendance upon the Prince Consort, no less. I trust the captain has a fat wallet and a strong constitution for he'll need it if the good doctor is to be let loose upon him. And that goes for the Prince Consort too,' she added thoughtfully.

Charlotte glanced up and saw a well-dressed, grey-haired man in the doorway, expostulating with Dr Perry who had made a belated appearance.

For a moment, Charlotte thought Miss Nightingale had a smirk on her face as she went on, 'The bearing of an archbishop,' was her whispered aside, 'and the soul of a petty clerk. The good doctor doesn't approve of intelligent women who are taller than he is himself.' Yes, however unlikely, Charlotte was convinced the great lady sported a broad grin. 'He doesn't approve of me,' she added. 'And he certainly won't take to you, my dear.'

A pompous-looking fellow, Charlotte decided, but he'll get no change out of Dr Perry so there can be no need for me to rush to Captain Penbury's assistance. She hid a smile as she took note of the captain's wife who was indulging in a small fit of the vapours on her own behalf with little success, as the assembled guests merely quickened their steps, averting their eyes as they passed by her.

'Oh dear,' Charlotte sighed as she realized nobody else was likely to do anything, certainly not Dr Perry who bent over the fallen sailor, took his pulse, barked a few chastening words, and took his leave. 'Do pray excuse me, Miss Nightingale but I must rescue the poor captain, not only from the doctor you mention, but from his own wife.' She bowed politely. 'It has been an honour to make your acquaintance.'

From the lady's frowning expression, Charlotte suspected her own timely escape bid had rescued her from being badgered for a donation, but Miss Nightingale pursed her lips and nodded, saying only, in what Charlotte felt to be an ominous under-tone, 'I shall write to you, Mrs Richmond.' The words were accompanied by an enigmatic twitch of her brows. After a moment, she continued, 'I knew your late husband, you know, when we were children; we were much of an age. On one occasion he tied me to a tree and left me there for hours. He was a bully and a coward and you are exceedingly well rid of him.' Charlotte could only bow politely and agree with this unexpected but only too accurate assessment of her late husband's character. As she administered common-sense to Mrs Penbury, along with a glass of brandy, she observed that Miss Nightingale had followed her.

'Oh, oh,' gasped Melicent, fluttering a hand to her meagre breast. 'Oh, my valves.' Charlotte stared in surprise and Melicent went on, 'I have valves in my heart, you know. They are a sore trial to me.'

'Nonsense,' Miss Nightingale interrupted fiercely. 'Everyone has valves in his heart. It's perfectly clear to me that there is nothing amiss with you, my good woman, apart from hysteria and a fit of attention-seeking.'

Charlotte tried to bite down the gurgle of amusement that rose to her lips, but was forced to feign a coughing fit before she set about pacifying the shocked patient. A few moments later, Lord Granville hove into sight with a smile for Charlotte, but upon realising that Miss Nightingale was at her side, hastily made some apology and veered off to the other side of the room.

'Dear me,' Florence Nightingale looked grimly amused. 'Poor Lord Granville, I seem to have terrified him.' She watched him go, 'However, he has a sanguine temperament and does not dwell on things. Out of sight, out of mind, as they say.' The great lady gave a brisk nod and turned away to seek further voluntary contributions for her nursing fund, leaving Charlotte to listen to Melicent's complaints.

Lady Granville, her fine eyes narrowed, had been staring thoughtfully at the stricken captain, her hand held to her heart, her face, first pale but now suffused with an angry flush. Now a frown further darkened her brow as she stared round the room but Charlotte could see no reason for the lady's dismay. Her husband, now safe from other women, was gossiping with some visiting gentlemen, and her long-suffering son was firmly clamped to her side. As Charlotte herself glanced around, all the while exhorting Melicent Penbury to compose herself, she saw Miss Nightingale pull out a small notebook from her pocket. Beneath the reddish-brown hair, the famous heroine's furrowed brow became smooth once more and a grim smile lightened her face as the august lady scanned the list therein, making pencil marks as she did so. It was evident that she was adding the sums written down and that the total had proved satisfactory. This task completed, Charlotte was amused to see that the lady had no further use for Finchbourne or its inhabitants. However, she had underestimated Miss Nightingale's determination.

'Another word, if you please, Mrs Richmond,' beckoned the great lady who, if she was much the same age as Charlotte's thankfully-deceased husband, could only be about thirty-eight, although illness made her look older. 'I understand you are lately come from India, and before that, from Australia?'

Charlotte submitted to a brief interrogation. Yes, she had been caught up in the Mutiny last year in India when her stepfather had sadly succumbed to a fever, and yes, she had indeed been married, and promptly widowed, shortly afterwards.

'But was there not some tale of your husband, Major Richmond, having been falsely declared dead?' Miss Nightingale's handsome eyes expressed a lively interest.

'Indeed yes,' Charlotte's response was brief and guarded. 'He was injured, but he was able to make his way home where he died of a fever.' Not for all the tea in China would Charlotte go into details of that return and death, nor would she be pressed upon her upbringing in Australia, however imperiously Miss Nightingale enquired. No, she thought decidedly, it is no business of anyone else if my mother and stepfather were transported, and not the free citizens they had claimed to be.

She decided to throw the lady a sop. 'My godmother was Lady Margaret Fenton,' she said casually, suppressing a smile at the image of that illustrious lady beating an importunate admirer about the head with her parasol. Meg had declared, in her impeccably well-bred accent, '*I may be a whore, sir, but I promised my brother, the earl, that I would be a circumspect whore. He would never allow me to stoop to an affair with a pork butcher.*' Charlotte stifled the bubble of laughter that threatened to escape her lips as she recalled Meg's afterthought. '*That is, unless the pork butcher in question were to offer me a very large inducement in guineas.*'

'I see that you suspect me of vulgar curiosity,' Florence Nightingale surprised her. 'Acquit me of that, Mrs Richmond, for I have a scheme in mind that could work to our mutual advantage.'

At that point, Barnard bustled into the room bent on jollying his guests into further excesses of food and drink and managed, by deafening her with his jovial bellow, to bully Miss Nightingale into tasting the wassail brew.

'Here we are, here we are,' he cried, seizing the silver ladle and starting to dole out generous helpings of the steaming, spicy liquid from the enormous silver bucket Lily had unearthed in the cellar. 'All the traditional ingredients,' he announced, though Charlotte was well aware that Lily and her cook, having despaired of finding a recipe, had concocted their own. 'Wine and spices and currants, slices of oranges and apples, um, other fruits, berries, you name it. What do you call 'em? Er, yes, raisins, that's right, you'll find 'em all in the Finchbourne Wassail.'

He looked so absurdly pleased with himself that those of his guests who were clustered around the dining-table laughed and shrugged and suffered him to hand them a glass. Charlotte, glad to see no evidence of rats or kittens swimming in this particular brew, looked askance at the cinnamon and spices floating on her drink along with odds and ends of candied fruit, but she nodded and smiled and raised her glass, so Barnard was satisfied. It was warming on a cold day, she supposed, though the taste of cinnamon was strongly dominant and that was not a spice she particularly relished.

'As long as it's hot and wet and alcoholic,' as her beloved stepfather, Will Glover, had once remarked, 'it'll do the trick.' That was when someone had handed him a glass of something resembling rum, distilled somewhere on a sugar cane plantation. Hot, certainly; the temperature had made a mockery of the thin muslins and sun-bonnets that Charlotte and her mother were wearing, and everyone who tasted the potion had become instantly flushed in the face. Wet also, and potent too, in spite of the cornucopia of berries floating on the amber liquid. Charlotte could recall, as clearly as though it were yesterday rather than ten years earlier, the startled widening of Will's blue eyes as the full force of the alcohol he had injudiciously gulped down, had struck him.

Soon most of the guests were willingly toasting the baby's health along with hearty greetings for Christmas and the New Year. Lord Granville was there, nodding and smiling, genial as usual, but still, Charlotte thought, peering round at every lady who came within his orbit. She had been watching Lady Granville skilfully circumvent her lord's every attempt to approach any female guest. He would bob up in one direction, only to find his wife appearing from another. It was like watching a dance, Charlotte reflected, deciding that his lordship was quite outflanked by his determined lady. Indeed, as Charlotte watched idly, the gentleman shook his head disconsolately, perhaps believing himself to be mistaken. He shrugged and allowed his wife to shepherd him towards Lily Richmond at the other end of the room.

The delighted Lily was not likely to give up her prize easily and Lady Granville left him in her clutches while, with young Oz in tow, she made her way to the small crowd clustered about the table. There, she fussed about giving the boy a taste of the wassail punch. Charlotte had just raised a glass to her own lips when she spotted the elder of Lily's new friends take a sip of the brew and wrinkle her nose. She murmured something to her sister who laughed and took the glass from her. Charlotte overheard her say, 'Well, I certainly have no objection to the taste of cinnamon, my dear Sibella; in fact I'll drink a second glass with pleasure.'

Charlotte heard Lady Granville exclaim aloud, though what she said was indistinct as Dr Chant chose that moment to lean forward and speak to his wife as she sipped at her drink.

'Pray take no more punch, Verena, it is very strong and cannot be considered a suitable drink for a lady in your position.' He bit off his remark, as she laughed in response, and continued. 'Besides, the carriage is outside now and waiting to take you and your sister back to Winchester. Pray do not delay, it will not do to keep the horses waiting in this inclement weather.'

'In my position, dear husband?' The young lady's blue eyes snapped in what looked like malicious amusement. 'As the wife of Prince Albert's trusted confidant? Or....' Yes, Charlotte thought, there was definitely malice there. 'Perhaps you meant to say – in my delicate situation, did you, my dear husband?' The glance she shot at him was arch and suggestive and her husband, about to turn on his heel, halted and stared at her, his face darkening.

Charlotte raised an eyebrow but young Mrs Chant only laughed carelessly and turned to her sister. The incident passed mercifully without the embarrassment of an altercation in public between husband and wife and probably no-one but Charlotte was aware of a momentary silence in the group of people in her immediate neighbourhood, as they looked at the young lady on hearing her husband's admonition. Melicent Penbury held her glass of punch to her lips, while one or two other guests looked up before they once more tucked in to more of the sweetmeats displayed on silver shell dishes.

Lady Granville, who looked a trifle pale, had resumed her expression of glacial indifference, moved to her son's side and Dr Chant, still poised to leave the group, stayed a moment longer, his eyes narrowed at his wife's careless peal of laughter as she drained her glass.

As she watched from the outskirts of the group, Charlotte was teased by a sudden thought that failed however, to make itself clear. The elder sister, Miss Armstrong, wore a slightly troubled look, quickly replaced by a resigned smile, and the only person present who looked completely uninterested was the fair-haired boy, Oz Granville, who was surreptitiously nibbling at the candied fruits laid out temptingly before him. Oz, Charlotte surmised, was patently unaware that he was the object of scrutiny, not only of his parents, for he was accustomed to that circumstance, but that the fashionable doctor had glanced at him several times, with pursed lips. Not only that, but the two visiting ladies were both acutely aware of the boy, although they tried to disguise that interest.

Charlotte was surprised when Lady Granville accosted her with a complaint upon her lips.

'Did you observe that, Mrs Richmond?' Her lips formed a tight line and her eyebrows frowned over her dark and disapproving eyes, as she stared at young Mrs Chant who was now donning her warm cloak. 'That young lady or perhaps the other – well, whichever one of them it was, I believe she snatched the glass I had thought to give my dear boy, Osbert.'

Charlotte turned a startled gaze upon her. 'I'm sorry to hear that, Lady Granville,' she felt she should apologise on behalf of her brother and sister-in-law, their hosts. 'I'm afraid I did not observe that, I think there was somebody obscuring my view at the time. What an uncomfortable thing to happen.'

'It is no matter,' sniffed the lady, evidently mollified by this apology. 'It is merely an example of London manners, I suppose, something that has made me both impatient and weary so that I was glad to take leave of the capital. I am most relieved that Lord Granville has decided to relinquish some of his London responsibilities so that we will be spending a great deal more time at home in Hampshire.'

Charlotte was glad to recall something that might interest the lady and deflect her complaints. 'I believe I heard somewhere that you are the creator of a wonderful mediaeval garden, are you not?' It was probably politic to avoid mention of her discussion with the Granville boy lest his mother take umbrage. 'I was so interested to hear of it. As you might not be aware, I was born and brought up in Australia so anything of historical, old-world significance is most intriguing to me.'

'Really?' Lady Granville's gaunt, but still-handsome features took on a lively expression as she turned eagerly to the younger woman, shaken out of her indifference by the reference to her pastime. 'I did not know that. Indeed, I should be delighted to show you my garden, Mrs Richmond, if you are sure that it would be of interest you? Do, pray, allow me the pleasure of inviting you to tea tomorrow at Brambrook Abbey. My garden is indeed my great treasure, apart...' her fond smile enlivened and lifted her sallow face from its habitual air of chill and ruined beauty as she beheld her son, 'apart, I should say, from my very *greatest* treasure, of course: my son Osbert.'

Her expression grew even more gracious as Charlotte turned to look at the object of Lady Granville's adoration and smiled in her turn as Oz – poor lad, she thought, no wonder he refuses to answer to Osbert – backed silently out of the room with both hands filled with sugar plums that he had grabbed from one of Lily's best silver side dishes in passing. Alas for his attempt at escape. In his haste to elude his parent, Oz bumped into Charlotte's bugbear, Melicent Penbury, and had to make hasty apologies while the other ladies, his father and Dr Chant all turned to watch him.

Pricked by conscience and feeling that, as a member of the family she owed a duty to her hosts, Charlotte was immediately at the ready to offer assistance, knowing that, years earlier, Melicent had lost a leg in an unfortunate carriage accident. This made her sometimes unsteady on the artificial one but on this occasion the former governess righted herself with the clumsy but willing help of the Granville boy, whose friendly smile was wiped from his face when Melicent began to gush.

'Why thank you, Master Granville.' The boy gave an awkward bow and was about to escape when Melicent, with the archness she always assumed in male company of any age, continued, 'What do you have to say about the dreadful event that occurred so recently in your own grounds? But there, young lads thrive upon such excitements, do they not?' Charlotte bit her lip in exasperation and made to move forward as the boy glared at his persecutor, his cheeks suddenly pale. He turned on his heel and walked away. Charlotte relaxed for a moment until she heard a sudden sound, a sharp intake of breath perhaps, or a slight groan. She whipped round, puzzled, and wondering if someone had been taken ill. Lady Granville was staring at the group still standing by the wassail bowl, her face looking unaccountably drawn and heavy, as she looked from one to the other then cast a glance in the direction of her son's fast-disappearing back view.

'Is something wrong, Lady Granville?' Charlotte's whisper was discreet as she wondered whether the lady was feeling quite the thing. Indeed, Charlotte considered, since the recent contretemps concerning the glass of punch, the older woman was looking distinctly unwell, a light sheen of sweat masking her face.

'No – no, thank you,' came the response, followed by a slight gesture, her fingers tightening on a handkerchief she clutched, as she reinforced the negative. Then she paused, still staring over at the other guests. 'No,' she said slowly, looking round at Charlotte, her expression very thoughtful, with narrowed eyes and tightly folded lips. She hesitated and started to speak again. 'No, indeed.' She glanced across the room once more and seemed to straighten her shoulders. 'I cannot say. It is just that....' She pressed the folded linen handkerchief to her lips for a moment, then shook her head once more, but Charlotte glimpsed an odd glimmer in the large dark brown eyes as Lady Granville, after a final, considering stare at Charlotte, turned away, muttering, 'Three times. I believe that is three times.... What can it mean?'

Good gracious, Charlotte thought, and stood politely aside to let the illustrious guest precede her. Wondering about that enigmatic little aside, she accompanied Lady Granville to find her outdoor wrappings, when something that had been teasing her about the lady's manner suddenly dawned upon her. Sarah Siddons, the great tragic actress; that was who was called to mind by Lady Granville's air of simmering anxiety. Not that Charlotte had ever been privileged to attend one of the lady's dramatic performances, but her godmother, Lady Meg, had certainly done so as a young girl.

'Astonishing woman,' Meg had told her, shaking her head. 'I had nightmares for weeks after I saw her as Lady Macbeth.'

There was no need to act as ladies' maid, for the nondescript companion must have been on constant watch and was on hand to shroud her mistress in a sumptuous sealskin mantle

'Pray do not forget, Mrs Richmond,' Lady Granville, who now resembled nothing so much as an enormous Arctic mammal, turned a surprisingly gracious smile to Charlotte, all tragic under-tones now vanished. 'I shall be delighted to show you my garden tomorrow and to give you tea. I believe you reside with Lady Frampton? Naturally if she would care to accompany you I should be delighted. Shall we say at a quarter to three? If you like to arrive a little early there will be daylight enough to take a brief turn round the garden, although sadly this is not the most favourable time to be looking at plants.' She took her husband's arm. 'Come, my dear,' she said firmly, as she beckoned her son to her side.

When most of the remaining guests had been waved on their way, Lady Frampton was happily enthroned in her favourite seat by the hearth and in no hurry to go home to Rowan Lodge, so Charlotte went in search of her hostess to see if she could be of any help.

A chance remark soon had Lily Richmond opening her eyes wide and turning up her already distressingly retroussé nose.

'What's that you say, Char? Barnard? Barnard, come here at once and listen to this, I never heard of such a thing.' Her light voice, with its little girl notes, was rising with indignation. 'Now look here, Barnard. Here is Charlotte telling me that she has been invited to take tea with Lady Granville tomorrow afternoon. What can have put such a notion into her ladyship's head?'

Charlotte sighed, recognising the signs of an impending tantrum, as an ominous frown drew Lily's finely drawn dark brows together and the rosebud lips formed a distinct pout. 'But, Lily....' she began.

'I cannot understand it,' Lily continued, ignoring the interruption, a tinge of ice entering her voice. 'Why her ladyship has not even invited *me* to take tea with her, and we are quite the most intimate of friends now. So why in heaven's name do you suppose she should she invite Charlotte, whom she has never seen before in her life?'

'Well, Lily,' Barnard Richmond weighed in with well-meaning goodwill, rolling an anguished eye nonetheless at Charlotte as he spoke. 'I daresay her ladyship means it as a compliment to you, my dear.' He floundered as he met Lily's scornful gaze. 'I mean, er, I expect she is merely being kind to our dear Charlotte.'

Charlotte hastened to his rescue. 'Of course she is, Lily dear,' she said in a soothing tone. 'Why, she is naturally aware that, apart from taking tea at the Deanery the other day, you are not officially visiting at the moment, because of dear little Algy being so very young. I believe Lady Granville only decided to invite me as a very poor second choice.' Lily's brow showed signs of looking less thundery so Charlotte persevered. 'It is only that she wishes to show me her garden, after all. I have observed that dedicated garden lovers will seize on the most unlikely persons to enthuse about their plants and walks and shrubberies and so forth, and I believe the invitation to tea was a mere polite afterthought. Besides, you must not forget that I am quite unusual in these parts; someone who has come from the other side of the world. She probably thinks I'm something of a curiosity. Like a talking pig.'

Charlotte was saved from Lily's astonished demand as to her meaning, by the appearance of Kit Knightley, whose conversation with Barnard had been interrupted by Lily's call.

'Pray forgive me, Mrs Richmond.' The gleam in his blue eyes indicated to Charlotte that he had overheard her surprising simile, but he merely smiled at Lily and bent over her hand. 'I must tear myself away from this felicitous occasion. I am glad to have seen my godson safely baptised and must thank you once more for doing me such a great honour in making me a sponsor.'

Mollified, Lily said her farewells and Barnard clapped his old school friend on the shoulder and muttered, with rough but sincere affection, 'My very best wishes to Mrs Knightley, my dear fellow. I hope to hear that she goes on well.'

The twinkle in Kit's eyes dimmed as he answered with a word-less nod and reached out a hand to clasp that of his friend. He turned to Charlotte and she read the distress in his face with an answering dismay. Kit's invalid wife, Elaine, was Charlotte's dearest friend in the entire world, and Elaine's health, which had always been precarious, had sharply deteriorated in the last couple of months.

'Come and see Elaine, Char,' he said, holding up a hand to stop the anxious flow of questions that sprang to her lips. There was a roughness in his voice as he added, 'I know it's Christmas and I expect you'll have little time to spare from the jollifications at the Manor, but…. Make it soon.'

Chapter 4

Next afternoon saw Charlotte set out in the brougham borrowed from the manor, ready to make a call in state upon her illustrious neighbour.

'Walk, do you say?' Lady Frampton was scandalised at the idea. 'Lord above, gal, what in the world can 'ave got into you? There's a murderer loose about the countryside, you could come upon him at any turn of the road. And anyway, you h'ought to know by now that there's a time and a place when it's not done to go walking about so free and easy as you do.' She shook her head in stern admonition. 'And going to visit 'er fine ladyship for the first time, is one of them times. No, Char, I mean it, I'll make Barnard put his foot down, you see if I don't. Besides, you'll give offence, make no mistake about it, and raise eyebrows too, if you swan in to Brambrook Abbey with your hem trailing mud and your boots in a state, not to mention your bonnet soaking wet. I know you like walking, though Gawd knows why you should is beyond me. But it ain't done, Char, mark my words.'

So here I am, sighed Charlotte, condemned to propriety. The manor groom clucked to the bay horse, so much more elegant and sleek than the fat pony she and Lady Frampton were accustomed to when they used the pony chaise. They set off at a sedate pace, skirting the green of Finchbourne village, and down Pot Kiln Lane opposite. It seemed highly unlikely that the murderer would be lurking around the village when surely he would have made off towards Southampton, say, to disappear into the busy alleyways near the docks, but she could not give Lady Frampton an anxious hour or two by disobeying her. Having reluctantly accepted the old lady's dictum that Charlotte must uphold the honour of

Finchbourne Manor and the Richmond family, she was arrayed in her second-best winter dress, a becoming golden-brown, silk and merino blend.

Charlotte's plain gowns were the despair of Lily Richmond. 'I'm tall and skinny,' she tried to explain to her sister-in-law. 'Although, if you insist, I'll admit to being just passable, I'm far too lanky to look well in feminine fripperies. It's all right for you, Lily, you're little; frills and flounces become you. I'd look like the village maypole decked out in that pink dress you wanted me to have.'

Gran approved today's outfit, the high neck trimmed with a ruched satin-ribbon which, like yesterday's dress, was pinned with Lady Meg's gold acanthus leaf brooch. To keep out the cold, Charlotte wore a warm coat and carried a shawl offered by Lady Frampton. 'My 'usband's second cousin's daughter sent it, silly wench, as if I 'aven't worn naught but black this thirty years. You take it, young Char, it'll go with that dress of yours.' The brown and yellow paisley swirls were not really to Charlotte's taste but she was glad of the warmth, and Gran was right: it did go with the brown merino.

If only Will and Ma could see me, she sighed, picturing their astonishment at her prosperous appearance. 'As fine as five-pence,' Will would have exclaimed, and followed it by circling round her, amused and admiring, and pointing out that Char 'was a proper lady now, and no mistake.' Ladylike, she corrected that laughing ghost. I am swathed in fur rugs against the cold and dressed as a lady should be, with due decorum and no vulgar outward display, but I'm not sure I'm really a lady, not yet. Her eyes danced at the memory of a younger, coltish Charlotte running barefoot along a deserted southern shore, scantily clad in a faded muslin dress that had seen better days. The amusement waned as she recalled herself to the present.

No more blissful, childish ignorance, she scolded herself; no more looking backwards and sighing for the moon, yearning for those who were dead and gone this many a day. This afternoon I am the young, respectable, widowed Mrs Richmond from Rowan Lodge, kin to the Squire at Finchbourne Manor, with a wardrobe full of becoming dresses, and I am off to visit a real, live lady. A ladyship, no less and, according to Lily Richmond, a lady who was descended from a long line of impeccably-connected but impoverished nobles, hence her marriage to the wealthy but undistinguished Lord Granville. (Lily had an encyclopaedic knowledge of the ins and outs of the nobility and enjoyed nothing more than poring over the London papers to discover who was engaged to whom and whether or not some long-awaited heir had yet made his appearance. As Barnard, with bewildered pride, had told Charlotte, 'Lily knows all about everyone in the stud book.')

When the carriage turned into the drive, Charlotte felt a slight shiver of apprehension but dismissed it at once, irritated at her silliness. Her eyes opened wide in astonishment as the brougham drew up before the front door of Brambrook Abbey. Someone in the not too distant past had manifestly fallen prey to an architect who favoured the Gothic style in country houses. Barnard Richmond had mentioned that the Abbey was a relatively new establishment, dating back a mere sixty or so years, so Charlotte had somehow convinced herself that she would see a red brick mansion, brick, and flint also, being prevalent amid the vernacular architecture of Hampshire.

Lord Granville's enormous and imposing home was more a castle than a house, bristling with turrets, awash with pointed windows and with gargoyles by the dozen, leering down from every gutter spout. The grey stone was forbidding so that the whole resembled something from *The Mysteries of Udolpho* and similar gothic novels enjoyed by Charlotte and her mother. The crowning embellishment was a shallow moat that looked suspiciously like a working portcullis and drawbridge. It was set in a stone portal over which the brougham was now clattering. There were even pikes, she noted with an amused grimace, set above the grim gateway, though mercifully none bore the severed head that would have seemed appropriate. A shudder ran through her as she recalled that however artificial the castle might be, it was no stranger to recent terrible events.

Once through the portal and away from the outer wall, there was a sweep of gravel, where the carriage came to a halt outside the house, though Charlotte thought it should rather be described as a keep. This was set upon a slight rise, overlooking a heavily ornate fountain, sprouting naiads and dryads and others of that ilk. Charlotte, gazing at it with a critical eye, trained by her knowledgeable godmother, decided it was a little late for the mediaeval period and was surely a baroque creation. As the groom opened the carriage door, Charlotte glanced around nervously and was relieved to see the massive, heavily-carved and studded oak door flung open to reveal Oz Granville standing at the top of the short flight of steps, a smile of hospitable delight on his fair, freckled face.

'You came after all, ma'am!' he exclaimed, running down to greet her, his hand outstretched. 'I did start to worry whether you would cry off.'

She felt sorry for the boy, all over again, as she had at the church on the previous day. What must his life be like if a mere courtesy visit from a neighbour could loom so large?

'Of course I came, you foolish Oz. I'm most intrigued at the prospect of seeing your Mama's garden and I'm only sorry to have to convey Lady Frampton's apologies. She likes to rest in the afternoons and after all, she is more than eighty years old, you know.'

And she's a cockney and not in the least interested in chilly winter gardens either. Charlotte concealed a smile at the dismay on the old lady's face when presented with the invitation. 'Wot? Parade myself round a garden in this weather? I'd catch me death of cold. No, you go and enjoy yourself but be certain to wear a flannel petticoat to keep you warm, and just be sure you don't sound too 'appy when you report on the visit to our Lily. She's still ready to poke out your eyes for getting an invite from 'er Ladyship before she does, don't forget.'

The butler now loomed towards her and tenderly divested her of her outer garments, then the boy, who had hopped impatiently from one foot to the other throughout these proceedings, led her through the vaulted and echoing Great Hall. This was a lofty, stone-clad place, double or even treble the normal height, and embellished with carvings in every possible nook and cranny. Well-tutored by her godmother, Charlotte recognised Norman dogtooth doorways, while a sulky winter sun fought with gas lights in the shape of antique torches as it shed pools of light on the marble floor from the brightly coloured stained glass in the windows. Enormous pieces of supposedly mediaeval furniture offered no prospect of comfort, had anyone dared to sit upon them.

Glimpsed through a wide-open, heavily-carved and gilded door, was a vast dining-room with a monumental table made from a massive slab of blackened oak perched on bulbous carved legs and surrounded by carved chairs that looked to combine ugliness with extreme discomfort. Through another door she saw a drawing-room, papered in black and gold. Oz Granville led his guest out of the hall to a smaller chamber where his mother, upholstered in purple cashmere trimmed with black velvet ribbons and flounces, and wearing a formidable lace cap also trimmed with purple and black, rose to meet them, laying aside a large, leather-bound volume as she did so.

'A history of England,' Lady Granville explained as she graciously accepted the apologies Charlotte presented on behalf of Lady Frampton. 'Or rather, a history of the Queens of England, one of my great interests, although I must confess that my garden absorbs most of my time.' Her fond glance at the flaxen-haired boy jigging impatiently beside her, showed where the bulk of her interests lay and Charlotte found herself warming to such an open display of affection. Lady Granville kept her son waiting for a few moments while she waved a hand round at the room. 'This is the morning-room, Mrs Richmond,' she explained. 'I find it so much more comfortable than the rest of the Abbey that I tend to spend most of my time here.' She drew Charlotte's atten-tion to the Chinese wallpaper and the ebony furniture, adding complacently that it contained the only chimney in the entire house that did not have a tendency to smoke when the wind was in the north.

Charlotte could well believe that, having observed the smoke stains on the stone lintels above the vast twin fireplaces in the Great Hall. She felt at a loss as she wondered whether condolences on the recent tragedy would be welcomed but, on reflection, she remem-bered that Barnard and Lily had said all that was needful, so she kept quiet. An attentive footman, clad in an immaculate livery of dark blue, appeared with Charlotte's outer garments, which he helped her to resume. He then silently bowed them out so obsequiously that his periwigged head almost reached waist level.

The lady of the house, now clad in her sealskin mantle, sailed haughtily through the door without a glance at the servant, but Charlotte was pleased to see that the boy grinned and made a kind of jaunty salute in thanks.

'*Always be polite to the servants, Char,*' had been her godmother's advice. '*They see everything, hear everything and know everything and can be a gold mine of information if they are so disposed.*' Meg had looked mischievous as she added, '*And believe me, they can cover up your misdemeanours too, if they like you.*'

Outside was a wide, gravelled walk, edged by a clipped yew hedge that reached to a height of about six feet, with a heavy wooden door set into an archway cut into the dense foliage.

'I keep the garden door locked,' Lady Granville remarked as she took an ornate key from her pocket. 'It is my private sanctuary and the gardeners only enter at my command.'

Looking through the entrance Charlotte saw something like a ruined castle at the far end of the garden, ivy-covered and sporting gaping windows at the top, arrow slits winding upwards around a circular tower, the whole surmounted by a crenellated battlement. A flagpole crowned the ruins and from it, a long, silken banner floated in the slight breeze.

Lady Granville said nothing but kept a watchful eye on her guest as she waved her through the archway. A smile of gratification lightened the severity of her features at Charlotte's exclamation.

'But … but it's Camelot!' She turned to her hostess with her hands lifted in a gesture that seemed to encompass the scene before her eyes. 'It's an enchanted garden. How wonderful.'

'It is almost my greatest treasure,' confided the older woman and exchanged a smile of comprehension with her guest as, once again, Charlotte read clearly the message as to what was, without a doubt, her most beloved treasure.

'I had no idea.' Charlotte was released from the spell that had held her poised in the arched gateway and she flitted about the garden, discovering more and more delightful surprises. 'I can't believe how colourful it all is, even at this time of year,' she said, waving her hand at the glowing scarlet berries on the holly tree in the corner and glancing up at the mistletoe, with its mother-of-pearl fruit, hanging in clusters from an apple tree. 'Surely some of these trees are very ancient, Lady Granville?' She looked at the holly again and then, doubtfully, at the apple tree as she spoke. 'But the garden must be of a more recent date, if you designed it yourself?'

Lady Granville shook her head. 'Indeed it is. I built the garden around the trees,' she explained. 'The apple tree is only about twenty years old, I planted it myself, but the other trees were here first, the holly and the Queen's Yew over in the corner.'

At Charlotte's look of enquiry, the other woman nodded. 'There is an old story that says Queen Eleanor of Provence, wife of Henry III, spent time visiting the abbey that is said to have graced this spot. It seemed a pleasant conceit to me, when I decided to design a garden to suit the mansion put up by my father-in-law, to call the garden after the queen and to stock it only with plants that grew in the olden days.'

Charlotte's eyes were bright as she continued her exploration, aware that her interest was giving considerable pleasure to Lady Granville, who looked, Charlotte decided, as though she needed to smile more frequently. 'Goodness,' she said, stooping to look at a long walk bordered with sword-like green leaves. 'What on earth are these? The berries are the most brilliant orange I've seen since my arrival in England.'

'That's called Stinking Iris,' explained Oz Granville, interrupting with a snort of laughter. 'If you crush the leaves and stems it stinks.'

Charlotte raised a sardonic eyebrow and allowed him to hand her a leaf which she obediently crushed, though declining, with a laugh, to hold it to her nose, until his pleading gaze made her change her mind. 'Another name for it is Roast Beef Plant,' he informed her as she wrinkled her nose at the smell. 'Mama likes it for the bright colours.'

'Oh dear, with such an unpleasant smell, you would expect it be poisonous.' Charlotte was surprised to see a frown eclipse her hostess's earlier amusement at her idle remark.

'I believe the roots should be avoided,' was the careless answer. 'I prefer not to dwell on that aspect of my plants, however. The beauty of the berries is sufficient for my pleasure though the flower itself is quite lovely, in varying shades of a brownish-purple and yellow.' Her enthusiasm was engaging as she eagerly drew Charlotte along the path to admire first this favourite, and then another.

'Osbert is quite correct,' she admitted with another of those doting smiles, 'when he says I am particularly fond of the brightly coloured berries. A garden in winter can be so bleak, after all, but with careful planting, I believe I have overcome that disadvantage.' She waved her hand in an expansive gesture. 'You see, Mrs Richmond? Small black berries on the ivy that clothes the ruins; scarlet berries on the honeysuckle along the vine walk; purplish red ones there on the St John's Wort. There are colours everywhere, as you so observantly remarked when you entered the garden.'

'Indeed there are.' Charlotte found herself being disarmed by the other woman's enthusiasm. There was a glow in her dark eyes that spoke of a passion and eagerness about her 'treasure', that showed an appealing side to the woman Charlotte had thought dull at first meeting. She turned eagerly to her hostess. 'My stepfather told me of a knot garden at his … his childhood home, but I gathered it was much more formal than this one.'

'Knot gardens were a later development in the art of gardening,' Lady Granville informed her and was soon well away on the history of planting, not noticing her guest's far-away expression as she looked back down the years. During an unusual period of peace and stability Molly Glover had decided to plant a garden, and she had been nettled by Will's amused criticism of their efforts.

'What do you know about gardens, anyway?' Molly had snapped in a rare moment of annoyance with her adored husband. Suddenly sobering, Will had stared at the straggling plants and answered wistfully, *'My mother loved gardening and it was her great pride that she brought back the gardens to life, particularly the knot garden, after my grandfather died and my father….'* Had he been going to say, 'When my father inherited?' Charlotte wondered, with a sigh and a shrug of her shoulders. No point in speculating about her irresistible but

unreliable stepfather's family. Hints, carelessly dropped and hastily brushed aside, had given her the distinct impression that Will's family were well-connected and wealthy, but then … she sighed again. Will had been a consummate actor, so it could all have been one of his games.

The garden was not large and because of the high brick wall surrounding it there was a feeling of tranquillity and silence, although it was not, in truth, very far from the bustle of the stables. When Charlotte found herself at the crossroads of two paths, the intersection marked by a sundial, she turned to survey the various segments of the garden. At the far end stood the ruin, stark and dramatically wreathed in ivy, with a spiral staircase, its artistically ruined windows open to the air in some places, and leading, she assumed, to the crenellated tower at the top. She was amused by the bravely-fluttering pennant, a surprising piece of whimsy on the part of her stately hostess.

'Does the tower date back to the abbey that you understood to be here in Queen Eleanor's time?' she asked with interest. 'It certainly looks very ancient, with those gaping holes in the walls.'

Lady Granville looked delighted but shook her head. 'That is what you are supposed to believe,' she said. 'In fact, the tower was erected around the turn of the century, some years after the house was built by my late father-in-law, the first Lord Granville. He was the only son of a wealthy mill owner from Lancashire, but the climate there never suited his wife, who came from the south. She claimed that the north was too prone to damp, I believe. He had turned gentleman and made sure of a title,' her ladyship's mouth primmed in evident disapproval of such a proceeding, 'so he stuck a pin in an atlas and determined to build a house to suit himself, wherever the pin landed. Sadly, his lady did not live to enjoy her new home, or the new tower, and expired shortly after she moved here when my husband was a child. However, my father-in-law lived to a great age and added many improvements and embellishments to the place.'

Charlotte nodded her thanks for this explanation and gazed round the garden. 'I believe I see your herb bed,' she said slowly, pointing to a plot edged with rosemary. 'And there are fruit trees along the wall, but what is that small enclosure over there? It looks for all the world like a seat made of grass.'

'Come and see.' Oz Granville had tired of kicking stones at the wall of the ruin, stoutly ignoring his mother's plaintive protests. 'Mama copied the idea from some old picture or other.' He stood back to allow Charlotte to see that the seats, arranged in a square with a gap for entry, were indeed covered in turf.

'Just as they would have been in the thirteenth century,' Lady Granville told her, clearly pleased with Charlotte's delighted comments. Suddenly her good humour vanished and she whisked her skirts aside. 'Oh, that wretched animal. Osbert, shoo that cat away at once, if you please.'

A rangy-looking ginger cat sidled up to Oz and was greeting him with delight. Charlotte surprised a guilty look on the boy's face as he tried to do his mother's bidding.

'Don't touch it,' the lady almost shrieked, all the while keeping well away from the animal. 'Filthy creature, you will catch fleas from it. I shall have the gardener drown it.'

'No, you mustn't,' cried the boy. 'It belongs to the children at the lodge. Please give me the key to the other gate, Mama. I'll get rid of it this minute.'

He ran down the garden, followed happily by the cat, and thrust it through the gate at the far end. Charlotte was surprised to see him hesitate as he looked outside, but all she could discern in the gloom was the castle drive, which looped round the garden wall at that point. Lady Granville was still glowering but regained her usual composure by the time Oz rejoined them.

'I was telling you about the ruins, was I not?' she turned to her guest. 'When I married I took great delight in furnishing the house in an appropriate style. My husband's father had lost heart when his wife died, so the furniture was of no great interest or value. I spent many years travelling round the country, visiting abbeys and priories, some in ruins and others which had been converted to houses, so that I might discover the correct tables, beds and chairs, and so forth.'

She pursed her lips, looking a little wistful, Charlotte thought, and went on, 'I became, if you like, a connoisseur of abbeys, I visited so many. I went to Fountains in Yorkshire, Gracedieu in Oxfordshire, Cleeve in Somerset, Walsingham....' There was an awkward little pause, then she said, again, softly, 'Yes, Walsingham.' As Charlotte looked at her, enquiry in her glance, she straightened up and nodded. 'Now, I must not keep you out in the cold,' she said, with a gracious smile. 'Osbert has a delicate chest so let us take a final turn about the garden and then we will go indoors for tea.'

Charlotte thought it was as well that Oz Granville's devoted mother could not see the scowl that briefly disfigured her son's face, but she made no remark and followed in the lady's wake. She was very glad of her warm clothes; the onset of twilight brought a freezing wind, though her hostess seemed impervious to the temperature.

Lady Granville led them to the vine tunnel and the trellises that supported more ivy, and drew attention to a hawthorn hedge, and another formed by the prickly shoots of sweetbriar. Where the land sloped gently away from the house, there was a stream that ran along the outer edge of the garden on the east side, bisected by a small, calm pool with a stone seat carefully positioned for contemplation. When the stream reached the ancient yew tree in the corner, it was culverted and ran, so Oz told her, down into the moat. He also told her that his mother believed the yew to be at least a thousand years old and Charlotte stared in astonishment and awe at the gnarled and twisted branches with their few withered red berries.

The names of the plants enchanted the young woman from the far side of the world. Rosa gallica, which Lady Granville informed her, was a red rose, emblem of Queen Eleanor, and which later became the rose of Lancaster; beside it grew Rosa alba, famed as the white rose of York. Seeing her interest, Lady Granville tossed some more names at her, at random: Rampion and Purslane, for use in salads; Herb Robert and Mouse-ear for medicinal use.

She broke off from her catalogue of planting, to cast a further anxious glance at the darkening sky and at her son and soon, with a brief apology, she hustled Charlotte and Oz back into the house to where tea awaited them in her sitting room.

'Next time you come to tea,' Oz told his guest, 'You must climb up to the battlements of the ruin. It's a splendid place to play at being besieged.'

Charlotte smiled assent. 'The battlements are really accessible then?' she asked Lady Granville. 'I supposed them to be mere make-believe.'

'Oh no,' Oz hastened to assure her before his mother could respond. 'There's a spiral staircase with arrow slits, and down at the foot of the tower Mama has a small room that is built into the wall.'

'I like to keep my gardening tools at hand,' Lady Granville nodded to Charlotte. 'The head gardener would prefer me not to work in the garden myself, but I find planting and weeding a soothing occupation.'

Conversation became general but Charlotte felt she had given satisfaction by the sincerity of her reaction to the garden and when even Oz had mopped the crumbs from his mouth with his napkin, Charlotte ventured a suggestion.

'I wonder, Lady Granville,' she said with some diffidence, 'If you would agree to something my brother-in-law has asked me to propose?'

Her hostess, still apparently under the softening influence of a guest whose interests chimed with her own, expressed mild curiosity, so Charlotte continued.

'Barnard wondered whether your son would enjoy a day out with him,' she said. 'Tomorrow is the day when he will be visiting all his tenants, his Christmas visit, you understand, and it occurred to him that as your lands march with those of the Manor, it would be an opportunity for your son to re-acquaint himself with some of the people. Barnard would take the greatest care of – of Osbert,' (she cast a brief glance of apology towards the boy, at the use of the hated name). 'And he is of the opinion that the farmers would be delighted to see him.'

Charlotte could see that Lady Granville was in two minds about the proposal.

'How kind of Mr Richmond,' she said slowly. 'Now we are to spend more time in Hampshire, it is in Osbert's interest to become known to the lower orders. It has to be tomorrow, does it? There is no chance that Mr Richmond might postpone the visits till after Christmas?'

'I'm afraid not,' said Charlotte; she looked demure and stretched out her foot to give Oz a surreptitious kick under cover of the table, as he had his mouth open to protest. He subsided at once with a grunt, looking at her in surprise, but quickly took her hint and remained silent. 'Christmas Eve is the customary day and my brother-in-law is a stickler for tradition.'

'Quite rightly so,' the lady appeared to be giving in with a good grace. 'Very well, Mrs Richmond, Osbert shall accept this kind invitation. My only regret is that his father and I must be elsewhere, as we are spending the day with the Bishop.'

Charlotte congratulated herself that her expression combined, very skilfully, pleasure at the treat Osbert's presence would bestow upon Barnard, together with regret that the Manor should be deprived of the presence of Osbert's parents. In fact, she had over-heard Lord Granville the day before, discussing the impending visit with the vicar.

She rose to take her farewell and at a moment when her hostess's attention was distracted, Charlotte managed to whisper in the boy's ear. 'Not a word,' she hissed. 'But Barnard tells me there will be ratting in the barn tomorrow, and I think you'll enjoy it. Try to smuggle some old clothes with you.'

Shaking her head at him as his face lit up in eager anticipation, Charlotte was at the entrance to the Great Hall when in scurried Lady Granville's companion, all aflame and aflutter with excitement.

'Oh, my lady,' she gasped, fanning herself with a gloved hand, as Lady Granville stared at her in well-bred distaste. 'Oh my lady! Such news, such terrible news. I am this moment come from Winchester, where if you recall, you said I might use the governess cart, and I have heard such distressing tidings.'

'Well?' Lady Granville's voice held no encouragement. 'You had better enlighten us, Cole. What has happened that is so dreadful?'

Unabashed, Miss Cole, whose ungainly loops of pepper and salt hair dangled beneath her unbecoming bonnet, caught her breath and disburdened herself of her news. 'It seems that one of the ladies who was at the christening yesterday – one of two sisters who were visitors to Winchester – was taken violently ill yesterday shortly after leaving Finchbourne, and now, after all remedies have failed, it is announced that she has *died!*'

Chapter 5

CHARLOTTE'S SHOCKED GASP echoed the sharply indrawn breath taken by Lady Granville as they stared in dismay at the companion. She, in turn, was gazing eagerly at her mistress, awaiting the lady's reception of this news. Miss Cole's mouth drooped once more as neither Charlotte nor her hostess spoke, so the companion rushed into further rattling speech.

'If you remember, my lady, I had been invited to spend the day with my acquaintance in the town, the one whose husband has an upholstery business there. We were partaking of a dainty and most excellent tea.' she paused, fondly reminiscent, before continuing, 'when suddenly, her good husband (a most respectable man, and quite the gentleman, I do assure you) burst into the room, with a hurried apology for the intrusion, and said, was it true that I had been a guest at the christening yesterday, for the young heir to Finchbourne Manor? Naturally I corrected him, explaining that my presence there was not in the character of a guest, but that I was, of course, in attendance upon your ladyship. He was most genteel in his apology for being the bearer of distressing news and he then went on to tell us the sad tidings that he had heard from one of his apprentices, just moments before.'

As she gabbled her news, Miss Cole stripped off her gloves and fanned herself with them, the plump face glistening and avidly pink with excitement and a kind of pleasure, her small eyes turning from Charlotte to Lady Granville. 'The apprentice has a sister, apparently, who is one of the maids at the lodging where the unfortunate lady passed to her maker.'

'Which of the sisters was it that died, Cole?' Lady Granville's manner was abrupt as she asked the question although to

Charlotte, she appeared, not surprisingly, to be a trifle pale and abstracted, and clearly shocked. 'And did your acquaintance inform you of the cause of this untimely death?'

Not one whit daunted by her mistress's dismissive reception of her news, Miss Cole hurried to reply, 'I gather it was the younger sister, my lady, a sweetly pretty young creature, with fair hair and such a dainty pink gown, married to a medical gentleman from London, I believe.' She shook her head in sad contemplation of such a premature end but Charlotte was aware of an undercurrent of almost gleeful excitement. 'I have no information as to what caused her sad demise.'

At that moment Lord Granville entered the room, only to stare in astonishment at the excited companion. 'What's this, what's this? Found another body, Cole? Hey?'

Ignoring his wife's expression of distaste at his ill-timed jest, Lord Granville listened in growing horror to the tale of woe. 'I heard tell that the grieving widower, together with the other young lady, is to set off to London this very evening,' Miss Cole told them. 'And who can blame them if they never return after such a tragedy.'

Lord Granville looked very shocked but at her last comment he looked thoughtful. He frowned, then nodded, and gave the companion a kindly pat on her shoulder, as he said, 'Well, well, that is probably all for the best,' before turning away to leave the room once more.

Charlotte dragged herself out of the horrified silence that had affected her. 'I must go home at once,' she turned to Lady Granville with an apology. 'Lily and Barnard will be beside themselves with anxiety and grief at this dreadful occurrence, so close upon the lady's visit to Finchbourne. I must see if I can be of any help to them.' She shook the hand that was held out to her and pressed her thanks upon Lady Granville. 'I have so much enjoyed my visit this afternoon, ma'am,' she told her warmly. 'I do admire your skill and vision so much. I'm so sorry to leave on a sad note, but...' she hesitated, and a glimpse of a fair head poking round the door encouraged her, 'I do trust you will still allow your son to visit the Manor tomorrow? Even in the midst of tragedy, I am quite certain that Barnard will not deviate from tradition, so he will collect

Master Granville at nine o'clock tomorrow morning. I'm sure my brother-in-law will look after him well.'

Her hostess nodded then gave a distracted frown. 'Now what did I.... Ah, I recall now, this shocking intelligence has made my wits go begging, but yes, I have caused the gardener to place two bouquets of hothouse flowers in your carriage, Mrs Richmond. A slight token of esteem for Lady Frampton and Mrs Barnard Richmond, in the hope that we may renew our friendship in the not too distant future,' she gave a satisfied nod as Charlotte offered suitable delight and gratitude, and added, 'and naturally I have had a posy prepared for you, my dear. That, however, is composed of some of my own favourite hyacinths. I fancy you are at one with me in preferring them and my gardener brings them on especially for me.'

Alone in the brougham, Charlotte heaved a troubled sigh and lifted her elegant little posy of white hyacinths to her nose, savouring the delicious scent. It had been a pleasant interlude, strolling round the unusual, jewel-bright little garden, lit by the pale winter sun, with the hitherto unbending Lady Granville suddenly transformed into a human being. What of this news though, that one of the previous day's guests at the manor had died? Hard upon the heels too, of the death of Lady Granville's maid.

That pretty, silken young woman, with her laughter and the mocking tilt of her head as she surveyed her fellow guests, to have died so suddenly! The afternoon's diversion was driven from her mind, but wait.... Charlotte had a sudden memory of the pompous Dr Chant trying to stop his wife from drinking so much of the wassail brew, only for the young lady to laugh and make some comment about her condition. Perhaps that was it; some unforeseen complication of early pregnancy.

It was an obvious and plausible explanation, but why, Charlotte wondered, did she feel such a weight of unease? There could be no connection between Lady Granville's maid, Maria Dunster's, unfortunate killing by the reported burly man and the sad death of a guest of the manor. It was a coincidence, nothing more. Still, she racked her brains to try to discover what it was that was making her feel so unsettled, so uncomfortable. What had occurred at yesterday's celebration to set her mind racing thus?

She directed the coachman to take her back to Rowan Lodge by way of the Manor, so that she could check on Lily's reaction to the news. Shock and sadness were inevitable, Charlotte thought, but knowing Lily, she believed that the young woman would also be entertaining a lively fear regarding the possible social stigma pertaining to a sudden death following so close upon a party at Finchbourne. I think I'd better make sure Lily isn't making poor Barnard's life a misery, Charlotte decided, though he'll surely be feeling that this reflects upon the hospitality of the house too.

'Char, thank God.' That was Barnard, his broad face a little less ruddy of hue than was usual, his manner a little less bluff and hearty. 'You will have heard the news? Good girl, I knew I could rely on you to come to our aid. Lily is in the drawing-room. Here, follow me and let me pour you a glass of sherry; we all need a drop of something to strengthen our nerves.'

Even in the midst of her distress, Lily could not fail to be gratified by the flowers Lady Granville had sent her and she sat playing with them in her lap after Charlotte had greeted her with a kiss of sympathy and a brief explanation of the bouquet's provenance.

'Have you any information on the cause of this sudden dreadful illness?' Charlotte sat down beside Lily and sipped thoughtfully at the sherry Barnard handed her. 'I assume her husband was at her side? Miss Nightingale told me that Dr Chant is most highly thought of in the Capital, so every precaution must surely have been taken. Poor young lady, she can have been no more than twenty-five or six, at the most, do you not think?'

'It was a sudden attack of biliousness,' Lily's spirits had revived sufficiently to allow her to join in the conversation. 'I received a short note not an hour ago from Miss Armstrong, the elder sister as I'm sure you will recall. She apologised for importuning upon me but she wondered if she might beg a bed from tomorrow, for a night or two. She has no other acquaintance in Winchester, apart from the Dean's wife and she could hardly impose on a cathedral dignitary at Christmas.'

Charlotte was startled. 'But Lady Granville's woman said that

Miss Armstrong and Dr Chant were returning to London this evening?'

'Oh, no,' Lily was adamant. 'She is quite mistaken; how *do* these rumours get around? Our kitchen maid brought home that, and several other tales, when she returned after her half-day in Winchester. I have the letter here, from Miss Armstrong, who states that Dr Chant informs her that his wife's body will be interred in Winchester at the earliest opportunity, and that he will be glad if she would vacate the rooms which his wife engaged last week, when the sisters arrived in Hampshire for a short holiday together. The rooms are wanted and tomorrow is the final day of their week for I believe they planned to return to London then.'

Lily looked sharply at Charlotte, her plump, inquisitive little face shorn of its usual artifice. 'I understand the rent for the rooms would be beyond Miss Armstrong's means, in any case. I also gained the impression that there is no love-lost between husband and sister and that this little vacation was arranged without the doctor's knowledge, still less his permission.' She pouted, 'Unfortunately, I did not have occasion to discover just why they don't get on.' She drew her fine, dark brows together, then continued, 'Dr Chant was not residing in the same house and Miss Armstrong says that her sister's sickness increased until she herself became alarmed and sent for a local doctor, but it was too late and the poor young lady's final breaths were taken sometime in the small hours.'

'Very sad, very sad.' That was Barnard, interrupting Charlotte who had her mouth open to speak. 'But Char, what if the poor lady died as a result of something she ate here? At young Algy's christening party?' He pulled out a large handkerchief from his pocket and mopped his brow, looking more like a doleful prize bullock than ever. 'I doubt I should ever recover from the mortification,' he announced, his voice tailing away in a doom-laden rumble.

'Dear Barnard,' Charlotte rose and spoke forcefully, giving him a reassuring squeeze to his beefy, muscled arm. 'Stop this fretting at once. Now, sit down, take another glass of sherry and listen to me. Good,' she nodded approval as the large, anxious creature obeyed her. 'First of all, I have not been ill and neither has Grandmama. Have you, Lily? Or Barnard? Of course you have not. Have you heard that anyone else has been taken ill after yesterday's party? There you are then.'

She smiled at him and went on, 'If there had been something amiss with any of the dishes you served yesterday, you would certainly have been inundated with messages about other guests also suffering. You know what Dr Perry is like; had he been called to attend any bedsides, he'd have been up here, hot foot, to demand a list of recipes and ingredients from Cook.'

She was glad to observe that the force of her argument had struck both Barnard and his wife, so that a degree of their distress was alleviated. 'You see? Besides, I overheard a brief exchange between Dr Chant and his unfortunate wife that will, I suspect, provide some explanation.' She hastily sketched out the scene she had observed, ending with, 'It seemed clear to me at the time that the lady was hinting that she was with child. Sadly, it seems only too likely that her death must have resulted from some irregularity in her condition.'

After dinner, Charlotte and Lady Frampton spent a comfortable evening alone at Rowan Lodge, in the cream-panelled dining hall that was their favourite place for relaxing and gossiping. The old lady, who found the stairs difficult these days, used the former dining-room as a bedchamber, while Charlotte slept in lonely state upstairs with a further room set aside there for her own pursuits. The large downstairs drawing-room served for their few formal gatherings.

'Well, I never,' exclaimed the old lady, when Charlotte had told her the sorry tale of young Mrs Chant's tragic end. 'The poor young thing, I recollect thinking what a pretty creature she was, to be sure, all dressed in pink.' She ruminated for a while then remembered something else, 'Mind you, Char,' she said, with a minatory nod. 'You say nobody else was taken ill, but what about Captain Penbury, eh? 'e collapsed, didn't 'e?'

Charlotte looked aghast. 'Oh, Gran,' she exclaimed. 'I'd completely forgotten about that. For heaven's sake don't remind Lily or Barnard.' Her brow puckered as she recalled the occasion. 'But the captain wasn't bilious though. It can't have been anything he ate for he wasn't ill at all, really. I think it was just a sharp attack of indigestion, although it did look like a heart attack at the time.'

'So it was,' nodded Lady Frampton. 'Indigestion, I mean. Silly old fool, he tells everyone he meets about that old musket ball in 'is belly, and I've 'ad to shut my ears time and again when 'e drones on and on about his bloomin' innards. What the devil did 'e think 'e was up to, stuffing himself with all that rich pastry, eh?' She gave a complacent nod as she bragged, 'My 'usband used to tell me, "'arriet, it's a pleasure to see you eat." It takes a stout constitution like what I've got to eat rich and 'earty, so it does.'

An odd memory struck Charlotte. 'Didn't Lady Granville complain that the captain had snatched a mince pie away from young Oz?' She pictured the scene and nodded. 'Yes, she did. She said nothing to the captain, but certainly she moaned about it to me, not that Oz gave two pins. He simply used the uproar at the captain's collapse, to pile his plate high with sugar plums, and make his escape.'

Lady Frampton made a face. 'That woman will make a milksop out of the boy, sure as eggs is eggs,' she grunted. 'As nice and sparky a lad as any you could wish to meet, but no, what must she decide but that he's delicate. Delicate my eye! She'll drive 'im demented one of these days, the way she 'overs over 'im, poor lad. Still, it's not to be wondered at; all those hopes come to nothing and then at last, this precious boy arriving safe and sound. Well over forty, I believe, before she found 'erself in the family way, at what must 'ave been 'er last chance.

'I've seen it before, you know. A "Change" baby he must 'ave been and her took poorly near the whole nine months, as is so often the way with older ladies. And 'is Lordship kept in London a lot of the time, seeing as 'ow 'e was in the Government at that time, though 'e's retired now.' The old lady shot her companion a malicious grin. 'Not that 'e was up to much then, too busy running after the young ladies, so I 'eard. But there, as to Lady Granville, well, it was more than enough to turn 'er into a fussy old hen with 'er one chick, I'm sure, and who can blame her.'

Charlotte listened with only half an ear, though with a moment's sympathy for Lady Granville; another memory was teasing her but nothing came to mind so she shrugged it off. It's none of my business, she told herself firmly and picked up her well-worn copy of *Persuasion* which she knew almost by heart. After her earlier life, always on edge lest Will Glover's schemes should come undone, followed by her desperate journey across India during the Mutiny, it was still a novelty and a treat to find herself at leisure to enjoy herself.

'Gran?' Even Anne Elliot's travails in Lyme Regis for once failed to keep her interest. She ignored Lady Frampton's disgruntled muttering as she pursued her thoughts. 'Who would inherit Brambrook Abbey and the title if – if anything happened to young Oz?'

'Now what maggot have you took into your 'ead, you silly wench?' The old lady cocked an eye at her companion and sighed. 'Oh, all right, let me see. I believe the house and money would go to some cousin or other, lives in Yorkshire and has never been near the place. But 'e's the son of some great-aunt of 'is Lordship, so there's no more Granvilles to inherit the title, and it would die out.'

She roused herself. 'You ain't got some bee in your bonnet about that poor old servant's death the other day, 'ave you? Because you can just stop that at once, you 'ear me, gal? That Maria Dunster was killed by person or persons unknown, the constable said so and so did the coroner, so don't you get all fanciful and start looking for something to connect it to this poor young lady's death. I won't 'ave it, Char, you mark my words.'

Tucked up in bed later that night, Charlotte nonetheless found herself reflecting on the christening party. *Stop this at once*, she told herself firmly, I cannot see any point in this conjecture, there was certainly no sinister stranger from Yorkshire in attendance. This is merely the product of an over-active imagination, no doubt brought on by drinking sherry at Barnard's insistence. Tomorrow will see an end to such fancies.

She frowned and nibbled at her thumbnail. Tomorrow would also bring a reluctant visit to Winchester. Somehow or other, Charlotte had found herself appointed to take the brougham into town in the early afternoon and rescue the bereaved Miss Armstrong, along with her bags and baggage and convey her to the manor to spend Christmas with her new friend, Lily. Poor soul, thought Charlotte, as she snuggled down under the covers. It won't be much of a Christmas for her but I suppose she can retire to her room if it all becomes too merry for, she yawned, I can't see Lily cutting down on the festivities. This is her first winter as lady of the manor and she has plans afoot, plans that are intended to dazzle the neighbours, even though young Algy's extreme youth will no doubt curtail several of his mother's more extravagant ideas.

Next morning Charlotte shivered awake to a sparkling frost on her windows and, for a moment, yearned for the warmth of her far-off childhood climate. With due consideration towards the solemnity of her task, she dressed again in her brown woollen dress and fished out her most sober bonnet ready for the journey. Her plan to visit Elaine that morning had been thwarted by a message from Knightley Hall advising her that Mrs Knightley was not up to visitors that day but hoped to see Charlotte on Christmas morning. Sighing, she busied herself about her usual tasks, wrote letters, did some mending, interviewed the cook, and listened once more to Lady Frampton's views on child-rearing as it should be applied to young Algy. At last she bade her farewell and set out at a brisk pace across the village and up the short drive to the manor and invited herself to luncheon.

Lily preceded her into the dining-room, waving to the footman who placed a chair for Charlotte. 'What a colour you have, dear Char,' she remarked, with a slight note of envy in her voice. 'You surely have not walked up from Rowan Lodge?' She turned to cast a glance in the mirror and pouted at her own rather pale complexion and pudgy cheeks.

'Certainly,' nodded Charlotte, as she tucked into some ham from one of Barnard's prize pigs. 'I think I'll make my way into Winchester fairly soon and rescue your unfortunate friend in good time. A private lodging house in St Thomas Street, you said, I believe, Lily? I'll bring her straight back here unless of course she has reconsidered and has other plans.'

'I doubt she'll do that,' said Lily, with a toss of her head. 'Her note was most urgent and it seems clear that she has nowhere to go at present, with Christmas on top of us now. Besides, from what she said, she has precious little in the way of funds.'

As Charlotte muffled herself once more in her pelisse and shawl while taking her leave, she threw a deliberate crumb of praise towards her sister-in-law. 'I am full of admiration, Lily,' she said, giving the other girl an affectionate hug. 'I'm sure Miss Armstrong will be eternally grateful to you for your generosity, particularly at this festive time of the year. You are quite the Good Samaritan.' There, she thought as she clambered into the Finchbourne double brougham and waved farewell to the gratified lady of the manor; that should help to ease Miss Armstrong's stay. Lily dearly loves to be seen as Lady Bountiful.

A shout from Barnard made her pause. 'Here, Char,' panted her brother-in-law as he galloped up to the carriage. 'I've written a note to Dr Chant, inviting him to stay a day or so if he finds himself detained in Hampshire. It seems only right and proper, poor fellow, it's not the time of year to be stranded in some hotel or other, particularly in the circumstances.' He thrust the note into her hand and hastened back to the stables saying, 'Got to get back to the ratting. It's going famously, the boy is in seventh heaven.'

Charlotte smiled as they swung out on to the main road, glad that young Granville was enjoying his sport. Dear Barnard, he would do what was right, if it killed him, bless him, even though Charlotte suspected that neither he nor Lily had taken to the new-made widower.

The coachman drew up outside a narrow, red-brick slice of a house in St Thomas Street in Winchester, a short distance up the hill from the cathedral, and just off the High Street.

'I'll wait, shall I, Miss Char?' asked the coachman who, like most people in Finchbourne, both manor and village, had adopted this informal method of address. 'Yes, please do,' Charlotte nodded. 'I'm hoping to be out quickly but if there looks to be some delay, I'll let you know.' She took a deep breath and climbed the two high steps to the door, where she seized the bell handle and tried to ring in a muted manner suitable to a house of mourning.

A subdued young maid showed her into the parlour and went in search of Miss Armstrong, but to Charlotte's dismay, she found that the stout, middle-aged gentleman standing in the bay window was the bereaved widower himself, Dr Chant. He gave her a curt bow and glowered at her but, after a cursory appraisal, he straightened up and advanced on her with his hand outstretched. Aha, she managed to conceal a sardonic smile, though her outward demeanour remained demure. He has recognised me as a part of the family at the manor and, moreover, has just noticed that my muff is sable and that my rig-out, though plain, is well-made and modish – or at least, as modish as Winchester fashions allow. Whatever grief he was feeling at the loss of the pretty wife who must have been at least twenty-five years his junior, it had not prevented him from brushing his straight grey locks forward so that it disguised his receding hair line, nor was his smooth pink brow furrowed by sorrow.

'I believe we met the day before yesterday, ma'am?' The voice was unctuous with a suitable touch of gravity and his hand, equally suitably, was warm but not pressing. 'I regret that I do not recall your name?' He stroked his neat grey beard then dashed a hand to his eyes, which, Charlotte was intrigued to see, held no sign of moisture or grief. Indeed, she was slightly shocked to observe that there was an air of unmistakeable interest about him as he discreetly looked her up and down. And his poor wife lying dead, perhaps in this very house, she frowned.

'I am Mrs Frampton Richmond,' she announced in a ceremonial way. 'I am here on behalf of my relatives at the manor to offer succour to Miss Armstrong and, of course, to you, sir, if there is any way in which my brother-in-law might be of service to you, in this sad time.' There, she thought, handing him Barnard's note. Honour is satisfied. Now, for heaven's sake let Miss Armstrong hurry up and let me go home.

Fortunately, the door opened at that moment and Miss Sibella Armstrong, slipped into the room. Now here, thought Charlotte, was yet another person who bore no sign of the ravages of grief one might reasonably expect. Miss Armstrong was indeed pale, and her expression anxious and unhappy, with her brow creased in a frown, but her blue eyes were not rimmed with red, nor was her handkerchief sodden with tears.

'Mrs Richmond,' she said, her voice composed and low. 'It is kind indeed of you to give me shelter at this sad time.' Her gaze flickered towards the doctor who stood aloof from the two women. 'The servant is carrying my luggage out to your carriage and I am quite ready to leave at once.'

'I am so sorry to hear of your sister's sad death,' Charlotte said quietly as she turned towards the door. 'I believe you will be comfortable at the manor while you collect your thoughts.' She gave a formal half-bow of farewell to Dr Chant, who responded politely though she was intrigued to note that his face darkened as he nodded distantly to Miss Armstrong. She, in turn, bobbed a slight curtsy but as the two women turned away, the doctor spoke.

'Mr Richmond has kindly invited me to stay for a day or so,' he said, hesitating a little. 'If I might accept, that would ease my difficulty. I have decided to have my wife's body interred here in Winchester instead of returning the – the coffin to London, but the undertaker tells me he can do nothing until the 27 December. Today being Christmas Eve, I am thus detained in Hampshire for a few days and would be glad to trespass on the hospitality of the manor later this afternoon.'

Charlotte concealed her lack of delight at this intelligence – she had hoped he would hasten to London to seek solace with his illustrious friends – and assured him of a warm welcome from the squire and his lady, all the while aware that the doctor's late wife's sister bore no sign of pleasure at this development and indeed, looked distinctly unhappy at the prospect.

As Miss Armstrong climbed into the Finchbourne brougham, Charlotte stood aside while one of the lodging house servants, a stout, elderly woman, panted back up the steps to the house.

'Why, thank you, ma'am,' the woman began, then, when she overheard Charlotte urge Miss Armstrong to make use of a fur rug that was lying on the carriage seat, she stopped short with an exclamation of astonishment.

'Why, surely I know that voice?' The woman peered up at Charlotte's startled face and frowned for a moment. 'Oh, I do beg your pardon, miss,' she began. 'For a moment I took you for a former mistress of mine, but she lives far, far....' She stared searchingly at the tall young woman beside the open door of the brougham and her broad face broke into a smile of delight. 'Well, I never did! I took you for Mrs Glover, but no, 'tis not, I see that, but…. Surely, it can't be you, Miss Char? All grown up and a real lady now? What in the world are you doing here in England, and looking so prosperous too? Is his reverence with you? And your dear ma, how does she go on?'

Charlotte stood frozen to the spot, staring at the servant. Her worst fears were realized. Here was someone from her childhood; someone who knew too much about her and who could ruin the house of cards that was the lovely, make-believe life she had built for herself.

Chapter 6

'GOOD GOD!' CHARLOTTE pulled herself together, resolutely banishing the feeling of dread, as she summoned up a smile. '*Bessie*? Bessie Railton?' She stretched out her hand. 'Surely it cannot be? What in the world are you doing in England? And in Winchester of all places?'

'Why, bless you, Miss Char, I mean, ma'am. I thought I'd like to see the old country once more before I die so when my last mistress died, leaving me a tidy little legacy, I hopped on a ship and here I am.'

Charlotte had herself well in hand now and her eyes narrowed. 'So what are you doing working in Winchester as a maid, Bessie, if you had a legacy? And how in the world did you recognise me? I cannot have been any more than twelve or thirteen, the last time I saw you.'

The older woman gave a gap-toothed smile and looked round hastily. 'Ah well, it was this way, Miss Char. I met up with a man who liked a bit of a flutter and what with one thing and another, by the time the ship landed in Southampton I found meself a bit embarrassed for cash. Luckily one of the passengers needed a maid for a while, so that tided me over and somehow or other I've ended up here. But tell me about your ma, dear? You don't look like her, of course, but my goodness me your voice is hers to the life, which is how I knew you the minute you spoke. How does she go on?'

'Ma – my mother died last year,' Charlotte said briefly and stiffened at the outburst of comment and commiseration. 'Mr Glover was offered an incumbency in India so I went with him, but sadly he died of a fever almost at once.' She bit her lip but it was better to get the next part over with. 'I married a major in the British army but he died as well so I am now living with his family in Finchbourne, a few miles down the road.'

'Well, what a how d'ye do to be sure,' exclaimed Bessie. 'And your poor ma, God bless her. She was a dear soul and his reverence too, and him so lively always.' She heaved a gusty sigh as she pressed Charlotte's hand with touching sympathy and wiped her eyes. 'Ah me, it's as well his reverence never came to hear of the trouble that befell his congregation not long after you left the town.'

Charlotte gave a shiver of apprehension, as Bessie continued. 'It was a gang of those rough diggers that were passing through,' she said, with disapproval. 'I heard about it from the grocer's wife, who used to write to me now and then. It seems those ruffians turned to and stole the funds that had been collected to build a new church, the rogues. Some of the townsfolk were all for chasing after his reverence and begging him to come back and help raise some more money, him having such a genius for it, as you might say. But there, they thought better of it, what with his poor mother being on her death bed, poor soul.'

Overriding relief was shot through with a pang of shame. That had been the first time Molly and Charlotte had encountered Will's methods and they had been shocked to the core to discover that the dying mother did not exist. Will Glover, Charlotte recalled, had been a man of great charm, eloquence and kindness, and she adored him along with everyone who met him, but there was no denying he had barely a moral bone in his body. Some of the games he played with other people's property gave the family some dreadful moments, she reflected, staring with unseeing eyes at the smartly-painted front door of the lodging-house. If only he hadn't had that queer kink in him, he could have risen to any height. Still, he was dearly loved in his lifetime, she gave a slight shake of her head and smiled inwardly, and he was sincerely mourned by her, in spite of his failings. There's many a great man could wish for no better epitaph, she supposed.

She pulled herself together and glanced at the carriage, and then at the sky, which had a lowering, yellowish look that boded ill, so she fished in her purse.

'Here, Bessie, I mustn't keep Miss Armstrong waiting, but you must come and see me as soon as you have a half-day off. We'll talk about the old days then.'

Bessie Railton eyed Charlotte's guinea with considerable respect. 'Right you are, Miss Char, ma'am, I mean. But....' she leaned closer to Charlotte and whispered. 'I'll be glad to talk to you, there's something funny about the other young lady's illness, but I daren't say anything or I'll lose my place and it's a good one. The mistress is open-handed and good to work for.' Her cheerful expression vanished as her brows met in a puzzled frown. 'I'd value your thoughts, Miss. I mean, ma'am. You always did have a good head on your shoulders, even as a child.'

'What do you...?' Charlotte turned to look over her shoulder at the waiting carriage and shook her head. 'No, I really must take Miss Armstrong home to my sister-in-law now, but listen, Bessie.' She took the maid's hand and gave it a squeeze, 'I live at Rowan Lodge, in Finchbourne, it's a village a little way outside Winchester, anyone will tell you how to get there. Oh?' at an exclamation from the older woman. 'You know the village? And I'm Mrs Richmond now. Come and see me as soon as you are able and we'll talk about this. And about old times too.'

The journey home was conducted in near silence with both women absorbed in their own reflections. To be sure, Charlotte did ask her companion if she was comfortable but on receiving a nod of assent, settled down to consider the implications of Bessie Railton's sudden re-emergence into her life.

All the old anxieties came flooding back and it was a relief to look out of the carriage window and realize that they were approaching the village of Finchbourne. Not long now, Charlotte sighed, politely concealing her relief. I'll just see Miss Armstrong safely ensconced at the manor and pass on Dr Chant's message to Barnard and Lily, and then I can withdraw discreetly and make my escape.

It was not to be that simple. To be sure, Lily received her bereaved guest with an air of overwhelming graciousness, assuring her that Barnard would be gratified to hear that the doctor would arrive later in the day, but Charlotte was instantly aware that some kind of crisis had ruffled her sister-in-law's customary iron-clad complacency. She was not left long in ignorance.

'Char,' Lily spoke in an urgent whisper once Miss Armstrong had been conveyed upstairs to a well-appointed room in the Queen Anne wing, with instructions to make herself comfortable and to have a good long rest. 'I know that you and Gran are to dine with us tomorrow and stay the night, but please – you simply must come and stay with us tonight as well, and for a few days over Christmas too. I shall go mad if you do not!'

'Don't be ridiculous, Lily.' Charlotte's response was swift and bracing. 'What in the world is the matter? I tell you quite frankly, my dear, that if you've been squabbling with Barnard again over the colour of the curtains for your bedroom, I shall persuade Gran that we won't even come up to the manor for our Christmas dinner tomorrow, let alone stay the night as Barnard wished. We'll eat bread and cheese instead.'

'How can you be so absurd, Char?' Lily was momentarily distracted from her plaint. 'As if I would ever be so foolish as to consult Barnard about an important thing like curtains, particularly when he suggested such a dull brown brocade. Besides, I never argue with my dearest husband.' She ignored Charlotte's sceptical eyebrow and hurried on, 'That's beside the point. The thing is, that dreadful Melicent woman is driving me to distraction. First she must feel faint, then she must complain of the stuffy atmosphere in her room and to cap that, she must announce in a very loud voice that she is sure Mrs Chant died as a result of some careless mistake by our cook yesterday.'

'Oh good Lord,' Charlotte almost groaned. This was just the kind of stupid gossip that she dreaded. Such a tale, embroidered upon as it would inevitably be, would destroy the peace of the manor and the village and almost break poor Barnard, her dear, well-meaning if bovine brother-in-law. 'I hope you scotched that silly idea very firmly, Lily?'

'Of course I did, and so did Barnard. Even Captain Penbury, to give him his due, roared at her that she must guard against starting a rumour so uncomplimentary to her kind hosts. But Char,' Lily was now clutching at the other girl's arm. 'Don't you see? Melicent Penbury is the worst cat imaginable and now she sees we are seriously disturbed by her maunderings, she'll give us no peace. And here we are, with Miss Armstrong already in the house and Dr Chant about to descend on us, and both of them grieving. How can we protect them from Melicent's dreadful scandal-mongering?'

Charlotte was intrigued and shaken to see that Lily, whom she had never before seen in the grip of any emotion other than rage or smug self-satisfaction, was actually shedding genuine tears.

'Char,' pleaded Lily. 'If only you and Gran would come tonight and stay in the house, I think I could support the next few days. I don't know how it is, but you seem to have the knack of keeping Melicent in her place. And you know what dear Gran is like about what she calls Melicent's silly megrims and fancies. Dearest Char, do say you will come to our rescue?'

Charlotte opened her mouth to refuse, while her mind squirrelled around in an attempt to dredge up an excuse, but before she could speak, Barnard Richmond bounded into the hall, with young Master Granville hot on his heels.

'Lily, my dear, and Charlotte too? Excellent, I'm glad to see you, Char. We have had capital sport, have we not, young Oz?' He rubbed his hands together and clapped the boy on the shoulder.

'Oh, Mrs Richmond,' Oz was beaming as he held out an extremely grubby hand to Charlotte. 'It's been absolutely splendid. Mr Richmond let me hold back one of the terriers and it only bit me the once. And at the command, I let it go and my word, you should have seen those rats run. I never saw anything like it in my life, it was first rate.'

'Yes indeed,' Barnard said, with a genial laugh. 'I think we had better go and wash our hands, Oz, and then I'm sure Mrs Richmond will have something good for us to stay our stomachs. I could eat a horse, I do believe.'

'Stay for a cup of tea, at least, Char, and a bite to eat,' pleaded Lily. 'You'll see how badly That Woman behaves.'

Charlotte nodded and slipped up to her own old room to take off her bonnet and tidy her hair. She knew Lady Frampton would be tucking in already to her own hearty tea, with no anxiety about

Charlotte's whereabouts, and she could see no help for it but to stand by Lily.

'I'm sorry, Gran,' later, at Rowan Lodge, Charlotte knelt beside the old lady and took her hand. 'I didn't have the heart to abandon poor Barnard to the atmosphere at the manor. What with Lily coming the gracious chatelaine and Melicent sighing and gasping, holding a plaintive handkerchief to her eye now and then, and all the while sending out her nasty little darts, I could picture murder being done at Finch....'

She gave a sudden tiny gasp and halted in mid-sentence. Fortunately Lady Frampton took no notice and was swift to scold over what she described as Charlotte's foolish nonsense, but Charlotte bit her lip, unable to dismiss an idea that now, insidious as a snake, refused to go away. Nonsense indeed, she shook her head and tried to pull herself together. Time enough to consider this foolishness when she had a moment to consider it when she was alone, which would probably not be until bedtime.

And that bedtime, she sighed, would not now be spent at Rowan Lodge as she had hoped. She had known that neither she nor the old lady could bear to see poor Barnard harried and chivvied out of his senses by a couple of warring women, so here they were, making the most of their last peaceful half hour at home before tackling the atmosphere up at the manor.

'Very well, Lily,' she had conceded. 'I'll persuade Gran that we should stay with you tonight as well as over Christmas Day as we planned. That should give you some respite from Melicent's behaviour – though I've told you before, all you need to do is give her a firm set-down. I warn you though, Gran may have some cross words to say about it, you know she likes to have plenty of warning before she has to make any change.'

She suggested that Lily send down a pleading message to Rowan Lodge and, as they had known she would, Lady Frampton gave in to the inevitable, albeit with a good deal of complaint. Before going home to oversee the removal and confronting a testy old lady, Charlotte had eaten her way calmly through the very good tea put before her at the manor and then volunteered to accompany Oz Granville on one final visit to the stable yard, and afterwards to drive him home in the pony chaise, or walk with him before the weather closed in.

'That sounds a capital notion, Charlotte, and I only wish I could make time to come along with the pair of you.' Barnard bellowed approval of this scheme, glancing wistfully at his womenfolk while young Master Granville looked pleased and opted for the walk. 'We've had a good, full day of it, have we not, young Oz? First we dropped in at all the farms and cottages, not staying more than a few minutes for we had a long list to see to, but I believe I can say the tenants were pleased with their Christmas parcels, and particularly gratified by a visit from their young neighbour here.' He nodded complacently as he downed the last gulp of ale from his tankard, ignoring Lily's pained glare at his refusal to drink tea. 'Aye, and then it was back here for the ratting which was a splendid affair. We must ask your Mama, Oz, to allow you to come along next time we mean to have a clear out. I'm sure she would want you to have that pleasure.'

The boy looked doubtful as to his mother's permission or pleasure, but was clearly sincere in his thanks to his host as he and Charlotte took their leave. Charlotte had tried to engage their bereaved guest in polite conversation, but with little success. It was hardly surprising, she sighed, as she nodded farewell to Miss Armstrong. The poor woman was clearly shocked and must be wondering what on earth was to become of her if, as Charlotte understood, she was between situations as a governess and without a settled home.

Sibella Armstrong had answered all Charlotte's efforts with a monosyllable or shake of the head, keeping her eyes lowered and eating very sparingly. She had suffered an introduction to the other house guests, Captain and Mrs Penbury, and had shaken hands with Oz Granville rather diffidently, turning away immediately to find her place at table, though Charlotte thought she saw Sibella slide more than one sidelong glance at the boy, her expression unreadable.

Oh dear, thought Charlotte. She's so very pale, I do hope she didn't think talk of ratting was inappropriate when she is so recently bereaved, but it couldn't be helped. She turned to the boy. 'Did you not promise to show me all the ghastly corpses?' she joked – and bit her tongue as the boy shivered. In view of the recent death of his mother's maid, her words were ill-chosen. Had he been particularly fond of the woman, she wondered, remembering that he had seemed disturbed at the previous day's party.

He rallied at once and ten minutes later she was granted her wish as Oz and the stable boy proudly conducted her into the barn to admire the 23 rats that had met their doom. Prior to that, Oz had insisted on showing her round the yard and some of the outer buildings as well.

'Look, Mrs Richmond,' he told her, pointing to a rough patch of ground behind the piggeries. 'That's where we started. Mr Richmond let me have his own best terrier, Willow, on a lead, and the men had hold of the others, then at the word, "Go," we all let the dogs loose. It was a famous sight, I can tell you.' His blue eyes sparkled at the memory and he brushed aside her enquiries as to the scratches and bites on his own hands. 'Oh yes,' he admitted carelessly. 'I did have gloves on, but they must have slipped off. It doesn't matter. You never saw anything like it,' he exulted. 'Willow was the best of the dogs by a long chalk, and I saw him wriggling through a gap, looking just like a snake. It was beyond anything!'

When Charlotte had been treated to a blow-by-blow account of what seemed like the death of every individual rat, Oz determinedly marched her back to the barn to display the deceased rodents, where she gave considerable satisfaction by her whole-hearted admiration.

'You're a great gun, Mrs Richmond,' he exclaimed looking at her in surprise. 'Most ladies don't seem to appreciate ratting. I know my mother wouldn't, which is why I was so pleased that you didn't happen to mention it to her.'

'I know,' grinned Charlotte. 'I'm an unnatural woman, but I've encountered deadly funnel-web spiders more than once, not to mention a swarm of locusts which is something I pray never to see again, so I have no qualms about getting rid of vermin.' She nodded to the boy, 'Remind me to tell you about the crocodile I once had to tackle; after that, rats hold no fear for me.' She glanced at the stable clock and then at the sky, which was looking dark and overcast. 'We must not stay here enjoying ourselves, Oz, it's time we set out for Brambrook Abbey or your mama will be getting anxious.'

Before they could set out, however, Barnard came hurrying out of the house. 'My word, Char,' he exclaimed. 'If I hadn't forgotten all about that murderous ruffian. He might even yet be skulking about the place as Lily reminded me.'

Charlotte opened her mouth to protest but was overruled. 'Here,' Barnard called to the stable boy. 'Fetch my grandmother's dog and my terrier, Willow, and accompany Miss Char to Brambrook Abbey and bring her back safe. Don't you let her out of your sight, mind.'

Resistance was futile, she could not let Barnard worry, so Charlotte smiled at the stable lad and gave in with a good grace as he followed closely upon their heels, Oz proudly leading the terrier and Charlotte herself taking Lady Frampton's stout old spaniel. By the time they had turned off Pot Kiln Lane and were walking up the drive to the Abbey, Charlotte and the Granville boy were firm friends and Charlotte had discovered the extent to which his mother's anxieties hedged him in.

'No,' was the doleful reply to a query. 'Mama won't let me play cricket. She says it's too dangerous as I might be hit by the ball.' He glowered at the idea. 'She can't seem to understand that I'm not stupid.'

'Well,' Charlotte temporised. It was no business of hers to criticise his mama. 'Perhaps when the warm weather comes we could get up some games of cricket at the manor? I know Barnard plays and so do some of the men about the place, there's always a cricket match in the summer – village against the manor.' She grinned at his sudden spurt of enthusiasm. 'I was away in Bath last year when they held the annual match but I doubt I'll be allowed to join in. Oh yes,' she explained at his questioning glance. 'My stepfather taught me to bowl straight and to hit hard. We practised on beaches and in fields and in the Outback, wherever he could rustle up a team.'

Oz had to be satisfied with the promise that she would certainly coach him, but he was doubtful if his mother would permit such a thing. 'It's not fair though,' he said. 'Papa wouldn't mind if I played cricket but, oh well....' He sighed and kicked at a pebble. 'Mind you,' he brightened up. 'At least my father did insist I must learn to ride,' he added, 'Mama didn't dare go against him about that, but she makes such a fuss there's not much pleasure in it.'

Charlotte sympathised but said no more, merely cautioning him with a laugh, not to let his mama hear about the refreshments he had been offered that morning. 'I don't believe your mother would like to know that you have been drinking sloe gin,' she grinned. 'And I'm quite sure she would be shocked to learn that you stuffed yourself with plum cake in almost every house. My advice is that you should be discreet when you tell her about your visits. As my old nurse used to say, *'what the eye don't see, the heart don't grieve over.'*

She drew in a sharp breath at that, remembering the startling encounter with that very nurse, Bessie Railton, only that morning. Was Bessie going to be a nuisance, fond as Charlotte had been of her long ago in Australia? Charlotte racked her brains. I don't believe Bessie ever knew of Will's 'eccentricities' she told herself anxiously. Wasn't it during that year when Bessie was housekeeper and nurse-cum-housemaid rolled into one, that Will was actually gainfully employed as chaplain to someone? She found a likely-looking husband just before we moved to the township that later suffered from Will's depredations. From Bessie's remarks, it seems that nobody thought of blaming Will for the theft. Perhaps it might be possible after all to be comfortable with Bessie, as an old friend? It would be such a comfort not to be afraid of a chance word, or a sudden memory that might destroy her peace.

As they approached the impressive drawbridge and portcullis at the entrance to the Abbey, Charlotte and Oz were hailed by Lord Granville as he emerged from round the corner of the house.

'What's this? What's this? Been on an adventure, hey?' He shook hands with Charlotte in the most genial fashion, clapping his son's shoulder in an affectionate way.

'I've been ratting at the manor, papa,' confided Oz, looking guiltily over his shoulder as the great oak door creaked open and his mother's anxious voice was heard within. 'It was first rate, we caught twenty-three rats, sir.'

Charlotte caught his lordship's small, twinkling blue eye and stifled a laugh. 'Here, Oz, I'll hand your old clothes over to the butler somehow. Let me have the bag.'

'No need, my dear.' Lord Granville whispered hastily as he relieved his son of the incriminating bag. 'I'll take it to the stables, lad, don't you fret. Twenty-three of 'em, eh? Upon my soul, I call that a triumph.' He nodded to his wife as he disappeared. 'Here he is my dear, safe and sound, and here is Mrs Richmond who has kindly delivered him back to us.'

Lady Granville took a moment to pass a gentle hand over her son's tousled locks before she came forward to express her gratitude to Charlotte. 'I was in my garden room,' she apologised. At Charlotte's pleasant nod, the lady went on to explain, 'I spend a great deal of my time planting and potting and drying seeds, you know. I hope to develop some strains of my own in future.'

There was a flurry of thanks and handshakes, with Oz giving Charlotte's hand a particularly grateful squeeze, while his mother expressed her relief at the safe homecoming of her treasure who was bubbling over with excitement about the people he had met on his outing with Barnard, as well as the other guests at Finchbourne Manor. Lady Granville halted in mid-sentence for a moment, listened and frowned and then, to her husband and son's evident surprise, she held out her hand once more to Charlotte.

'My dear Mrs Richmond,' she said with a smile that, though cordial enough, seemed to Charlotte to be a little strained. 'I have just had a thought. Were you aware that Boxing Day will be Osbert's eleventh birthday? St Stephen's day, of course, as it is otherwise known and indeed, Stephen is his second name for that very reason. I wonder if you and Lady Frampton, and Mr and Mrs Richmond at the manor, would care to come here for a birthday tea party on that day? I will give orders for a special cake to be made and I am sure Osbert would be delighted to play host.'

Her son stammered his thanks and turned to Charlotte with glowing eyes. 'Oh, please say you'll come, Mrs Richmond, and everyone else too. It will be famous sport.' He turned to his mother anxiously. 'But, Mama, did you not hear me say that Mr and Mrs

Richmond at the manor have guests staying in the house? They might not like to leave them.'

'But naturally, Osbert,' his mother tapped him lightly on the arm. 'I shall send a written invitation to the manor entreating Mrs Richmond to be sure and bring her guests as well. It would not do for anyone to be left behind, you are quite right.'

As Charlotte, chatting amicably to the stable boy about the snow which was forecast, walked briskly towards home along Pot Kiln Lane under the darkened sky, she was hailed by a familiar voice.

'Char? Is that you? I thought I could not be mistaken.' Kit Knightley hurried to catch up with her, calling to his retrievers to behave themselves as they bounded up to the terrier and spaniel, then leaped up at her in delighted welcome.

'No, don't worry, Kit,' Charlotte laughed, bending down to greet the dogs who were both old friends. 'Have you been walking by the river? I see these two gentlemen have been swimming, cold as it is.' She straightened up, only to step backwards when the dogs shook themselves over her.

'Indeed they have,' Kit agreed, falling into step with her. 'If you were any other young lady, I believe I should feel obliged to remonstrate with you about going abroad at such a time without someone more formidable than that skinny lad as protection.' She could hear the amusement in his voice as he added, 'However, as I am quite aware that you could probably rout any evil doer with one hand tied behind your back, I shall be wise and leave well alone. Besides, the dogs would kick up a racket enough to scare off most suspicious characters. So then, Char? How goes it? Are you happily settled at Rowan Lodge now? And getting on well with the old lady?'

'Oh yes.' She turned a smiling face towards him in the gloaming. 'Gran is the delight of my life, you know. Having lost what little family I had of my own, I cherish the one I acquired so unexpectedly and I love them all so much, even Lily.'

He smiled and asked, 'Has everyone recovered from the shock you caused by painting all the rooms in pale colours? Elaine was most entertained by the furore but she wasn't surprised; she said you were craving for light and space after your Australian upbringing.'

'She was quite right,' Charlotte nodded. 'Oh yes, they were shocked to the core and Gran refused to let me do the same with her rooms, so she is snug in her crimsons and dark blues, while I relish the light in every other room.' She grinned reminiscently. 'I suppose you heard what the blacksmith's aunt said? "They say 'tis like a place where you'd lay out a corpse, natural for decent folks." Sadly she died before I could invite her to see for herself.'

She walked along a little way then turned back to him, her expression grave. 'Tell me, Kit, how does Elaine go on? I was sorry she was not up to a visit today, I long to see her. I'm hoping to call on her tomorrow morning, for a brief Christmas greeting if you think it would tire her?'

'She'll welcome your visit,' Kit assured her. He hesitated then shrugged, 'She's not at all well, Char, I cannot pretend otherwise. Dr Perry refuses to commit himself to a prognosis, saying with truth what I can observe for myself, that her condition varies greatly from one day to another and the morphia keeps the pain at bay, for the most part. Yesterday, for example, she was busy about her room, wrapping up small gifts for all the servants, yet today, perhaps not surprisingly, she had to keep to her bed.' He stalked ahead, swishing his stick at the bare straggles of brambles along the hedgerow, carefully not glancing at his companion, as he said: 'Come tomorrow, Char. You know how much she … she loves you. You won't do her any harm and who knows? A visit might take her out of herself.'

They continued in silence until Charlotte roused herself from her introspection. It would do Kit good, she decided, if he had something else to think about, so she told him about the dramatic events following upon the christening of his small godson.

'Surely you are making it up?' Kit looked aghast as – after a moment's hesitation – she confided in him the disturbing comment made in farewell by Bessie Railton. 'No, of course not; I beg your pardon, you would not do that, but what are you saying, Char? A young woman dies of a sudden indisposition, you start to feel uneasy because Lady Granville is an obsessively cosseting mother and says someone pushed the Granville boy so that the curate ended up feet first in an open grave? It's far-fetched, my dear girl, there can be no connection. No, Char,' he spoke with authority. 'This is mere speculation from an overwrought woman who has been seriously overset by an actual murder at her own door. You're not giving this any credence?'

She said nothing and he frowned at her, 'Forgive me, Char, but is it possible that you are pining for some excitement? You know Elaine told me of your adventures in Bath and you are living such a quiet, restricted life with the old lady; does it pall after tripping over dead bodies and uncovering a murderer? I know you value your secure and tranquil life but surely, after your adventurous youth, there must be times when you find village life interminably boring?'

'I don't know.' She spoke frankly and hunched her shoulders as they halted at the gate to Finchbourne Manor. 'You're quite right, of course, life *is* very dull sometimes, even though we have our little card parties and other such revels. Oh, Kit,' she held out her hand in farewell as she shook her head and smiled at him. 'You may be right to suggest I'm hankering after excitement, but even so, call me foolish indeed, but I do have a real sense of unease. And there's something else; something that struck me yesterday when the Waits were singing and everyone was eating and drinking, but for the life of me, I cannot remember now what it was.'

Chapter 7

A LETTER WAS waiting for her when Charlotte walked into the drawing-room at Rowan Lodge and found Lady Frampton resigned to their impending removal to the manor. 'What's this?' she frowned. 'I don't know the handwriting.'

The old lady shrugged her massive shoulders. 'It was delivered by hand an hour or so since,' she explained.

'Good God!' Charlotte had briefly scanned the short missive and now raised startled hazel eyes to her aged relative. 'It's from Miss Nightingale, of all people.'

'You don't say?' Lady Frampton swivelled round in her chair to stare. 'Well, girl, get on with it. What does she want with you?'

'She's offering me a situation,' announced Charlotte, looking blank. At the old lady's astonished outcry, she nodded and went back to the letter. 'I know, it sounds ridiculous, doesn't it? But apparently she is serious. Listen to this, Gran: *"I was impressed by your sensible behaviour and quiet competence in an emergency and would be glad to make use of these qualities which are sadly lacking in most young women I have encountered. As you may recall, I mentioned that I am collecting funds with the aim of establishing an order of nurses so that the disastrous inefficiency of the hospitals, as demonstrated in the late war in the Crimea, may be avoided in future.*

"With this in mind, I wish to offer you a senior post in an administrative role, as yet to be defined, in the proposed nursing organisation. From enquiries I have made, I understand that you have no ties other than your late husband's family at Finchbourne Manor, so I am confident that you will see the good sense of accepting my offer.

Believe me, yrs, etc, etc...."

'What in the world am I to make of that?' Charlotte looked up from the letter and was dismayed to see that the old lady was looking upset. 'What is it, darling Gran? Are you not well?'

'No, no, me dear,' the old lady patted her hand and gave a mighty sniff. 'I'm well enough. T'was just the thought that you might be goin' off to join 'er 'igh and mightiness.'

'You foolish old lady,' exclaimed Charlotte, fondly embracing her grandmother-in-law. 'As if I would dream of doing such a thing. Lay that fear aside at once, I could no more work with Miss Nightingale than I could work with Melicent Penbury. But it's quite flattering, is it not? I suppose she means me to work at this new hospital at Netley that the Queen has just opened? Just fancy: I am sensible and quietly competent!'

'And so you are, me dear, but don't tell our Lily or she'll be jealous as a cat.' Lady Frampton, beaming with relief, was now ready to appreciate the situation. 'Whatever you do, don't mention the new horspital to Miss Nightingale if you meet 'er again, she can't abide it. Probably because they won't build it the way she told 'em to.'

'Put it out of your mind, Gran,' Charlotte reassured her with a smile. ' I admire Miss Nightingale, of course I do, but I'm far too independent and downright stubborn myself, to buckle down under her iron rule. Why, I thought Lady Granville a terrifying enough woman when I first encountered her, but in comparison with The Lady with the Lamp, she's a woolly lamb.'

Dinner at the manor proved something of an anti-climax as far as Charlotte was concerned. Barnard's bluff hospitality masked the abstraction of their two unexpected guests and Lily was happy to be queening it over a full table. Lady Frampton's temper improved visibly as she tucked in to a hearty helping of roast beef, preceded by an array of what the old lady stigmatised as 'kickshaws'. Nonetheless, Charlotte observed with a smile, her dear relative sampled every dish so that by the time the pudding made its appearance, Lady Frampton was positively mellow.

By tacit consent, the death of Maria Dunster was not mentioned, any more than that of young Mrs Chant, and Captain Penbury must have had a word with his irritating wife because the lady was on her best behaviour, nodding and smiling at everything her host said. I don't know which is worse, sighed Charlotte, Melicent being a cat, or Melicent in this odiously compliant mood.

It lasted a mere half hour until Lady Frampton made some remark about the handsome new carpet in the bedroom she always used at the manor, nodding her thanks to Lily.

'Do you not find there is a risk of accident, Lady Frampton?' Melicent turned to the old lady. 'Not having the carpet nailed down, I mean? I always think there is something a little shabby about a room that has the boards showing.'

Lily swelled angrily and was about to demolish her infuriating guest when, to her surprise, Dr Chant stepped in to her rescue. 'I think you will find, Madam,' he addressed himself to Melicent, icily polite, 'that there is a considerable risk to health where carpets are nailed down, with the accumulation of dust and other noxious irritants. Besides, persons of quality, such as our gracious hosts, are aware – as perhaps you are not – that a house of great antiquity such as Finchbourne Manor, which dates in the main from Tudor times, needs no tawdry decoration.'

After that, it was war. Entirely ignoring Melicent, who was gobbling like a turkey cock, with an angry flush in her pasty cheeks and a lock of lank dark hair flopping on her brow – and the astonished but gratified expressions of his hosts – Dr Chant ate his dinner with an air of dignified abstraction and bowed himself away to his bed after the meal, leaving Barnard and the captain to take their port in gentlemanly isolation, safe from the their womenfolk. Miss Armstrong, who was understandably pale and had picked at her food, did not hasten away quite so quickly, but followed Lily and the other ladies to the drawing-room.

Melicent spent five minutes sobbing on the window-seat, then finding herself ignored by the other ladies, she tried another tack, throwing out spiteful little remarks about the medical guest and attempting to elicit sympathy for the way she had been spoken to. When she began on the topic of the death at Brambrook Abbey, Charlotte was about to intervene, very reluctantly, when Lady Frampton beckoned the former governess to her side.

'You will be silent,' she said shortly. 'It ill becomes you to make so much noise in a house where you are a guest. I advise you to recollect your station and to mind your manners. The villain is long gone, the inquest dealt with that poor woman's death and she 'as been buried, so let 'er lie in peace. And you can stop that slanderous gossip about the doctor too, this instant.'

After that, Melicent clearly determined to behave herself so she limped over to the grand piano and announced that she would entertain the company by playing some seasonal music. She then launched into a mercifully quiet rendition of the fine but lugubrious old hymn, 'Behold the Great Redeemer makes, himself a house of clay'. Charlotte was unable to persuade herself that it was a particularly tactful choice in the present circumstances, but glancing across the drawing-room, she surprised an unmistakable glint of amusement in Sibella Armstrong's eye. Attracted and curious, she moved unhurriedly over and sat down beside the guest.

'I would ask Mrs Penbury to play something more uplifting,' she murmured, 'but I'm afraid it might set her off on to her symptoms again, if she is interrupted, and I simply can't bear any more details.'

The other girl bit back a smile. 'I shouldn't have laughed,' she said. 'I'm sure she means well. Please don't worry, I wasn't upset by the gloomy music, it's just that it reminded me of a wedding at my father's church. Edward, my brother, used to stand in if the organist was indisposed, and he played that hymn because the bridegroom was a Mr Clay.' The fleeting smile was in evidence once more, 'Father was furious but the bridal pair took it as a compliment.'

The slight flush that had animated Sibella's face now ebbed and Charlotte said quietly, 'I do hope that you will have a real rest while you are at the manor, Miss Armstrong. I know Lily and Barnard are anxious to make your stay as comfortable as possible at this difficult time.'

'Thank you, everyone is so kind.' The lighter mood had vanished and there was a slightly awkward pause while Miss Armstrong sat looking at her hands, linked together in her lap, and Charlotte racked her brains as she tried to think of something unexceptionable as a topic of conversation, but found herself reduced to further condolences.

'If I can be of any assistance,' she began. 'Perhaps I could write to tell your relatives the sad news, to spare you?'

That produced a faint smile of gratitude. 'Thank you, but my sister and I were the last of our family.' She bit her lip and looked away, a faint colour staining her pale cheeks, a frown creasing her brow.

'The last?' Charlotte was all sympathy and the other woman nodded, then in a sudden burst of confidence, she said, 'There were three of us. My brother was the eldest, and then I, four years younger. Verena was born when I was five years old, but sadly my mother died a few days later. As I said, my father was a clergyman in Northumberland, near Corbridge, but he died of heart failure when I was seventeen.'

She acknowledged Charlotte's murmur of sympathy and continued, clearly finding some relief in the telling. 'My sister was away at school at the time and her godmother, a cousin of my mother's, agreed to adopt the child, paying for her education and undertaking her presentation at Court. The lady died shortly after Verena's marriage to Dr Chant, a little over six years ago.'

'And your brother?' Charlotte wished she had held her tongue when Miss Armstrong's face darkened.

'My brother emigrated to Australia eleven or twelve years ago,' was the terse reply, followed by a look of consternation as Lily exclaimed in surprise,

'Why, what a singular coincidence,' she cried. 'Did you not know, Miss Armstrong, that our dear Charlotte is herself an Australian? Perhaps she and your brother are acquainted?'

Charlotte hastily interrupted her. 'Goodness, Lily. Australia is a very large continent. It is highly unlikely that Mr Armstrong and I should ever have crossed each other's paths.' Heaven forbid, she told herself, that I should find myself saddled with yet another potential source of embarrassment. It's bad enough that I have met up with Bessie once more, fond of her as we all were.

Her dismay was clearly shared by Sibella Armstrong, who said quietly, 'We heard of my brother's death a year or so later.'

With relief, Charlotte passed over the thorny topic by diverting Lily on to a recital of what could be expected on what would be her first Christmas Day in England, but she found herself wondering about young Mr Armstrong and his sister's reluctance to discuss him. She might still be grieving for him, of course, but as Charlotte well knew, relatives of a transported felon would often embroider the journey and refer to it as 'emigration'. Indeed, she was in the habit of doing so herself, when questioned about her mother, her godmother, and her stepfather and their presence in the Antipodes.

The company broke up early. Although in the rudest of health, Lily was still a very new mother who, to Charlotte's surprise, had refused to employ the services of a wet nurse. Charlotte liked Lily all the more for this, considering, with a smile, that should she ever find herself in a like situation, feeding the infant herself would make escape so much easier. Oh well, she grinned, while Lady Frampton announced frankly that she was ready for her bed, not much danger of finding myself in that kind of predicament, and – certainly for the present – no need to think of escape.

Miss Armstrong bade everyone a quiet goodnight and Charlotte followed her and the Penburys up the oak staircase. They turned towards the older part of the house, while Charlotte politely conducted the guest to the room next to her own.

'Pray do not hesitate to knock on my door if there is anything I can do for you,' she told the other woman. Miss Armstrong nodded her thanks and turned into her room, looking suddenly drained and weary.

As she blew out her candle, Charlotte frowned. Perhaps I *have* met Mr Armstrong at some date, she pondered. If so, it might explain that odd sense of recognition I felt when I saw the late Verena, though we had scant conversation. She shrugged and snuggled down under the covers. Twelve years ago I was a child, she thought. I could easily have met him and forgotten his name, but still find his face drawn to mind. I wonder….

Next morning, Christmas Day, a groom rode over with an invitation for the entire family at the manor, including Lady

Frampton and Charlotte, along with any guests, to attend Oz Granville's eleventh birthday tea on Boxing Day.

'Thank heavens,' Lily whispered. 'Imagine how awkward it would be if she had not invited them too.' At that moment, Sibella and Dr Chant entered the dining-room so Lily informed them that the Finchbourne party would be taking tea with a neighbour the next day. Charlotte purloined the letter and grinned to herself as she read the stately phrases. She recalled her own description of the lady, when discussing her with Lady Frampton. A 'woolly lamb', was it not? She could scarcely have chosen a less appropriate description for a woman whose air of haggard grandeur emphasised a character whose nature was reticent in the extreme. Still, compared with Miss Nightingale, Lady Granville was almost a human being.

Charlotte was drawn to Lady Granville because of her two obsessions: her son and her magical garden, but she was wary. I'd better be careful, she mused. She certainly won't like it if I become too friendly with Oz. I must not arouse any maternal jealousy as I fancy she could be a difficult customer and perceive slights and liberties where none was intended. Her colouring is quite un-English. I must ask somebody if those dark, haunted eyes and olive complexion suggest any Italian or Spanish blood. If that were so I might even find myself involved in a vendetta of some sort.

I shall be circumspect, she told herself briskly; I do hope Oz will be pleased with his birthday present. The fearsome pocket knife, complete with all manner of attachments had been among the effects of her late, and decidedly unlamented, husband and although she had protested with heart-felt sincerity that she had no need of such mementoes to remind her of Frampton, her sister-in-law Agnes, now wife of their vicar, had pressed the box upon her. It had proved simpler to accept it and stow it away in a dark cupboard at the manor, than to make any further fuss, and now here was the knife, the perfect present for an eleventh birthday.

Charlotte suddenly remembered Miss Armstrong who must also be given a gift. The other woman would not expect anything and was highly unlikely to have provided herself with gifts for her hosts, but an embroidered linen handkerchief was an unexceptionable little gift and Charlotte had provided herself with a new one for Christmas Day. Luckily Lily had decreed that presents were to be exchanged after today's early dinner so there was time to wrap it in silver tissue paper

'I'm going to walk over to Knightley Hall this morning,' Charlotte announced to Lady Frampton before breakfast. 'I begged a slice of bread and butter from the kitchen, so I'll forego breakfast here. I'm only going to offer the season's greetings to Elaine and Kit, and I'll be home in plenty of time to smarten myself up in time for church.'

'Season's greetings, hey?' The old lady reached out to press Charlotte's hand with hearty sympathy. 'Poor souls, it won't be much of a Christmas for them, I fear, not from what I 'ear of Mrs Knightley's state of 'ealth.' She glanced at her dear companion's face and nodded, noting the sudden pallor and the grief that darkened her hazel eyes. 'You'll feel it very much, me dear,' she added, with kindly affection.

'Yes,' was all Charlotte could say as she hastily rose from her chair in the old lady's room. She went to find her outdoor garments, along with the tiny nosegay she had fashioned from sprigs of rosemary and a spray of yellow winter jasmine from the garden. It was a small enough present, she sighed, but what could you give to a woman who was dying?

'So you enjoyed your visit to Brambrook Abbey?' Elaine Knightley looked so fine-drawn and delicate that Charlotte was hard put to disguise her concern, though she knew that any reference to her friend's health would be quite unacceptable.

'I did,' she agreed. 'I really accepted the invitation to please young Oz, but I found Lady Granville much less daunting than I had anticipated. Do you know anything of her history? She told me her husband's father had built the Abbey and that he was a mill owner from Lancashire, but I know nothing of her own background.'

'I believe her mother was French and...' Elaine frowned as she marshalled her thoughts, 'her father was English, Viscount something or other, I don't think I ever heard the name. Lady Granville was brought up at her mother's home in Provence where I presume they returned after Napoleon's defeat. I do recall someone telling me that she provides the respectable lineage in the partnership, while his lordship is the one with the money.

'A great deal of money too, from what I've heard, so nobody has ever wondered that she put up with his rumoured infidelities, though I believe it was said that she did so with an ill grace. I gather though, that when she finally managed to bear a living child, her nature seemed to soften and that she and her husband have since been on much happier terms.' For a moment Elaine's delicately lovely face wore a shadow and Charlotte knew she was thinking of her own still-born child.

'I have a conundrum for you, Elaine.' The sorrow on her friend's face was too much and Charlotte cast about for some new diversion. 'I must tell you something very disturbing.' She recounted the various mishaps that had troubled Lady Granville at the christening, along with the sadly unexpected death of young Mrs Chant the next morning.

The diversion worked perfectly. Ignoring her weakness, Elaine Knightley sat upright on the chaise longue agog with interest. 'My dearest Char,' she exclaimed, looking round to call for fresh coffee. 'What a perfectly dreadful thing to happen and on top of that shocking murder last week. What is the village coming to? That poor young woman and her sister too, bereaved so suddenly.'

'Kit thinks I'm yearning for adventure,' Charlotte confessed. 'Oh, he was very polite and concerned but I know he believes I'm exaggerating all the little coincidences and seeing murder on every side, because of my experiences in Bath.'

'Kit talks a great deal of nonsense,' was the caustic reply. 'He knows very well that you were nervous and shaken for weeks after our stay there, but....' Her eyes narrowed as she looked at her visitor, 'Your life *is* very quiet, Char. However, perhaps it is about to liven up with the arrival of this old acquaintance from Australia?' She narrowed her eyes. 'Is that – forgive me, my dear, but you have told me something of your early life. Are you likely to find yourself embarrassed by this elderly servant's reminiscences? For you know I will do whatever still lies within my power to help.'

'Dear Elaine....' Charlotte was touched and gave the thin hand a loving squeeze. 'How like you to offer, but no, I don't fear Bessie's tales. She knew us at a time of relative prosperity and of quite unparalleled propriety, so there are no secrets to be spilled by her.'

No, she made a face, shamed again by the memory. It was fortunate that Bessie's departure to Tasmania, with the large and handsome vagabond who had swept her off her feet, had occurred just before Will Glover tired of being respectable. *'I'm sorry, Molly,'* he told Charlotte's long-suffering mother, when she realized he had absconded with the church building fund, cajoling her with the smile he knew she found irresistible. *'But living a life of stifling respectability has definitely begun to pall upon me. What do you say? Shall we seek our fortune over in the goldfields? I hear there are rich pickings (of every description) to be had around Ballarat.'*

There had certainly been gold, easily picked up, though not through sweating in the fields – that was hardly Will's style – by a handsome and charming Anglican clergyman (albeit a former convict posing as such). Charlotte recalled her mother's gritted teeth as Will blithely set himself up as vicar to a mining township.

Much better not to bring those days to mind, she sighed, and hastened to reassure Elaine Knightley that she would be safe from scandal.

'Goodness,' she exclaimed. 'I nearly forgot. You'll never guess what has happened, Elaine. Miss Nightingale has offered me a situation!' She explained about the letter and told of Lady Frampton's dismay on hearing of the proposed post. 'I told Gran I had no intention of accepting,' she said with a sigh. 'But even though it's true what I said, that Miss Nightingale would surely be the most difficult of employers, I must confess that I'm more than a little tempted.'

'I can see that,' said Elaine, to Charlotte's surprise. 'You still don't feel entirely at home here, do you?' She reached over to clasp the other girl's hand. 'I've seen that look on your face sometimes, in an unguarded moment, when you look as you did when you first arrived at the manor. Alone, fiercely independent and as wary as a hunted hare.'

'You know me too well,' Charlotte admitted with a slight smile. 'I've promised Gran that I won't accept and I sent a polite refusal to Miss Nightingale only this morning, by way of one of our stable lads who has gone to see his mother on the Embley Park estate. Of course I shall stick to my word, I can't hurt Gran, but yes, I confess that I've been rather tempted. Perhaps Kit is right about me? I don't seem to have a true purpose in life and I am restless, but...' she brightened and gave a light laugh, 'I don't think I'm so bored that I'm reduced to seeking out non-existent murderers so, for the present, I shall continue to be a companion to Gran and to help Barnard with the place, as well as spending Christmas trying to prevent practically everyone else from strangling Melicent Penbury.'

Elaine leaned back against her pillows looking exhausted, but she opened her eyes and waved Charlotte back to her seat, when the younger girl rose to tiptoe out of the room.

'No, don't go, please, Char. I'm well enough for the moment. I was just wondering about you, my dear.' Her grey eyes were larger than ever in the delicate face, now so much more fine-drawn than even a few months ago when they had first met. 'It sounds a worthy enough purpose, to look after Lady Frampton, and I know that the old lady is a splendidly cheerful companion, but still.... Is there nobody else? Nobody you could call a kindred spirit? It's a lonely life after all. However fond you may be of Lily and Barnard at the manor – and indeed, they of you – you will need a friend in the coming months, dearest Charlotte.'

Charlotte's eyes filled with tears but she said nothing and sat looking down at her hands, while she fought back the sob that threatened to choke her. It was painful beyond measure that it should be Elaine who recognised the gap that would soon yawn ahead of her, but out of love and respect for her friend, Charlotte made no comment other than to summon up a tremulous smile and say, 'I have little hope of making Miss Nightingale a bosom friend, I fear, though I do rather like the look of our visitor, Miss Armstrong. She is bearing her troubles with dignity and I respect that in her and I believe I've surprised a glimpse of mischief once or twice, when Melicent Penbury has been particularly trying. Miss

Armstrong has an unexpected dimple that came into view when Gran was berating Melicent last night. I can and will befriend her for a day or so, but it will not answer in the long term for the poor girl must begin to look for a situation as soon as Christmas is out of the way and her sister safely buried.'

She knuckled her tears away with a sudden glimmer of amusement. 'I must say that Lady Granville is proving surprisingly sympathetic, astonishing as it might seem.' At Elaine's exclamation of surprise, Charlotte nodded. 'I know. It's hard to picture it, is it not, but she is so enthusiastic about her wonderful garden, that it's difficult to recognise the normally stately lady. Besides,' her smile was reminiscent, 'She is so utterly devoted to her son that I can't but be charmed.'

'I believe his arrival was the greatest joy to her,' Elaine remarked. 'I was newly married at the time and I know Kit's mother, who was a friend of hers, felt exceedingly anxious during the long wait before his birth. It was said locally that the lady took to her bed for near the entire time, with visitors strictly rationed lest they bring infection to the house, so anxious was she to avoid disappointment. In fact, I believe she was conveyed very gingerly and in easy stages to a small place near Bournemouth for the last month or so, to benefit from the pinewoods and the sea air and that was where she was confined. It's no wonder she is so besotted with the boy.'

She looked nostalgic. 'It's one of the places Kit took me to a year or two ago after someone had praised it to him as being the perfect place for a cure. So it might be, for someone else,' she shrugged. 'It's very restful and if you want some society there's a lending library and an assembly room. The pine walks are charming but I don't imagine Lady Granville saw much of them.' She looked thoughtful. 'You could do worse than take her for a friend, Char. I doubt Lord Granville enters into her pursuits. I gather he likes a peaceful life at home and lets her rule the roost but otherwise, from what Kit tells me, spends most of his time shooting and hunting, and riding about the estate.'

'I was interested in what she told me about her passion for old abbeys,' Charlotte said. 'I can't remember all of them, but she certainly mentioned Gracedieu and Walsingham.' She broke off abruptly at a sudden shadow on her friend's face. 'What is it, what did I say to upset you?'

'Nothing, you foolish Char. How could you know that for centuries Walsingham was a place of pilgrimage for barren women? I believe there is nothing to see, these days, but women still go there to pray. Lady Granville was one of the fortunate ones.'

Elaine was looking weary so Charlotte said no more, and prepared to take her leave, pausing only when a thought struck her.

'Heavens, I almost forgot.' She turned a sparkling smile towards her hostess. 'The vicar received a letter yesterday from his sister, Dora. You recollect her, I'm sure? It was you who reconciled me to her marriage to our neighbour.' Elaine nodded, looking keenly interested. 'It seems that Dora is to present her husband with a token of her affection in July. They are in Italy at present and she announces that she is in splendid health and clambering about a multitude of ruins. She cannot imagine why her sister-in-law has made such heavy weather of what is, after all, a perfectly natural state. Poor Agnes, who has suffered every discomfort under the sun, is sunk in gloom and guilt at her own incompetence.'

'Good God!' Elaine's eyes brightened with a slightly malicious sparkle. 'Who would have thought her husband brave enough to demand his conjugal rights,' she giggled, 'and how typical of Dora to sail through with no trouble. I do hope though,' she clapped a hand to her mouth and looked aghast, 'I hope Mrs Penbury has no such news? Surely everyone in sight would be obliged to suffer each pang and twinge along with her?'

Charlotte bent to kiss her. 'What a prospect. I feel guilty always, because that woman makes me uncharitable in spite of her infirmities, but I've heard nothing of the kind so far, thank God. Captain Penbury would surely demand a *couvade* in honour of his resident musket ball, should his wife announce an impending event.

'Now, I really must leave you to rest. I have to go home and tidy myself in time for church. I must also make sure Gran is not in a panic about which present she intends for which person.'

'That reminds me … before you go, dearest Char,' Elaine was holding out a small box from the table at her side. 'A little something for Christmas and to thank you for my sweet-smelling little nosegay. Open it, do,' she urged.

'Oh, Elaine....' Charlotte gazed in awe at the small but lovely emerald and pearl brooch that nestled in faded velvet. 'This is far too precious, you should not....'

'Indeed I should,' said Elaine decidedly. 'It belonged to my grandmother and has no great value, the emeralds are small and the pearls the same, but she was very dear to me, as are you. It's very old, it was her own grandmother's originally and now I want you to have it, dear Char, to remind....' She broke off abruptly. 'It's yours now, so no more protestations if you please.'

Charlotte nodded wordlessly, obediently pinned the brooch to her dress, and kissed her friend affectionately. As she picked up her shawl, Kit Knightley put his head round the door and smiled when Elaine called out to him, 'What an opportune arrival, Kit. You are just in time to escort this dear girl downstairs, for she insists on leaving us.'

'I suppose you are determined to walk back to the Manor, Char?' Kit offered his carriage but showed no surprise when Charlotte laughingly refused, saying she had obeyed Barnard's orders and the stable lad was waiting for her. 'Barnard is quite right but in any case I insist upon walking down the drive with you to see you safely off the premises.'

They conversed on unexceptionable subjects but neither broached the subject that tormented them; the increasing frailty of the woman so dear to both. It would have been a betrayal of Elaine, to discuss what was only too plain to see that, barring a miracle. She would be dead within weeks.

When they reached the carriage gates at the end of the drive, Kit Knightley hesitated.

'Char,' he said with some hesitation. 'That tale you were telling me, your old friend's fears and Lady Granville's morbid fancies...' he frowned and shook his head. 'Although I cannot believe there is a word of truth in any of this whole tarradiddle, I can't help being anxious on your behalf. Will you promise me –' he broke off in mid-sentence and looked across at the nearby copse of silver birch trees, their bare branches silhouetted in a delicate tracery against the pale winter sun. A frown creased his brow. 'The thing is, Char, there is trouble enough coming and I cannot spare the time to worry about you too.'

She pressed his hand in wordless sympathy and as she turned to walk across the heath track, Kit swallowed and said, abruptly, 'I've sent a note down to the vicarage, Char, offering Percy Benson an apology. I won't be at church today, I am not in the mood for festive celebrations.' He nodded to her and added, 'I hope you have a happy Christmas, Charlotte.'

Chapter 8

'AH, THERE YOU are, Char, come along there, come along.'
Barnard was fidgeting and frowning as he put his watch
back into his pocket, as Charlotte hurried down the ancient
blackened oak staircase, fastening her glove buttons as she did so
and smoothing down her golden brown skirts. 'Will you drive
Gran and Miss Armstrong in the pony chaise?' He cast a furtive
glance across the hall to where his guests were beginning to
assemble, and sighed as he caught a question in Charlotte's
twinkling hazel eyes.

'Look here, Char, Lily says I must make sure the doctor and his
sister-in-law don't sit together. She, Lily, says they're at daggers
drawn,' he whispered, looking vexed. 'So what with that, and
making sure Melicent doesn't fuss Gran into an apoplexy, Lily
thought…. The trouble is though, we were going to use the
brougham as well as the landau, but the wretched stable cat has
just had her kittens in it,' he confided, looking harassed. 'I don't
like … harrumph…' he cleared his throat sheepishly, trying to
disguise his tender heart, 'that is, the stable lads don't like to
disturb her, though I promise it'll be cleaned up before
tomorrow's visit to young Oz's party. I thought you might drive
Gran and Miss Armstrong? The weather's fine so we can pile rugs
and wraps round to keep out the cold.' He shot her another rueful
grin. 'You'll save my life and even if you're a bit chilled, you'll
still have the better bargain. I wouldn't wish Melicent on my own
worst enemy, though old Penbury's a good enough fellow. I hope
he'll keep his wife under control if Lily and I take them, along
with Dr Chant.' He mopped his ruddy brow and shook his head.
'Upon my word, Char, I had no idea what a damned – harrumph!

Beg your pardon, what a thorn in the flesh that woman has become.'

'Faint heart,' Charlotte laughed at him as they went outside to where the carriages were drawn up and waiting. 'I'll do what you want if you promise me two things.'

The Squire of Finchbourne glanced anxiously down at her and Charlotte gave him a little push. 'First of all it's up to you to break the news to Gran, and secondly, I'll need you to help hoist her into the chaise.' She grinned as he nodded in eager agreement. 'It's fortunate that none of us is addicted to modishly wide crinolines. Off with you then, and don't worry. If it comes on to rain or snow, the carriage can do several trips to carry us all home.'

The old lady was in fine fettle as the pony chaise set off smartly down the drive with Charlotte at the reins, all three ladies well wrapped up.

'I declare, young Char,' she announced. 'I like this frosty weather, so I do. Did I ever tell you about the time London's river froze over? 'Igh jinks we all 'ad then, I can tell you, my gal.' She stared with approval at the rime silvering the leaves of the magnificent red-berried holly by the gate, and nodded with satisfaction. 'I feel it in my bones,' she went on. 'We'll 'ave some snow to make it a real Christmas.'

'Oh dear, I hope not.' Miss Armstrong, tucked up to her chin in a large plaid rug, shivered and looked apologetic. 'I do beg your pardon, Lady Frampton,' she said, 'but I have to set out for London in a day or so to seek a new situation and I should much prefer to do so in fine weather.'

'But Miss Armstrong,' Charlotte gave the other girl a startled look over her shoulder. 'There's no need for such haste. I know Barnard and Lily are hoping you will remain at Finchbourne for some weeks to give you time to recover from your sad ordeal. Pray do not talk of going to London yet.'

Sibella nodded her thanks, looking unconvinced, and Charlotte had no time for discussion as she drew up beside the lych-gate. It was time to set about the business of decanting Lady Frampton from her carriage; no easy task but Barnard came to the rescue and the Finchbourne party set off past the tombstones leaving Charlotte chatting to Dr Perry and his wife who had come up to her at the gate, while Sibella lingered to pat the pony.

Lady Granville, her sealskin coat partly obscuring a strikingly unbecoming maroon plush dress, oozed graciousness as she greeted her neighbours at the church porch. Pleasantries were exchanged and Lord Granville, bowing with some ceremony, offered his arm to Lady Frampton, which old-world courtesy clearly gave her considerable pleasure. Oz Granville, in his Sunday best, made an awkward bow to the old lady and to Lily, then slipped back to greet Charlotte just as she turned to watch two parties of villagers.

Those decked in their festive best headed towards the church while the others, more soberly attired, turned off towards the Ebenezer chapel at the other end of the street. A plump woman stood out among these decorous worshippers, her bonnet gaily trimmed with red berries. Charlotte stared, eyes wide and incredulous, at her old friend Bessie on the arm of a pillar of the community. Charlotte wondered why, bearing in mind that Bessie used to have a *penchant* for a charming rogue, she should take up with the baker, a non-conformist lay preacher.

Miss Armstrong still stood beside the pony, talking quietly to him, while Dr Chant tried and failed to engage Dr Perry in conversation and Miss Cole was in everyone's way as she fussed and flapped her handkerchief about. Oz was eagerly telling Charlotte about the ride he and his father had taken earlier that morning while the Granvilles' groom lounged nearby with his fellow, the groom from the manor, when there was a sudden commotion, screams and shouts and the squeal of an outraged, frightened animal.

Charlotte and the grooms jerked around followed by the boy as they rushed to the fat pony which, startled out of its placid nap, had started up with a loud neighing and tried to gallop forward. Mercifully, the chaise remained upright and its weight had no doubt acted as an anchor on the pony.

'Miss Armstrong, are you hurt?' As the groom seized hold of the reins and began to soothe the pony, Charlotte reached Sibella who was looking white and shaken. 'You brave girl. You held on to the reins even though you might have been dragged under the wheels or the pony's hooves. Here, let me support you over to the wall, you can lean there and catch your breath.'

'No, please....' Sibella Armstrong had herself in hand now and a faint colour crept back into her ashen cheeks. She moved her right shoulder experimentally and Charlotte saw her wince, but the other woman recovered quickly. 'It's all right, Mrs Richmond, truly. Just a wrench, and that will heal.'

'A wrench?' Charlotte felt the injured shoulder with firm, but gentle hands. 'I'm surprised it's not dislocated but no, you are quite correct, but what in the world happened? The pony is the quietest beast in the world, too indolent to rise to a trot, let alone bolt.'

'I scarcely know,' Sibella was as puzzled as Charlotte. 'I was petting him when suddenly he reared up with a scream of fear, or perhaps pain, and tried to gallop off. Mercifully I managed to grab the reins and try to drag him to a halt. The rest you know.'

Amid the anxious and inquisitive babble, Charlotte suddenly made out a familiar complaining voice.

'Yes, indeed, do see to the young lady, Dr Perry. I do assure you that *I* am mercifully unharmed, though nobody as yet has taken the trouble to enquire after my health, being far more preoccupied with that of the horse.'

'Pony.' There was an audible mutter from Charlotte's left and she turned to raise her brows at Oz Granville. 'Not a horse,' he added severely, with a glare at his mother's companion as he faded into the background.

'There was a dog too,' Miss Cole added as she flounced up the steps to go into the church to wait upon her employer. 'Yes,' continued the companion, over her shoulder to Charlotte who was waiting for Dr Perry to confirm her own diagnosis. He helped Miss Armstrong up the steps and Charlotte took the other girl's arm in hers for extra support.

'There was certainly a dog,' reiterated Miss Cole. 'It ran under the horse's legs, which was what startled it and set it off.'

'Poppycock,' hissed Oz, glowering, as he appeared once more beside Charlotte. 'There was no dog in sight, I'd have spotted it if there had been. I like dogs,' he declared. 'Papa agrees I should have one, but Mama thinks it would bite me.'

The ineffable scorn in his voice roused Charlotte's sympathy but this was no time for idle chit-chat. Leaving the groom to settle the old pony, Charlotte walked into church, giving an arm to Sibella Armstrong who, though less pale, was visibly trembling.

'Pray allow me to sit here at the back, Mrs Richmond,' Sibella's murmur was insistent. 'I'll be better able to collect my thoughts here in this quiet corner.'

Charlotte made no protest but nodded sympathetically as Sibella crept to the far end of the last pew. Her own thoughts and prayers were a complete muddle. This was the second Christmas she had spent since the deaths of her mother and stepfather and the day brought home to her how much her life had changed.

This time last year, she reflected, I was fleeing across India, living on my wits and desperately trying to reach a boat for England, and here I am: settled, prosperous, loved and … lonely. She bit her lip and bent her head in prayer, urging whatever deity might be watching over her, to give Elaine Knightley peace and freedom from pain, even though Charlotte knew what that would mean. She prayed that Kit Knightley might have the strength to bear up during these last days, weeks perhaps and then…. She cast that thought aside. What Kit's future contained was no business of hers. All that mattered was Elaine's comfort.

But what of poor young Mrs Chant, she wondered, turning her thoughts with an effort. Why do I suspect that there is something untoward about her death? For I was uneasy about it before I encountered Bessie with her tale of something amiss; and something about Verena Chant made me sit up and take notice, but the Lord only knows what it was. Too much seems to have intervened since then for me to remember details.

Her brother-in-law, Percy, climbed the pulpit stair to preach his first Christmas sermon as the new vicar but no doubt primed by his wife, he kept his homily mercifully short, unleashing his congregation promptly so that they could see to their dinner and enjoy a day of rejoicing.

As she made her way outside, Charlotte whispered to Sibella

that she should remain in her shadowy corner. 'Do rest a while longer, it will be an age while the congregation mills around outside the church door, and you'll find it fatiguing.'

She slipped outside just as the parties from Brambrook Abbey and Finchbourne Manor were taking leave of each other.

'We shall expect you, and naturally your guests, at half past three tomorrow,' Lady Granville glanced round curiously as she spoke graciously to Lily Richmond. 'My husband did have a fancy for an old-style dinner to celebrate Osbert's birthday, but we decided that a tea party would be more appropriate.'

She went on her way with Miss Cole flapping along behind while Lord Granville and Oz shook hands cordially with everyone. The boy smiled eagerly as his father and Barnard went into a conspiratorial huddle. 'I'll send word, Richmond,' murmured the older man. 'We'll arrange another rat hunt in the next week or so, this time on Brambrook land. The boy had capital sport with you and I mean to see that he gets another crack at ratting.' He touched his hat in a farewell salute and hastened after his wife.

'Now, do come along, Master Osbert, your mama will be waiting for you.' The interruption came from the officious companion, who had returned to harry the boy. Charlotte glanced over at him in sympathy and smothered a gasp at his expression. The woman had not stayed to see if her instruction was obeyed and Oz was glaring after her, with a look of distress on his pale face.

'Oz?' Charlotte brooked no denial, pulling him gently to one side. 'You *must* tell me what is wrong? I've seen before that Miss Cole disturbs you, what has she done? Tell me, or I'll be forced to speak to your father, it cannot be right for you to be so anxious.'

'Dunster,' his whisper was hurried, as he glanced apprehensively over his shoulder. 'There's a hidey-hole under the bridge; you know, the bridge over the moat? Nobody else knows about it and I like to sit there. The cat from the lodge comes there too and lets me stroke him.'

'Yes?' Charlotte touched his shoulder gently and Oz nodded, clearly trusting her. 'You saw Dunster? You don't mean, surely – oh, Oz, you didn't see her … killed?'

115

'No, oh no,' the fearful look was back on his face and he looked round again to make sure there was nobody in hearing. 'I didn't, but I heard Miss Cole puffing and panting so I peeped out, it was raining and she couldn't see me. M-Mrs Richmond – she came out of the garden door, not up the drive from the main gates at all.'

'You'd better call me Char,' she told him absently, 'though not when your mama can hear. Let me understand this, Oz; if you saw Miss Cole, you surely must have seen the burly stranger she bore witness to?'

She took his hand and gave it a reassuring squeeze.

'No,' his eyes were anxious as he looked up at her. 'That's just it. I didn't see anyone at all, only Miss Cole, and I didn't hear anything either, apart from the usual noises from the stables. I was hiding under the bridge with the cat and then I heard her puffing away. That was when I saw Dunster lying by the door to Mama's garden, with blood all over her and Cole in a great hurry just coming out of the door and running across to – to look.'

At that moment there was a hail from Lord Granville at the Brambrook carriage, and Charlotte waved in response. 'You must go, Oz,' she urged and gave him a brief hug. 'You're certain Dunster was already on the ground when Miss Cole came out? Very well, don't mention this to anyone else and we'll talk about it when we get a chance. I'm sure there's nothing to worry about but I can see it was upsetting for you. I promise you we'll get to the bottom of it very soon.'

The boy seemed reassured and ran off to join his parents, looking much more cheerful. Pursing her lips, Charlotte glanced down the road to see if the chapel-goers were also making their way home but their minister was made of sterner stuff than Percy Benson, she thought, and was known for the length and power of his sermons. In the midst of the commotion with the pony, she had glimpsed Bessie staring across at the throng outside the church, but it was of no use to wonder about her presence in Finchbourne.

The story the boy told sounded fantastic but she had no reason to doubt his word; he was an observant lad and clearly disturbed by what he had witnessed. What an odd tale it was! How could Dunster, the maid, be suddenly dead and covered in blood on the drive if Oz had heard no sound of a struggle? And why, if all this were true, had Miss Cole lied on oath at the inquest, firstly about coming up the drive from the main gate, and then about seeing a stranger running off from the scene? She shook her head and went to collect Sibella from the church. It was time to obey her own advice and put the conundrum aside as she entered into the spirit of Christmas with her family.

Barnard held old-fashioned notions about dinner time on festive days, though at other times he gave in with an ill grace to Lily's pretensions to fashion and ate at a later hour. Today there was still a faint hint of light in the sky when the manor guests sat down to eat and Charlotte drank her clear turtle soup with a guilty nod to the memory of faraway beaches and dusky nights when Will Glover had taken her to watch the giant turtles lay their eggs. She recalled too, a day when she had stood guard over newly-hatched turtles and protected them from marauding gulls as they staggered unsteadily towards the sea.

'Don't get sentimental about animals, Char,' Will had warned her, serious for once, as he mopped up the tears that trickled down her sandy cheeks. 'The time may come when you will be glad to eat anything – anything at all – and be grateful for it.' Well, he'd certainly been right about that, she reflected, remembering the near-starvation she had endured in her flight across India during the Mutiny, so now she finished her soup without demur.

A roast goose and a great rib of beef were soon disposed of and Charlotte was glad to observe that Captain Penbury, who was sitting next to her, was for once exercising restraint. The last thing we need, she told herself, is for him to suffer another episode of severe indigestion, if that's what it was. Almost without volition she glanced across the table at Sibella Armstrong. Now why do I associate her with our naval hero's indisposition, she asked herself.

As the pudding was brought in, held aloft and flaming, by Hoxton the butler, Charlotte suddenly remembered. *Oz Granville!* She almost exclaimed the boy's name aloud, so great was her astonishment as she sent her thoughts back to the scene beside the wassail bowl. That was it, she exulted, glad to have identified the connection that had been niggling her for the last forty-eight hours or so. I was watching Oz tucking into candied fruits when I glanced across towards Verena Chant. She was smiling at her sister and at me, and even though I can't think why it didn't register properly with me at the time, I was amazed at her fleeting likeness to the boy. Yes, Charlotte pondered the similarities with increasing eagerness and little interest in the rich plum pudding now being served and put in front of her. And when Oz looked up at me at that moment and *he* smiled too – their smiles were practically identical.

'Char? Charlotte, I say.' Barnard was calling out her name. 'Bless me, the girl is in a daydream. Come, Char, eat up your pudding and see if you have the ring or the coin in there, nobody has found them yet, nor the thimble. We shall all have to have second helpings, eh?'

Pulling herself together Charlotte forced herself to join in with the merriment but found no sign of anything in her pudding except the currants, raisins and other fruits that she expected. Others were more fortunate.

'Well, bless my soul.' Lady Frampton held up a silver thimble. 'There's my fate, ain't it? I'm to die in single blessedness. Well,' her several chins wobbled as she wheezed, laughing heartily, 'I've 'ad my fun, so I 'ave and it would be a brave man as took me on nowadays!'

'Miss Armstrong? What is that you're trying to conceal under your spoon?' Melicent Penbury looked distinctly put out. She was not the centre of attention, that place went by right to Lily, as hostess. Unlike Agnes, daughter of the manor and the vicar's wife, she had no interesting condition to give her importance, and here was Sibella Armstrong taking the place of honour as the lone woman in need of comfort and assistance, a place Melicent was accustomed to fill, despite her present status as a newly-married woman.

Sibella bit her lip and managed a faint smile as she caught Charlotte's sympathetic eye. 'It is the ring,' she murmured, but if she had hoped to turn away the kindly and inquisitive comments of a table full of increasingly cheerful and rosy diners, she was to be disappointed.

'By Gad, ma'am,' thundered the captain, banging the table with delight. 'A marriage, I see. Who will be the lucky man, hey? Hey?' With the dreadful timing of the truly tactless, he continued with a knowing smile. 'Sadly, I am out of the running these days, but have we a single man at table?' He stared round at the other men, his weather-beaten face agleam only with interest, but as his eye fell upon Dr Chant, so recently bereaved, the captain gave a sudden grunt of pain and turned an indignant stare upon Charlotte.

'I'm so sorry, Captain Penbury,' she apologised. 'I had a sudden cramp in my foot, did I inadvertently kick you? How very clumsy of me, I do beg your pardon.'

Barnard Richmond now rushed into the breach, his jovial face creased with anxiety on behalf of a guest's feelings. 'Here,' he cried, holding up a coin. 'See what I have, I am to be rich. That'll be a lark, won't it, Lily?' He caught Charlotte's eye and grinned with relief at their having jointly averted a grievous social gaffe. 'I heard the other day that there are railway surveyors at large locally, so perhaps I am about to make my fortune selling land to them.' His shoulders shook as he roared with laughter but only Charlotte was privy to the slight flicker of his left eyelid as he glanced at her. She knew that negotiations for the sale of several otherwise unproductive, distant acres for the new railway line were already well underway, for he had consulted her, having a good deal of respect for her opinion.

'Presents now,' decreed Lily. 'If we have to wait until the gentlemen finish their horrid cigars, we shall wait forever. Hoxton? Please hand round the basket of gifts.'

Charlotte was relieved to see that Miss Armstrong had a respectable heap of small gifts in front of her – more handkerchiefs, some ribbons, a length of lace for trimming a gown or hat, and that even Dr Chant was opening a box of fine cigars. Her own haul offered some surprises. Certainly there were gloves, some books, a fan, handkerchiefs, ribbons and laces for her too, together with a beautiful cashmere shawl from Lily and Barnard, but underneath was a small parcel that had clearly arrived in the post.

She undid the wrapping and opened up the brief note she discovered inside, while Lily, with undisguised curiosity, asked,

'Whoever can be sending you presents by post, Charlotte? You have, after all, little acquaintance outside Hampshire.'

'It is … it is a pair of emerald bracelets,' Charlotte looked up, with a dazed expression. 'From, from the lady I told you of, the one I met in Bath.'

'Really?' Lily's eyes glittered with envy as she examined the sparkling jewels in a slender setting, complemented by a delicately engraved tracery. 'Of course, I recall now. She turned out to be some kind of relative of yours, did she not? She must be a lady of some consequence.'

'Aunt Becky, yes,' Charlotte's response was a little absent as she scanned the accompanying brief, loving note. Not for the world would she ever reveal to Lily the true relationship that lay between her and the elderly lady she had met so unexpectedly during that summer's visit to Bath. She pulled herself together and looking up, saw that Lady Frampton was watching her in some anxiety. Charlotte looked down and realized that there was one present remaining and that one an official-looking document. As she opened it up under Lady Frampton's eager gaze, she saw the old lady hold a finger to her lips.

'Oh, Gran…' Charlotte stared in astonishment at the deeds of a pair of London houses and as Lily rose to gather her ladies to retire to the drawing-room, Char flung her arms round the old lady who had become so very dear to her. 'I had no idea,' she whispered. 'What a generous thing to do, you're the most wonderful old lady in the entire world.'

'You're a woman of property now, me gal,' the old lady spoke gruffly, always her way when she was deeply moved. 'You keep quiet about it though, it's nobody's business but ours, though Barnard knows. It ain't much, but Kensington is getting all the rage now, so the rent will make you decently independent, me dear. Call it an instalment of your in'eritance if you like, that pair of 'ouses was a gift to me from my dear late 'usband on my fortieth birthday. 'E'd have approved of you.' She blew her nose loudly and tapped Charlotte on the arm with the fan that was Char's present to her. 'And 'ed 'ave loved a daughter like you, Char, as much as what I do.'

Overwhelmed by the old lady's generosity, Charlotte slipped upstairs and tucked her gifts into a drawer, then splashed water from the basin to cool her flushed cheeks. Gran had given her the thing she had craved for so long: independence and respectability. Lady Frampton might speak dismissively of the value but even Charlotte's ignorance of London did not prevent her realising that a pair of town houses in Kensington was a magnificent inheritance.

Impossible after such generosity to consider, even half-heartedly, Miss Nightingale's offer of a situation; Gran would be hurt beyond bearing, though she would never mention it, so it was as well that Charlotte had despatched her refusal.

It was too much to take in at this moment, so she swung her new shawl around her shoulders and admired herself in the mirror. Clever Lily had chosen well: the shawl had a background of soft cream and the paisley pattern was predominantly green, just the thing to wear with her festive gown of dark emerald silk. With a wistful smile she slipped her new matching bracelets on to her arms, then her glance fell on Elaine Knightley's emerald and pearl brooch and Charlotte's eyes filled with sudden, anguished tears. Here am I, she half sobbed; healthy and loved and now with a truly independent income, honestly come by, for a change, while Elaine, whom I love so dearly and who is so good to everyone, Elaine is…. It was no use, the word would not, must not, be spoken and Charlotte shook her head. No time for grieving now, she shivered. Lily has a party of very mixed guests and she is relying on me to help her entertain them.

Downstairs, Lily was doing her best to dispose her awkward group of ladies around the drawing-room. Lady Frampton was happily ensconced beside the fire, with her fat old spaniel, Prince Albert, wheezing contentedly at her feet, as he kept an eye on his mistress should she slip him the odd titbit.

Melicent, Charlotte saw with a sigh, was at the pianoforte again. Lily had reluctantly asked her to play, backed up by the vicar's wife. Miss Armstrong had taken herself off to a seat to one side, and Melicent's playing was better than nothing, as neither Agnes nor Lily could boast of much talent. Anything, Charlotte thought, to stave off yet another war of words between Melicent and Dr Chant, who had taken to sneering at every ailment that the former governess claimed to have contracted. (*'Cholera, madam? I take leave to doubt it, but let us hear your symptoms. Did you suffer from high fever and dysentery?'*) Charlotte had thrown herself into the breach at that time, incurring the displeasure of both combatants, but receiving heartfelt gratitude from Lily who had been privileged to mediate over their heated discussions on increasingly revolting symptoms and ailments.

Half an hour of Christmas music, enhanced by some uncertain arpeggios and the occasional wrong note, passed the time and when Melicent stopped for a rest, Charlotte made an effort. 'How splendid, Melicent. It must be delightful to be able to play.'

'Do sing to us, Char.'

Oh dear, that was Agnes, attempting, with clumsy kindness, to give everyone a chance to shine. She lowered her voice and looked moist-eyed in the direction of the bereaved guest. 'Something quiet and in keeping, of course, but I know I can trust your taste.'

'I've told you before, Agnes, I have no accomplishments.' Charlotte was firm and turned away with a nod to Melicent. None, apart from cooking a plain dinner, sewing a plain seam, and, as she had confessed to Oz, killing a crocodile that had Will by the leg. Better not admit to that, she told herself, with an inward smile, and as for her voice – well, Will Glover had certainly taught her many songs but there were few that would pass muster in a lady's drawing-room. The ladies present tonight would be shocked beyond belief were she to burst into a chorus of one of the songs she had learned at the gold fields and the only respectable song that sprang to mind was *The Wild Colonial Boy*, which was a trifle too close to her own history for comfort, not to mention whatever had become of Sibella's brother.

Before Agnes could press her reluctant sister-in-law further, the double doors were flung open and Barnard ushered in his gentlemen. Evidently, the brandy and port had flowed once the dining-room was free of the hampering presence of the women folk. Barnard's bluff face was always ruddy and jovial but tonight he was in the highest of good humours, while Percy Benson, the vicar, whose build was slight and his complexion wan, now sported bright red cheeks and a silly smile. His wife, pursing her lips at the sight, said nothing but waylaid him and forced him to sit quietly beside her.

Captain Penbury was another man of habitual high colour but Charlotte was relieved to see that he looked none the worse for wear. Mindful of Elaine Knightley's mischievous suggestion, she shot a thoughtful glance at Melicent Penbury and was reassured; if Melicent were with child, the entire population of Finchbourne would know by now.

Dr Chant also had a heightened flush and seemed to have recovered from the deep gloom that had wreathed him earlier. His glance swept the drawing-room with the practised ease of a man used to winnowing out those members of society who might be of use to him. His gaze passed over Lady Frampton, to Charlotte's secret amusement, knowing that the old lady's enormous wealth would have the doctor solicitously at her feet, if only he knew of it. The vicar and Agnes clearly held no prospect of social advancement, apart from their relationship to the manor, while the Penburys, man and wife, were beneath his notice. Charlotte did suspect him though, of deliberately provoking Melicent for his own amusement, a circumstance which reinforced her conviction that he was not overwhelmed by grief.

On overhearing Melicent's peevish complaint that the manor was draughty, he had solemnly told her, 'You are quite correct, madam, to fear. It is well known that many persons take cold from the injurious currents of air that seep through window and door frames. Remember the adage, "When the wind comes upon you through a hole, it is time to make your will and take care of your soul." You would do well to take to your bed and recall those wise words.'

The doctor now made his way towards Lily, clearly bent upon charming her, but the butler entered at that moment, bearing cake and wine. Baulked of his prey, Dr Chant shrugged and turned towards Charlotte, who was sitting beside Miss Armstrong just out of reach of the ferocious heat of the roaring fire.

'I hope I do not intrude?' He sat down with a nod at Charlotte, his smile turning to a hastily-disguised scowl as Melicent Penbury tripped over to them, with a girlish squeal of laughter.

'Oh, do pray allow me to join you, dear Mrs Charlotte, I so rarely have the opportunity to converse with ladies. The women in our little town you know, very worthy persons of course, but....' she shook her head. 'One does miss the company of refined people of one's own kind.'

'Oh, do just call me Charlotte,' Char begged, casting about for an innocuous topic. 'I believe there are rumours of snow in the air. How delightful, I have never encountered snow before, it will be a new pleasure.'

'I did not think it ever snowed so far south,' said Sibella quietly. 'I was brought up in Northumberland so it was never a novelty.'

'Have you visited this part of the world before?' put in Melicent, her eyes alight with curiosity as Sibella hesitated and stammered a little, a fleeting colour staining her pale cheeks.

'Indeed not,' she said decidedly. 'Winchester is quite unknown to me,' she added. 'It was a whim of my sister's, I believe, that led her to choose the city for our short holiday.'

'A whim?' With a snort of laughter that contained little humour, Dr Chant broke into the conversation. 'Believe me, my dear Sibella, nothing your late sister ever did was by a mere *whim*,' there was a scornful twist to his lip as he went on, 'her every action, rather, was the result of calculation, believe me.'

Charlotte stared, while Sibella looked away, biting her lip and Melicent Penbury sat up, eager at the prospect of dissension. The doctor continued, 'But your brother must have known this part of the world quite well, must he not?' Dr Chant leaned back in his upholstered walnut chair, thumbs tucked into his waistcoat, watching his fellow guest as he went on, 'After all, he was employed as secretary to Lord Granville both in London and in the country. My dear late wife,' he allowed himself a moment of solemn remembrance by bowing his head, but Charlotte detected a note of sarcasm. 'Yes, Verena told me her brother was very well-regarded by both Lord Granville and his lady. Sadly, I fear the young man left their employ rather hurriedly and under a cloud.'

The malice in his expression was pronounced as Sibella shrank back in her chair, her face drained of colour. Melicent, who had been turning from one to the other with an avid interest, now joined in the conversation.

'Good gracious me,' she said, with her usual gasping, breathless manner. 'Is that the brother you told us had emigrated to Australia, Miss Armstrong? How sad it is when families are rent asunder by misfortune. When was it that your brother left these shores?'

Short of causing a diversion by dancing a hornpipe, Charlotte realized there was little she could do to protect Miss Armstrong from this interrogation. Besides, she was intrigued; the circumstance of the brother's employment by the Granvilles seemed a startling coincidence, bearing in mind the way his sisters had stumbled into a slight acquaintance with young Mrs Richmond from the manor. That thought slipped into her mind and without knowing quite why, she asked:

'Did your brother resemble you, Miss Armstrong? I did not think you and Mrs Chant were very much alike. Family likeness is sometimes very marked, other times it is barely noticeable. For example, I do not resemble my late mother at all, as she was small with fair hair and blue eyes, but I lately met an old servant who insisted that our voices were almost identical. What do you think, Melicent? You must have observed many instances of this in your various charges.'

Her praiseworthy attempt to broaden the discussion resulted in a faint smile from Sibella but Melicent sat bolt upright in an attitude of outraged dignity and Charlotte remembered, too late, that the former governess resented any reference to her earlier occupation.

Dr Chant still wore that expression of bright-eyed malice. 'I believe Edward Armstrong bore a very close resemblance to his sister Verena,' he said, shooting a glance at the silent Sibella. 'Not merely in facial appearance but in character also. In any event, he was not to be trusted and was despatched to Australia in an attempt to avoid a scandal, where he later died, and in answer to your question, madam,' he bowed to Melicent, 'I understand that his departure took place about eleven or twelve years ago.' The sarcasm was clearly apparent now to Charlotte as he added, 'As I said, he left under a considerable cloud.'

Chapter 9

CHARLOTTE BLESSED THE manor's infant son and heir whose angry wails had the effect of breaking up the party rather earlier than she could have hoped for. Agnes sent for her cloak and, after the customary quarter of an hour of fussing, succeeded in tearing herself and her slightly befuddled husband away from her ancestral home and back to the vicarage. Lady Frampton was always ready for her bed, and had indeed been nodding away beside the fire for the last hour, while the ill-assorted guests made no objection when Lily whisked herself anxiously away to the nursery to assuage little Algy's hunger, leaving Barnard hovering uncertainly between the drawing-room and above stairs.

While Lily was saying goodnight, Sibella whispered urgently to Charlotte, 'I really cannot go visiting tomorrow, pray help me to explain to my kind hosts.'

'Oh, of course,' Charlotte nodded in sympathy. 'I'll stay at home too,' she began, when Lily burst in on the conversation.

'What's that, Char? Barnard, come here at once.' She was agitated. 'Here is Miss Armstrong saying she won't go out to tea tomorrow and dear Charlotte offering to stay at home with her.'

A chorus of dismay and disapproval soon had Sibella shrinking into her chair but it was Barnard's exclamation that clinched the argument.

'That cannot be right, Char; I tell you what, I'll send a note to say that none of us will attend.'

Sibella bowed to the inevitable and insisted that she could not spoil the family's fun and Charlotte hastily took her to one side, lest Lily should carry on the discussion.

'I understand that you feel awkward at the prospect of meeting the

Granvilles, but there will be so many guests there that you will not be remarked upon,' she assured the other girl. 'Lady Frampton will take you under her wing and you may sit quietly out of the way of the festivities. Nobody will make you feel uncomfortable, I promise.'

It was a relief to escape to her room, away from Dr Chant's barbed remarks and Sibella's discomfort, although Melicent Penbury looked to have enjoyed her evening, darting little questions here and there. Charlotte frowned as she recalled Sibella's awkward attempt to deflect the intrusive interrogation.

'As I mentioned, I am from the North,' she had explained reluctantly. 'As I explained last evening, my father was a parish priest and my mother was connected, rather remotely, to the local gentry.' She sighed and lowered her eyes. 'When Papa died, my brother Edward inherited what money there was, with instructions to take care of his sisters.'

She paused and Charlotte shot her a wry glance. 'Oh dear, that sounds fraught with difficulties; it didn't work for Elinor and Marianne Dashwood, did it,' she suggested and was rewarded by a brief smile of understanding.

'I'm afraid it was like that,' admitted Sibella. 'My brother was not – was never very good with money.'

She was interrupted by a snort of knowing laughter from Dr Chant and by an exclamation from Lily who had moved over to join the other women. Bristling, Lily exclaimed, 'You mentioned someone called Dashwood, Charlotte? And you know them too, Sibella? How can that be, are they a local family? I was under the impression that I was acquainted with all the local gentry, so I cannot understand it. I should like an introduction but the name is unfamiliar to me.'

She glared suspiciously at Charlotte who hastily said, 'It's a book by Miss Austen, Lily; just some people in a book.'

Charlotte undressed rapidly, anxious to leap into bed and to forget the uncomfortable evening. She was putting her dark brown hair into its neat night-time plaits when there was a tentative tap at the door.

'Miss Armstrong?' She was startled but hospitable as she ushered the other young woman inside. 'Are you still anxious about attending tomorrow's party? I'm sure we can find you a veil if you would like that. Here, come and sit by the fire, it's bitterly cold everywhere, Barnard says he thinks it will snow tomorrow.' Aware that she was babbling in her surprise at this overture, Charlotte sat her guest in the warm while, still shivering slightly, she flung her new shawl around her own shoulders.

Still without speaking, Sibella warmed her toes at the small, bright fire. Charlotte sat quietly, wondering what could have prompted this unexpected visit, but willing to wait for enlightenment.

'I'm sorry,' Sibella made to rise, but Charlotte put out a hand to stop her. 'It's not the party, I'll do as you say and sit quietly out of the way.' She shook her head, 'I should not have – but you did say I might come and I....' She hesitated again then clearly made a decision. 'The thing is, Mrs Richmond – well, Charlotte then – I don't know what I am to do and I wondered if I might confide in you to some extent?'

At Charlotte's nod, Sibella went on. 'Thank you, you see I am singularly alone now and you – you have been so kind and so sympathetic, I believe I can talk to you. It's all so difficult....' She composed herself and took a deep breath. 'First of all, I should perhaps give you a clearer picture of my family circumstances. As I said this evening, my brother and sister and I were orphaned quite young and Verena was adopted, on an informal basis, by a distant cousin of our mother's. It was not ideal; our old governess had married late in life and she offered to take my sister under her wing and bring her up.' Sibella sat frowning at the fire and Charlotte waited quietly for her to continue. 'It would have been so much better for Verena, in many ways, if she had remained at her boarding school in Newcastle. However, her new guardian was a wealthy, childless widow who led an empty society life and she took Verena out of school and installed her in the London house, so delighted was she to have a real-life doll to dress and indulge and parade amongst her friends and acquaintants. Verena was already showing signs of beauty, even at a little under thirteen, and she became what her adoptive mother made her: another vapid, vain society flibbertigibbet with not a notion in her head apart from clothes and fashion and compliments.'

She wiped her eyes on her sleeve and gratefully accepted the handkerchief Charlotte held out to her. 'As a child, she was sweet and loving, but everything changed. I helped a neighbour with her children for some months until I decided to seek a position as a governess in London to be near my brother and sister.'

Charlotte was sympathetic. She too had considered employment as a governess, though in the end she had given in to her mother's pleas, looking away in shame as her erratic but charming stepfather carried on his career as a confidence trickster. But no longer, she reminded herself firmly; these days I am a respectable widow and no-one is any the wiser.

'Edward obtained a post with Lord Granville as a junior secretary,' Sibella was saying. 'One of our Northumbrian neighbours used his influence with his lordship. It was a godsend. Edward's career until then had been unsteady, to say the least. He tried university but was sent down for some misdeed that I was never informed about, then he joined the army briefly. He took – borrowed – the jewellery my mother had left me and sold it to purchase a cornetcy but that did not answer either. Again, it was never explained to me, but I suspect he was ... that he....' She pulled a face. 'At any rate, the position in London dropped into his lap at an opportune moment and he seemed to be making a go of it. So much so that he sent me my train fare to London and said he had found me a post as a governess.'

She paused while Charlotte poked up the fire and added some coal, saying with a shiver, 'I have never been so cold in my entire life as I have been these last few weeks. There, that's better. Do go on.'

'It was a happy time,' Sibella smiled faintly. 'My charge was a well-behaved small girl who was a delight to teach and at that time Verena was thriving under the cosseting she was receiving, while Edward seemed happily settled with Lord Granville. So much so, indeed, that he speedily became the pet of the household, with her ladyship being particularly fond of him, and inviting him to dinner whenever they were a man short.'

'Did you meet the Granvilles too?' Charlotte asked.

'Oh yes,' Sibella nodded and looked away. 'They were so kind; sometimes they allowed Edward to invite me to their receptions. It was a wonderful time – but he threw it all away.' She gritted her teeth. 'He was – he was a womaniser, although I had no idea of it at the time. Did I say that he was exceedingly good-looking? Well,' she faltered. 'You saw my sister, the resemblance was very marked and I was told, in no uncertain terms, that he had betrayed a young society lady by making up to her. I also learned afterwards that in order to satisfy the demands of the several women who were the objects of his attentions, he altered bank drafts, just a little at a time, so that his theft was undetected, but he grew too careless, too arrogant. He was discovered when he attempted to obtain money for some sensitive information he had gathered at the government office where Lord Granville was a junior minister.'

'Forgive me,' Charlotte broke in as Sibella's voice faltered into silence. 'But I did not observe you in conversation with the Granvilles. Did they not acknowledge you? How uncharitable, when this was none of your doing.'

'The Granvilles were bitterly hurt and disappointed,' Sibella explained. 'Lady Granville particularly, for she overheard Edward laughing as he described her as a "tiresome old woman".' She frowned and sighed. 'It would be unthinkable to expect them to renew the acquaintance and I do not wish to do so. I never expected to see them again, it was a terrible coincidence that Verena chose to visit Winchester; I supposed they would be in Town. Besides, they were kind at the time. To avoid scandal, they sent my brother packing without prosecuting him, although they would have been completely within their rights. Verena's guardian refused to allow me to see or speak to my sister again, and even forbade me to write, while my employer was an acquaintance of Lady Granville's and I lost my position also because of the shame. I was tarred with the same brush, as it was said that I must have been aware of Edward's behaviour, which was a complete and odious lie. I knew nothing of what he had done and it was a very dark and difficult time for me.'

'My poor dear,' Charlotte was all sympathy and took the other girl's cold hand in her own as Sibella blushed and stumbled awkwardly over the explanation, not meeting her eyes. 'It must have been dreadful, but it is surely a comfort to know that you were reconciled with your sister before her untimely death.'

Just after midnight, when Charlotte had been lying in bed for more than an hour listening to the wind whistling about the windows of the ancient manor house, she gave up her attempt at sleep and reached out to light her candle. Shivering, she wrapped her new shawl around her and was about to snuggle down into her pillows once more when she noticed that the fire was very low. No wonder it's so cold in here, she grumbled, and scrambled with considerable reluctance out of bed. Mercifully there was plenty of coal and kindling set ready in the hearth and she blessed the efficiency of the household.

I've never been so cold in my life, she thought, but at least I have a fire and I'm safely tucked up in a beautiful house with every luxury to hand. She recalled a conversation with Will:

'If you ever have to be a beggar, Char,' he had said, 'Try to make sure you are not destitute during an English winter. Poverty is easier by far to cope with in a warm climate, believe me; I've tried both and there's no comparison.' He had laughed at her expression and continued, 'I mean it, Char. If there's water and the occasional insect to hand, you won't starve.' He had hesitated then, 'Mind you, I've been fairly close to starvation in the Outback and I have to admit that the hunger was pretty terrible. If it hadn't been for those ants and that timely lizard....'

Charlotte smiled and shook her head now as she recalled her childish shriek of disgust at his suggestion, but shivering, she could understand what he had meant about the cold weather. She tended the fire until there was a good blaze going, with the flames crackling and sparks flying up the chimney, then she scuttled across the polished floorboards to pull the curtains closer. With a gasp of amazement, she stared out at the garden as the clouds parted and the moon sailed majestically into view. Clear as day, she saw that the wind had died down and that snow had cloaked the earth with ermine.

'Oh, how magical,' she exclaimed and gasped as she spotted a pair of roe deer picking their way on dainty feet across the snow-covered grass as they headed for the refuge of the woods.

Scrambling back into bed, Charlotte knew that sleep was far away so she reflected on the day's happenings. She shied away from thinking of Elaine Knightley, frail and gallant and surely almost on her deathbed. The idea was too painful, so her thoughts hurried onward to the startling incident at the church gate. Why had the fat old pony suddenly taken it into its head to try to gallop off like that? It had led a pampered existence, as befitted an elderly equine gentleman, with a comfortable stable in the yard of Rowan Lodge and the run of the paddock that ran alongside the lane, whenever it fancied a spot of exercise.

Miss Cole insisted that there was a dog in the case, and kept to her story. Everyone else seemed to have shrugged and accepted that as the cause of the incident, but Charlotte had seen no dog and neither had Oz Granville, whose temper had been sorely tried by the officious behaviour of his mother's companion. Sleep was beginning to overtake her when Charlotte suddenly exclaimed aloud, 'Bessie! What in the world was Bessie doing on Finchbourne village green?'

Bessie had looked startled, Charlotte now recalled, at the name of Charlotte's village; perhaps the smith's brother had something to do with that. Had she been near enough to the scene at the church gate to have witnessed anything untoward?

It was no use; Charlotte's eyelids drooped as she dozed off with one thought lingering in mind: *I wonder if Bessie saw a dog?* It was surely nonsense but she took the notion into her dreams.

Breakfast next morning brought another letter from the persistent Miss Nightingale. The butler handed it ceremoniously on a silver salver, bowing as he explained, 'The stable lad brought it back with him from Embley Park, Miss Char, ma'am, I mean.'

There was a slight, awkward pause as Charlotte nodded her thanks and took her letter, aware that Lily was staring with an outraged frown at the missive in her hand, while Barnard and his guests eyed her with covert curiosity. Oh well, gulped Charlotte; in for a penny, in for a pound. *I had rather Lily didn't know about this but it's unavoidable now.*

She ducked her head in polite apology and slit open the envelope.

It was as she feared: Miss Nightingale was not going to take no for an answer.

'*I believe you have not fully considered the advantages to you regarding the position I offer, dear Mrs Richmond…*' ran the letter. '*It would therefore be a great kindness on your part if you would do me the honour of visiting me for tea the day after tomorrow at three o'clock. I am persuaded you will then see clearly in which direction your duty lies.*'

A royal command, no less, sighed Charlotte, then she assumed an expression of honest surprise and dismay and prepared to admit to what Lily would surely take as a clandestine correspondence, deliberately undertaken in order to put a slight upon herself.

'Miss Nightingale wishes me to attend an interview in a day or two,' she explained briefly. 'She is offering me a situation.'

'A *what?*' To Charlotte's surprise Barnard bellowed the question, his face reddening in evident anger. 'What the devil – harrumph, I beg your pardon, ladies – but what the deuce makes her do such a thing? Damn it, it's an insult to a lady of your standing, Char, and to me. Makes it look as though you have no family to look after you, blast the woman. She always was a nuisance when we played as children, wanting to take the part of Robin Hood herself, and such like. Quite ridiculous.'

'But Barnard…' Charlotte was touched at his outburst. 'I'm sure she doesn't mean it as an insult. In fact, I think she intends it to be seen as a compliment.'

She turned to answer a question from Lily who, in the face of Barnard's roar, had bitten back the sharp comment that she was about to make. 'I don't know why Miss Nightingale formed such an opinion of me, but it appears she thinks I would be a suitable candidate for some administrative post within her proposed nursing order.' She shrugged. 'Naturally I have no intention of taking up any such offer,' she said, glancing at Gran who had mercifully said nothing. No need for Lily to know that the offer had already been made earlier and rejected, though clearly Miss Nightingale had no intention of giving up. 'I'll write a polite note to her later this morning,' she told Lily with a slight smile. 'I'm far too comfortable here in Finchbourne. She'll have to look elsewhere for her candidate.'

A thought struck her and she shot a covert glance in Sibella Armstrong's direction. Well, why not? The other woman was quiet and sensible, well read and with a pleasant nature and a sense of humour, Charlotte surmised, when not overwhelmed by circumstances. Perhaps she'd postpone her reply until she'd had a chance to talk to Sibella.

After breakfast, the plan was that such members of the household who were so inclined should walk down to the village to see the hunt go off.

'In former years,' Barnard explained, 'the meet has been at Knightley Hall but this year, well...' he shrugged helplessly. 'Anyway, the upshot was that back in the autumn, Kit and I discussed whether the manor would take it on this year, but Lily said....'

'*Barnard* decided,' Lily looked daggers at her hapless spouse. 'And I agreed with him, that the Boxing Day meet would be too close upon the heels of our dear little Algy's arrival, so for this year only the meet is at The Three Pigeons. They'll be going off at about eleven o'clock and as the snow has settled and the sun is shining this morning, we can walk down; it should be a splendid sight.'

Amid the murmurs at the table, Charlotte took the opportunity to whisper to Barnard, 'Didn't you want to ride yourself then, Barnard? Surely Lily would have let you off the leash just for this morning. I know how much you love hunting.'

He shook his head. 'Not fair to leave her with such a houseful,' he murmured, rolling his large brown eyes as he looked from Melicent and her captain, to the doctor, by way of his grandmother who was still addressing her usual gargantuan breakfast. 'Don't you worry, Char, there'll be hunting a-plenty later. Besides,' he turned suddenly serious. 'I didn't like ... in the circumstances. I mean, Kit's a very old friend and somehow it doesn't seem right to be....' He shook his head and looked surprised but pleased when, after casting a surreptitious glance round to make sure Lily wasn't observing them, Charlotte stood on tiptoe to plant a hearty kiss on his cheek.

'You're such a good man, dear Barnard,' was all she said, with an affectionate pat on his arm.

Just before eleven o'clock, Charlotte was consulted by Lily in a panic.

'What do you think, Char?' she hissed, beckoning Charlotte into her room. 'Will this shawl be sufficient to keep me warm? I should like to wear the sealskin mantle dear Barnard gave me yesterday, it cost a guinea, after all, but I would not wish to outshine Lady Granville, you know. I remember she was wearing something very similar at dear Algy's christening.'

Charlotte blinked at this unusual consideration for another's feelings, but hastened to reassure her sister-in-law. 'It's freezing outside, Lily,' she said firmly, nodding as Lily's maid helped her mistress into the new coat. 'You must wrap up as warmly as possible, think of the baby. Besides, Lady Granville isn't the sort to worry anyway. She's so secure in the knowledge that her ancestry goes back to Adam and Eve that she's probably too well-bred even to notice what we wear.'

Despite Lily's brave speech about walking down to the village, Charlotte was under no illusion; Lily had no intention of taking a brisk walk, today or any other, and as a new mother she had the perfect excuse, so she bundled Melicent Penbury into the brougham which was now clean and gleaming having been vacated by the stable cat who had conveyed her three kittens else-where. Lily nodded kindly at Miss Armstrong's polite but definite refusal, and bullied Charlotte into abandoning the walk she had planned.

'Nonsense, Char,' she snapped as the brougham set off at a careful pace down the icy drive. 'Of course you must come with us, what would it look like? The manor must be represented. Gran is excused attendance, of course, and Miss Armstrong, no doubt correctly, feels it would be inappropriate to make a public appear-ance at a sporting event though I'm relieved she's said no more about missing the party this afternoon.' She gave a disparaging sniff, 'I see that unbridled grief does not interfere with Dr Chant's enjoyment of the day's entertainments.'

Charlotte knew better than to answer Lily's pronouncements but inwardly she was surprised. So Lily didn't like the doctor either, that was interesting. Dr Chant, as a society darling who numbered

Prince Albert among his distinguished patients, should have been in high favour with his hostess, but that was apparently not the case. There was no opportunity to question Lily about this though, as they had arrived at the village inn.

Lily began to fuss again about her bonnet and coat while Charlotte helped to manoeuvre Melicent down the awkward step, just as Captain Penbury bustled forward to add an arm to his lady's aid, saying, 'Now, now, my dear. You must take care, we must not forget there may be a murderer still in the vicinity.'

On cue, Melicent set up a shrieking and gasping and Charlotte glared at the captain. 'I doubt, Captain, that any of us would be the target of an attack in the midst of so many.' She gave Melicent a withering stare and glanced round the village green, ducking her head back into the brougham.

'Do hurry up, Lily. I can see more people arriving, hacks and hunters alike and there's quite a throng outside the front door of The Three Pigeons. It won't do for you to be late.' She gave a sigh as she realized Lily was still anxiously inspecting herself in a tiny hand mirror. 'For heaven's sake, Lily. Remember that you are the great lady of Finchbourne village now and it's your duty to be on show. Besides, if you don't make haste, you'll find Melicent Penbury playing the hostess and greeting all the local dignitaries. And you don't want that, I know.'

The ploy worked and the two young women made their brisk way along the slippery pavement to the village inn, just in time for Lily to elbow the egregious Melicent out of the way.

'If you please,' she hissed, stepping with careless malice on Melicent's one good foot and causing her to yelp in pain. '*I* am the mistress of Finchbourne Manor, and it is *my* place to welcome everyone. Remember your place, Mrs Penbury, and kindly remain in the background.'

Charlotte took a few judicious steps away from this confrontation, although she noted with concern that Melicent looked very pale and that tears stood in her eyes. Oh dear, sighed Charlotte, feeling guilty. I wonder if her leg is paining her? I know she wears a harness for the artificial limb and it must surely chafe unbearably at times. She moved towards the other woman, but felt an involuntary spasm of relief as Melicent turned away and headed, her limp definitely more pronounced than was usual, for the cluster of local dignitaries. Charlotte went to stand by the horse trough, admiring the gathering of horses and huntsmen, but contented herself with a nod and a wave when she spotted Oz Granville and his parents. Time enough for polite conversation later today; besides, Oz was wearing an expression of mulish obstinacy from which she surmised that he had hoped to join the hunt. No fear of that, she grinned to herself as she turned aside; Lady Granville would never permit her darling to risk his neck in such a dangerous pursuit.

Barnard was soon absorbed into a group of men all wearing concerned frowns and pacing up and down as they glared at the snow-covered village green. I wonder, mused Charlotte, I know nothing about hunting in these wintry conditions, but I'm not sure I should like to take a horse out today. What would it take to make them cancel the meeting: a further fall of snow, perhaps?

Captain Penbury was outside the inn, injudiciously draining a glass of port handed to him by one of the hunt servants. Lily, she realized, had routed her enemy and was now in eager conversation with some of the more illustrious neighbours, so Charlotte was free to remain in the background and enjoy herself, but she shook her head with a frown as she watched the captain accept a second glass. This meant yet another set of complaints about his old war wound, she sighed and looked round for the captain's lady. True to form however, Melicent, who had been rebuffed – or worse in her eyes – simply ignored by the gentry, was now hanging about outside the inn, full of her own woes about her social standing, rather than concern for her spouse's state of health.

'My dear Mrs Frampton Richmond,' she fussed as she limped towards the younger woman. 'I should be grateful if you would have a quiet word with Mrs Richmond about her manner to me. She forgets that I am no longer a mere governess, to be slighted and put upon, but am now the respected wife of a gallant naval gentleman. It is too much, too much.' She dabbed at her overflowing eyes with a tiny lace-trimmed handkerchief. 'And I am so sadly sensitive that my delicate feelings are lacerated by the unkindness of more brutish persons.'

Charlotte was about to return a soothing answer, when she was hailed by Kit Knightley.

'Kit, what a pleasant surprise. Do excuse me, Melicent, I must go and ask how Mrs Knightley goes on.' She extricated herself from Mrs Penbury's clutches, to shake hands with Kit and to put her enquiry to him. 'Barnard explained about the Meet so I didn't expect to see you today. You are not hunting yourself?' she asked, noting his suit of country clothes, covered by a warm coat.

'Not today,' was the response, then he added, 'Elaine insisted I put in an appearance, but I shall take myself back to the Hall directly they are off. She's not at all well.' He looked away and Charlotte murmured in sympathy. 'I'm afraid, Char,' he said simply and looked away as she gasped, eyes filling with tears. He stared over the heads of the swelling crowd and took her hand once more. 'I must speak to Barnard,' he said. 'Don't come tomorrow, Char, she had a bad time yesterday evening and a sleepless night, but all being well, she'll be glad to see you the day after. I expect I'll put in a brief appearance, for form's sake, at the Granville lad's birthday affair this afternoon.' He turned to go, but looked back at her soberly, 'I promise to send for you at once,' he told her, 'If she should ask for you, or, or if Dr Perry thinks ....' His voice tailed away and he left her watching after him, her excitement at the bustling scene before her vanished, as her feelings of dismay echoed, in a small way, his despair.

She pulled herself together. It would not do to break down in tears; her task today was to act as lady-in-waiting to Lily, who however, was happily occupied with her neighbours. Melicent was now clinging to her husband's arm and in no need of attention, so Charlotte hugged her shawl more warmly round her shoulders, over her stout cloth coat, and began to walk round the village green to inspect the first snowfall she had ever encountered.

Brrr, even as she shivered in the still, cold air, she was enchanted by the beauty of her surroundings. Finchbourne Manor was handsome enough at any season, with its original Tudor parts, and the mellow brick of the Queen Anne wing tacked on to the side, but today, viewed from the other side of the green, with the pale sunshine lighting up the snowy whiteness, she was lost for words. The village too, was lovely, with its ancient church, and the cluster of cottages and villas looking picturesque amid the snow-covered bushes and gardens. There were icicles too, hanging from the cottage eaves and decorating the lych-gate, and the trees were weighed down with snow. A few minutes' walking about though, was more than enough to make her turn back towards home, until her name, called out, made her whip round to stare at the woman trudging gamely along the street.

'Why, Bessie,' she cried, hurrying towards her old friend. 'What a pleasant surprise, I'm so glad to see you, I hoped we might meet. Do come inside somewhere and get warm.'

The Three Pigeons boasted a small back parlour and Charlotte ushered her old friend in there, noting with relief that a fire had been kindled in the grate. The landlady brought in hot coffee and when Charlotte was satisfied that Bessie was comfortably settled, she began to ask eager questions.

'That's right, Miss Char,' was the response to a query about the blacksmith's brother. 'He's a nice enough man, to be sure, and I did think he might do for me.' Charlotte hid a smile, remembering Will's amusement at this phrase of Bessie's. *'I've lost count,'* he had whispered to his wife after one of Bessie's romances, *'of the number of men who were going to "do" for Bessie. Let's hope none of them ever does so, but she does take some foolish risks.'*

The trouble was, Charlotte recalled now, that even at a tender age she had recognised her nurse's fatal weakness. Bessie Railton fell in love at the drop of a hat and the objects of her affections were always utterly unsuitable. Having heard rumours in the village, Charlotte was sure that the blacksmith's brother was yet another.

'Yes, indeed,' Bessie nodded sagely. 'He's been making up to me for a week or two and he even brought me over to stay with his brother last night. I thought for sure he'd be down on one knee by today.' She sighed gustily and Charlotte patted her hand in sympathy. 'Aye, I even went to chapel with him yesterday, and a tedious affair that was, to be sure.'

'But, Bessie,' Charlotte frowned. 'The blacksmith attends the village church, so why does his brother go to chapel?'

'That's the rub,' Bessie sighed once more. 'T'was his late wife as was chapel and he took to it like a natural, jumping up and down praying out loud, he was, all through the service. And that went on for an age too, just when I was hoping for my dinner and my stomach grumbling as it was.' She shook her head. 'He won't do,' she announced. 'I'd rather have his brother any day. He's a real man, he is, the blacksmith.'

'And so is his wife,' Charlotte interposed hurriedly. 'Her arms are even brawnier than his, so give up that idea, for she has a temper to match. But tell me, did you by any chance see anything of that incident at the church gate yesterday? You saw our old pony shy and try to take the chaise with him?'

'Lord above,' Bessie looked aghast. 'If I didn't go and forget all about that. I should say I did see something and I was just going to run over to help when some young lady – I didn't see her plain, her bonnet hid her face – caught the pony and saved the day.'

'Well?' Charlotte was in a sudden agony of curiosity. 'What was it that you saw? One of the ladies said there was a dog that went under the traces and startled the pony, but I didn't see it.'

'A dog? No, that there wasn't, but besides the lady that caught the pony, there were two people standing close to it and I reckon one of them must have jabbed a pin into the poor creature's flesh the way it reared up and squealed. I couldn't see precisely but what I do know is that one of them patted the rump and the other the neck, both at the same time though I doubt that was by design.'

'But, but that's hardly conclusive,' Charlotte was disappointed. She had built so much on Bessie having seen the whole thing. 'You say you saw two people? Could you describe them?'

'You may not think it's likely, Miss Char,' Bessie folded her lips in a determined pout. 'But I say there was nothing else that could have upset that fat old pony. No dog, no sudden noise, nobody running about silly-like, just those two people touching it.'

'Very well,' Charlotte was reluctant to suggest her mother's former maid might be romancing, so she asked again, 'What did the two people look like, were they in conversation?'

'There was a man, a gentleman, for I could see his clothes. Trouble is, Miss Char, I didn't see his face clear for he was blocked from my view most of the time by the gentry that stood nearby. No dear, they didn't speak; he was by the pony's rump and ignoring the lady. I doubt he'd have been happy at being left to the mercies of some plump spinster, for that's what she was and no mistake about it. She was dumpy and dowdy, dressed in black and fussing about all the time with her hat and her hair and her handkerchief. And her showing off, a-patting that pony as if she liked him, whenever she saw anyone glance her way.' She hesitated and looked puzzled. 'I've seen that one before somewhere,' she frowned. 'But for the life of me I can't remember where it was. And not long ago either.'

Charlotte and her visitor stared at each other as Bessie repeated, 'I know it doesn't seem possible, Miss Char dearie, but I'm certain sure that one of those two did something to make that poor pony try to gallop off with his carriage dragging along behind him.'

Chapter 10

REFRESHED BY HER coffee, Bessie heaved herself out of her chair and announced that she must be getting back to the baker.

'For,' she admitted with a rueful grin, 'whatever my feelings about my gentleman friend, I can't deny that the ride he's promised me back to Winchester will be very welcome. After that, well, we'll see, but don't you worry, Miss Char,' with a nod and another smile. 'I'll stay well away from the blacksmith. You're right about his missus and it won't do to go looking for trouble.'

Suddenly Charlotte was startled by a loud outcry from her old friend. 'If I won't go and forget my own head,' Bessie exclaimed. 'There, Miss Char, sit you down again for another minute, if you please, while I tell you what it was that struck me when that poor young lady was ill.'

Her former nursling stared with equal dismay. Charlotte had also forgotten until this moment Bessie's murmured words at the door of the guest-house in Winchester a few day's previously. 'Goodness,' she agreed. 'Yes, of course; you said, did you not, that there was something odd about Mrs Chant's sudden illness? But I understood that it was put down to a sudden, unforeseeable consequence of her situation?'

'Situation indeed,' the older woman gave a snort of indignation. 'I've looked after ladies and children off and on for more than thirty years, Miss Char, and I think I can claim some knowledge as to whether a lady is in a promising way or not.'

'Not?' Charlotte put the question in some surprise.

'Not,' agreed Bessie, warming to her topic. 'The young lady certainly looked poorly when they arrived at their rooms, at one moment flushed, and then pale as a ghost and feeling faint. So I stepped in and offered to look after her, tucked her into a bed with a couple of hot bricks to warm her, and made her drink a nice hot cup of tea, nothing more, but tea is a great comfort.' She shook her head. 'The illness came on fairly rapid after that and a sad night we had of it, what with bouts of terrible sickness and cramps. Poor lass she certainly suffered, but just a few hours after midnight, it was all over.' She sighed and dashed a hand across her brow. 'That wasn't what I wanted to say though, Miss Char. It's this idea that it was all to do with her being in the family way, for that's the reason that has been put about.' She shook her head, 'And my mistress is more than thankful to lay the blame well away from her own house. Well, I could not discuss this with anyone else, you understand, my dear, but you being a married lady, I can say quite plain, that was not the case. If you'll excuse my speaking about such matters, that young lady had her courses that day. I was sponging the sweat off her in an attempt to cool her down and make her comfortable, so before you say anything, I'm certain sure what it was, and that there was no question of her miscarrying that night.'

'But, Bessie…' Charlotte was frowning and wondering how she could frame her question delicately, when she was interrupted.

'Now, Miss Char,' Bessie spoke decidedly. 'As I just told you, I've seen enough young women to recognise any sign you care to mention; besides, I know she wasn't in the family way because I asked her straight out, and she told me there was no question of it. And no need for you to look at me like that, for I'm sure she spoke the truth and no reason to lie, for she was too frightened and I could tell she trusted me. I was wondering if we should try ipecacuana in case she'd eaten what she ought not. It's a powerful emetic, as you know, but violent retching would have done her no good if she was that way. She managed to gasp that she was not, but by then it was too late to try it in any case.

'So, my dear, there it is. I wasn't easy in my mind when they told me word was going round that the lady's death was a consequence of being in a delicate situation. That she wasn't, poor girl.'

'Her husband was there when I came to fetch Miss Armstrong, had you seen him about the place before that?' Charlotte wondered what Bessie thought of the bereaved husband, aware that she had so far encountered nobody who could be said to like him.

'Never saw him then, and never seen him since, not to my knowledge, dearie.' Bessie was quite definite. 'He wasn't staying there, you know, and he hadn't been to call upon his wife, or at any rate not when I was about the place, for it was a doctor from Winchester that attended her, a well-respected local man, they told me. I didn't see him then and I wouldn't know him if I saw him now, for I was up half the night with the poor young lady and only went to my own bed a couple of hours before dawn.

'Most days my duties keep me up on the bedroom floors and I always use the back stairs anyway. It was only by chance that I was downstairs when you arrived, Miss Char,' she explained. 'The house was upside down with the poor young lady's illness and death, so when I'd snatched a few hours' sleep, I got up and helped my mistress out as best I could.'

Conscious that Lily would heartily disapprove gossiping with a servant, however long their acquaintance, Charlotte saw her visitor to the inn door and along to the smithy, a slight frown marring her forehead as she struggled to assimilate Bessie's revelations. As she hugged the old woman and sent her on her way, Bessie hesitated and looked back. 'There, if I didn't remember something after all. The gentleman had a beard,' she said. 'I remember now. The one I saw standing by the pony yesterday. The one that could have prodded the poor beast.'

A beard? Charlotte waved farewell and decided to go back to the manor. There was no sign of the stable boy, her appointed protector, but the road to the manor hid no secluded nooks where the murderer might lurk. She left a message for Lily with the coachman and set off, walking at a brisk pace, taking a childish delight in jumping in frozen puddles to see the ice crack. The wind had risen again and although there had been no further snow after the heavy overnight fall, the sun had gone in and there was a biting chill in the air. It was not the day to be standing around in idle conversation, even had the village not been still rife with the fear that a murderer lurked behind every bush bent upon rape, slaughter and pillage.

A beard? Thawing out as she huddled over the fire in the deserted morning-room, Charlotte made a mental review of all the gentlemen who had been anywhere near the lych-gate on Christmas morning, starting with Barnard, who sported a pair of dashing curly black side whiskers that gave him something of a military air, and of which he was secretly inordinately proud. No, not Barnard, she was quite decided on that; he was too much of a horse lover in any case and would never have made the pony bolt. Besides, if he had been close enough when it happened, he would have seized the reins himself. No, certainly not Barnard.

Who else? Percy Benson had been hovering in the vicinity, greeting the members of his flock but the thought died in an instant. Percy did have a regrettably unbecoming straggle of a beard; he had started it on his honeymoon in the summer, apparently in an attempt to make himself look more impressive. Agnes had confided to Charlotte that she admired her husband's new whiskered look and that the vicar intended to allow his beard to grow to biblical proportions. Charlotte maintained a diplomatic silence regarding her views as to whether the beard was a becoming adornment. It was her considered opinion that Percy looked less like an Old Testament prophet than a man being attacked by a singularly moth-eaten ferret.

Who else had been there? Lord Granville went straight into the church and in any case, was another who favoured the military style, though his flourishing silver side-whiskers were rather more in the mutton-chop style. Captain Penbury, who sported a mahogany tonsure surrounded by a halo of grey curls, was clean shaven apart from two curious tufts of grey hair high on each weather-beaten cheekbone. 'Slovenly things, beards, y'know, dear lady, they catch crumbs. Admiral Lord Nelson,' he had boomed at her once, 'his lordship, of blessed memory, never wore a beard, and what was good enough for Horatio Nelson, is surely good enough for Horatio Penbury, hey?'

Charlotte frowned again. Kit Knightley had not been at church and besides, Kit was clean-shaven too and Dr Perry, although he wore a tidily trimmed grey beard and moustache, had been nowhere near the lych-gate at the time. Nobody else, male or female, known or unknown, bearded or not, had moved away from the vicinity of the pony chaise towards the gate, so that meant.... She stared blankly at the glowing coals. The only candidate she could think of was Dr Chant, with his smooth pink cheeks adorned by a neat grey beard. He must have been the man Bessie had observed, and of course Miss Cole was the plump and fussy spinsterish woman.

At first it seemed highly unlikely that Bessie could have seen what she claimed, but Charlotte remembered her mother's words, *'Bessie may have the world's worst taste in men, Will, but you must agree that she is as honest as the day is long. I doubt if she could tell a convincing lie, anyway, she would turn red as a beetroot and get in a terrible fluster.'*

Just then, she was interrupted by the entrance of Dr Chant himself. Seeing her seated beside the fire he came forward, all geniality, and rubbing his hands together at the blaze.

'Good morning, good morning,' he cried heartily. 'And how is Mrs Richmond today?'

Startled, Charlotte replied politely that Mrs Richmond was very well, while common courtesy demanded that she invite him to take a chair. 'You also found it too chilly at the meet, did you, Dr Chant?' He looked startled so she explained, 'I was shivering so much that I slipped away and came home before the others. I confess I was surprised that the day's hunting was not cancelled, but I suppose the going was softer than it first appeared.

'I'll ring for some refreshment,' she told the doctor, wishing he would go away but sadly aware that he was settling himself comfortably in Barnard's favourite chair. 'That will ease the chill. I believe you know that I've lived all my life in warmer climes than this, so the degree of cold has come as a shock, beautiful as the snow undoubtedly is.'

'Indeed, indeed.' The doctor seemed bent on being charming as he embarked on a description of London life, with particular reference to his own place in society, along with mention of his own rising popularity. 'His Royal Highness, the Prince Consort has been gracious enough to call, more than once, upon my skills,' he told her and looked satisfied as she expressed her admiration. 'You walked back from the village?' he asked and, at her nod, went on, 'I have noticed that you have a long, elastic stride, my dear young lady, and your glowing health confirms a theory of my own, that walking is of benefit to the fairer sex.'

Charlotte could only bow her thanks, but inwardly she giggled. A long, elastic stride? Honed, no doubt, by a lifetime of running away from the equally long arm of the law after the pickles her stepfather had landed them all in.

But what on earth is going on here, she wondered. Has Dr Chant settled upon a prosperous young – and clearly very healthy – widow as the next Mrs Doctor? She recalled her first conversation with him, at the lodging house in Winchester when she had suspected him of viewing her with admiration. And his poor wife not even in her grave yet!

She shot a covert glance at her unwelcome companion. No, she mused, with a decided shudder, I cannot like him. He has a pompous little tilt to his head so that he seems to be looking down at people all the time, in spite of being of slightly under the average height. And his little neighing laugh grates on me.

Before she could interrupt the flow of placid self-congratulation, Charlotte was startled when he suddenly enquired, 'Are you well-acquainted with Miss Nightingale? I must say I was considerably impressed to learn that she has singled you out in such a manner; she is notoriously fastidious in bestowing her friendship and patronage. Perhaps I might call upon you when you have moved to the capital?'

'I have no plans to move to the capital,' Charlotte protested with rising indignation. 'I do not intend to accept Miss Nightingale's offer, flattering as it may be. In fact I have another...' she stopped herself from announcing that Sibella Armstrong would be a better candidate for the position. Time enough for that when she had sounded out the forlorn governess and gauged her reaction to the plan. 'I am not in the least acquainted with Miss Nightingale, though she *is* a friend of the family.'

This conversation was beginning to irritate her, but how to turn it to phrase the question that was burning in her brain. I suppose I cannot simply ask him straight out if he jabbed something at the pony to make it panic, she sighed, but then she brightened. I can at least try to turn his thoughts in a more suitable direction.

'I regret so much that I did not have the opportunity to become acquainted with your late wife,' she said, with a grave sympathy. 'It is tragic indeed, to think of such a lovely young woman so suddenly lost to all who loved her.'

'Ah, yes, yes of course.' Dr Chant blinked for a moment then accepted his cue and assumed a solemn expression. 'Verena was a lovely creature, there can be no doubt of that. But I fear we were not hap– she was not....' At Charlotte's raised eyebrows, the doctor shook his head and made play with his silk handkerchief. 'Excuse me, my dear young lady,' he harrumphed then, finding no further expressions of sympathy or admiration forthcoming, he gave up the attempt and finally took refuge in a series of heavy, heartfelt sighs, accompanied by meaningful and mournful glances.

Now what did he mean by that, Charlotte mused. '...she was not...' Not what? And 'we were not hap–' Again, what had he meant to say? They were not happy? And that Verena was to blame?

At that moment, relief, in the shape of Hoxton the butler, arrived.

'Miss Char,' he said, respectfully. 'Her ladyship's dog has unfortunately managed to fall in the duck pond.' At her cry of dismay, the butler held up his hand. 'No, miss, madam I mean, the dog is quite safe. I believe he was chasing a rat when the ice gave, but one of the grooms hauled him out and he's safe and sound in the barn. I merely felt you would wish to be informed, her ladyship being so fond of the animal.'

Charlotte leaped to her feet and made her excuses to her unwelcome companion. 'I must go at once, do forgive me, Dr Chant.'

She hastened to her room to fetch her coat and employed the same explanation when she encountered Melicent Penbury on her way downstairs. Melicent, it appeared, had noticed Charlotte's disappearance from the village and taken it as licence to follow suit. She had persuaded the coachman to convey her up to the manor since Lily was not ready to abandon the gathering.

'We must have a comfortable, cosy little talk, my dear Mrs – er, Charlotte, must we not?' That was Melicent's opening gambit.

'After all, we have scarcely had a chance to renew the friendship we embarked upon during our delightful stay in Bath.'

'That would be most pleasant.' Charlotte's answer was mendacious. 'We must certainly arrange to do so, but alas, I have to make an urgent visit to the barn. Hoxton?' She turned to the butler who was again at hand. 'Mrs Penbury is chilled, would you bring her something warming to drink, please?' And to Melicent, 'Do, pray, excuse me.'

Phew, Charlotte's whistle was unladylike but heartfelt, while all thought of enquiring after Melicent's increasingly painful-looking limp vanished uncharitably. There had certainly been no friendship between herself and the damply drooping former governess. Indeed, Charlotte had often scolded herself for her most unchristian dislike of the other woman. And to what portion of their time in Bath did Melicent allude to as 'delightful'? Charlotte smiled and sighed as she slithered aside to allow one of the stable boys to pass her in the yard as he dragged a toboggan full of logs and kindling towards the house. Last summer's visit to Bath had provided her with some unforgettable new friends indeed, but the over-riding impression she retained was of danger and death. Had Melicent conveniently erased those memories?

She satisfied herself that the dog, Prince Albert, was uninjured, although the racket he set up when she appeared was loud enough to denote fire and pillaging so, after petting him for a while, and taking a cautious peek at the new kittens, she wondered whether to make her way back down to Rowan Lodge to look for Lady Frampton's knitting which had been left at home. As she hesitated, Charlotte heard a clattering and turned to see the baker's horse and cart drive into the cobbled yard, drawing up at a peremptory exclamation from its passenger.

'Miss Char, Miss Char, dearie!' Bessie Railton leaned down to greet her former nursling. 'I won't hold you up a minute, my dear, and I'm off to Winchester myself so I can't stay,' she nodded briefly at the smith's brother who touched his hat to Charlotte. 'I just remembered something I meant to tell you.'

She wheezed and nodded but refused to alight and rest for a moment. 'There, I'm all of a dither, but it was preying on my mind, and I felt I had to come and tell you. Now what was I, oh yes…. That matter we were discussing, dear. I recalled where I saw the plump, fussy lady before. T'was a few days ago and I'd gone into the Cathedral to take the weight off my feet. It's quiet in there and out of the rain and cold. Anyway, there I was, not quite dozing, when in came the two young ladies; the one that died and her sister.'

Charlotte listened with interest but did not interrupt the flow, recollecting how easily in her childhood she had been frustrated when Bessie lost the thread of a story.

'Yes, indeed, and they took a stroll round the aisles, the younger one talking quite unsuitable for such a place and the other one telling her off. They were talking about the christening – that'd be here, of course, and saying that they meant to go.' She whisked a handkerchief from her capacious muff and mopped her brow. 'Nothing to remark upon there,' she said sagely, 'but I wasn't the only one listening that day. When I heard the door open and the ladies come in, I sat up, and set about tidying myself, ready to carry on with my errands, and I looked across and spotted that plump lady I told you of. A fierce scowl there was on her face as she watched those two young ladies make their way out of the place.'

'You must be talking about Miss Cole,' said Charlotte, almost to herself. 'She fits the description you gave me of the scene when the old pony was upset and she could well have been taking a rest in the Cathedral. I know she has a friend in Winchester whom she visits now and then. She was scowling at the young ladies you say?'

'Indeed she was,' Bessie was emphatic. 'I watched her, as I said. At first she was just nosy, like me, eavesdropping on a chance-heard conversation, but then she perked up when one of them mentioned a christening at Finchbourne Manor.' Bessie opened her eyes wide at Charlotte's gasp of astonishment. 'She did, Miss Char, true as I'm here with you. That was when she turned and took a proper look at the two of them and my word, she was taken aback. I could tell that from where I was sitting. Quite white, she went, and out came some smelling salts and her handkerchief and she set to fluttering away. No, Miss Char, dearie. I've no idea what it was that struck her so about those two ladies, but struck she was, and not in a happy way. If looks could kill, they'd have dropped like stones, the pair of them, poor young things.'

Charlotte's urgent further questioning brought no conclusion. Bessie was adamant that she had seen Miss Cole react in shock to the advent of Verena Chant and Sibella. She also insisted that she had witnessed either Miss Cole or Dr Chant do something – on this point she admitted to being unclear – to upset the pony outside the church gate. And no, it had not been possible to observe whether Miss Cole's venomous glance in the cathedral had been aimed at both sisters or at one in particular. 'It did seem to me that she recognised one or both of them,' was all she would say as she took her leave.

It was likely, Charlotte thought, that Miss Cole's distaste was reserved for Sibella. The woman must have known about the errant Armstrong brother's betrayal and would probably extend her disapproval to the sister closer to his age.

After a brief visit to take some carrots and sugar lumps as a gift to the Rowan Lodge pony in his temporary lodging at the manor stables, Charlotte, her brows knitted in a thoughtful frown, trudged back to the house, remembering that the butler's immense dignity made him take a dim view of the family lowering themselves in his eyes by using the back door. Accordingly, she took the long way round to the front of the manor, noting absently that while a snow-blanched landscape might be picturesque to behold, it was less delightful when you had to slip and slide on an icy path or find yourself drenched by a fall of snow from an overhanging branch. As she struggled to gain a foothold in some places, or reached out a hand to support herself by holding on to a branch, she tried to arrange her thoughts.

I wonder if Kit Knightley is correct, she sighed. Am I allowing silly fancies to run away with me? But Kit knows I am not prone to such flights and he also knows I've encountered a real mystery or two that could not possibly have been attributed to an over-active imagination. She shook her head in dismay and marshalled her anxieties.

Lady Granville had been adamant that someone had attempted to harm her son, firstly by pushing the throng of churchgoers so that Oz should have been the logical person to fall into the open grave, had he not been young and spry enough to slip out of the way. But why should anyone attempt such a thing? And what was it meant to achieve, in any case? Even if Oz had tumbled into the gaping hole, it was only six feet deep and the likelihood was that a young, healthy boy would have found it great sport to be covered in mud.

After that had come the incident with a mince pie. According to his mother, Oz had just reached out a hand for a pie when Captain Penbury barged in and snatched it up. Shortly following this act of greed, the captain had collapsed to the floor, writhing in pain; pain that was later put down to indigestion.

The spaniel was well enough, though dejected after his impromptu bath, so Charlotte brought him back to the house and shooed him into the drawing-room where Gran was drowsing by the fire.

Safely in her room, she shed her outer garments, tidied her hair and sat down to warm her toes at the bedroom fire. There had been no indication that Captain Penbury was suffering from anything but indigestion, so what had Lady Granville feared? Charlotte bit her lip. The only conclusion she could draw from the lady's anxious whispers was that someone intended harm to her son. Did that mean she suspected poison?

'That's ridiculous.' Charlotte leaped up from the low slipper chair and paced round the room, trying to make sense of it all. It *was* indigestion, Dr Perry said so. She paused to consider. Yes, he did, and I would, most emphatically, trust Dr Perry with my life.

Once the ridiculous notion had planted itself into her brain however, it refused to take itself off. She argued with herself, citing the nonsensical nature of such an idea, but was dismayed to realize that the fear remained. But if Lady Granville thought there might be poison in the mince pie, who could have put it there? She scowled at her reflection in the looking glass as she came up to it. And what about … the suspicion struck her with the force of a blow. The wassail cup! Lady Granville had been most strongly exercised over the theft, for such she had designated it, of the glass of hot punch she had marked out for her son.

Charlotte tried to picture the scene at the table in the manor dining-room. The boy had been there, of course, as had his mother. Was Lord Granville there too? In the background, perhaps. She went on with her exercise of enumerating those present. Dr Chant was in attendance and frowning at his wife about something and Miss Cole was certainly there, hovering alongside her employer, to that lady's evident irritation. Who else? Charlotte had a sudden half-buried recollection of a little scene that had been played out, of Verena Chant laughing gaily and saying to her sister, something like, 'Well, I certainly have no objection to the taste of cinnamon, my dear Sibella, in fact I am rather partial to it....'

Charlotte shivered in spite of the cosy warmth of her bedroom and she stared at the wall, her thoughts squirrelling round in her head as she suddenly had a clear picture of her stepfather telling one of his stories.

Will Glover, sitting on a barrel that served as a stool, table, and sometimes even a makeshift altar in that far away, long ago little township on the edge of the Bush; Will causing the ladies present to shiver deliciously as his voice sank to a whisper....

'It was when I was serving as secretary to the Bishop of – oh, well,' there had been a gurgle of laughter in his voice, 'Perhaps you'd be better off not knowing which bishop it was.' That was said with a suspicion of a wink that thrilled his audience into a hushed silence. 'Where was I? Oh yes; well, I had been at his lordship's palace for a week or so and I started to wonder how it came about that there were so many dead cats around the place? I spotted one in the drawing-room, poor creature, while another was stretched out dead as a doornail in the Library, and a third that had breathed its last in the morning-room. When a fourth cat turned up in the Bishop's bedroom, though luckily his lordship had not yet retired so was unaware of the tragedy, I set about investigating.'

Charlotte paused in her anxious pacing round the room. Will's voice rang so clearly in her ears that it seemed unthinkable, unbearable, that she should never see him again. She banished that thought; no time for tears she reminded herself. Will had squeezed his wife's hand and caught his stepdaughter's eye across the bevy of breathless townswomen who were hanging on his every word and with the smile that won all hearts – and, she reminded herself

– emptied the contents of all pockets into his own, he had explained. '*It transpired,*' he said, '*that the new cook was a fanatical free-thinker and had determined to rid the world of all clerics, one by one, beginning with my bishop. However, he apparently had small faith in his ability as a poisoner, so he set about practising on the resident cats. Hence the pitiful corpses that littered the premises.*'

The old memory made her wonder. Was it possible that Lady Granville was correct in her suspicions? Could someone have poisoned a glass of hot punch, intending it for the Granville boy, only to see his or her intention thwarted by Verena Chant's partiality to the taste of cinnamon?

But they said, didn't they … that poison was a woman's weapon? Charlotte found herself staring blindly out at the snowy garden while she thought furiously. Bessie Railton's testimony pointed to Miss Cole as the culprit, but culpable of what, precisely? Frightening an old pony? Trying to poison a child?

It was all too ridiculous, but a frown creased her brow. Miss Cole had appeared so opportunely on the scene where Lady Granville's maid lay so inexplicably dead. Inexplicably, that is, if Oz were correct in his insistence that he had heard no sound of a scuffle, seen no sight of a killer running off. Could there be a connection with that crime and with the death of a visitor to the manor?

Charlotte was almost thankful to hear the bell summoning the household to a cold collation in the dining-room, to stay the pangs of hunger until the tea party they were to attend in honour of Oz's birthday later that afternoon.

As she went slowly down the main staircase, with its fearsome array of weaponry and festoons of evergreens, holly and ivy, a great bunch of mistletoe hanging from the chandelier, Charlotte was unable to dismiss the memory of the Finchbourne wassail cup. She pictured Barnard proudly brandishing an ornate silver ladle and Lily beside him, beaming with pride at her houseful of important guests. There was the wassail brew itself, a concoction of heated wine and sugar, flavoured with a variety of spices and with fruit floating on the top.

Did that mean that the wassail punch had been tampered with?

She frowned again, fiercely, and tried to dismiss the only conclusion that made any sense. If indeed *anything* made sense, she added
as a silent rider.

It was possible. She would only admit to a possibility, nothing
more, that some person unknown had managed to slip a dose of
poison into the glass of punch intended for Oz Granville. And if
that were true – if there were any possibility, however slight, that it
could be true – then Charlotte Richmond would be very, very
angry.

Chapter 11

THERE WAS TO be no respite for Charlotte after the meal. Today she was clearly doomed to be the recipient of intimate exchanges, but as it was Sibella Armstrong who came to sit timidly beside her with a confiding air, it would be interesting, she concluded, rather than tedious.

In spite of the usual gargantuan breakfast that was served every morning at the manor and the promise of another, almost certainly large meal at Brambrook Abbey during the coming afternoon, Lily had insisted upon providing her household with more sustenance at midday. Knowing the impossibility of persuading Lily that she was not hungry, Charlotte nibbled at a slice of bread and butter and, refusing Barnard's offer of a glass of wine, a brandy to keep out the cold, a tankard of ale (this last suggestion accompanied by a hearty laugh), she allowed Lily to pour her a cup of tea instead.

'Did you hear the news, by the way, Char?' Lily suddenly asked when her guests were all supplied with food and drink. 'Young Oz mentioned to Barnard that Lady Granville's companion, that rather tiresome Miss Cole, has unaccountably taken it into her head to hand in her notice and take herself off to some friend's house some-where in London.'

'What's that?' Charlotte raised her head in surprise and carefully put down her cup of tea. 'How extraordinary! I was under the impression that Miss Cole had been a permanent fixture in Lady Granville's household for many years, that in fact she is some kind of distant relative of her ladyship? What in the world can have possessed her to take such an unexpected course? Do you suppose there's been some kind of quarrel and that Lady Granville might rather have dismissed her companion?'

'I believe not,' Barnard took up the story, reaching for a large slab of Christmas cake to sustain him for another hour or two. 'Young Oz was most definite. He told me that his mother was in a fine taking late last evening when she discovered that Miss Cole had packed up her bags and taken herself off without so much as a by your leave. Apparently, her ladyship was not disturbed when her companion failed to appear at dinner, because Miss Cole had complained of some trifling indisposition – which was quite a frequent occurrence, Oz remarked.'

'Indeed,' burst in Lily. 'It turns out that Miss Cole left a short, ungracious note to her ladyship, and will send for her trunk as soon as her circumstances allow.' Lily shook her head, her round pink face reflecting excitement mingled with sympathy. 'Imagine! According to her note, Miss Cole has received an extremely advantageous offer of a position with a former employer who now resides just outside Paris. The wretched woman means to stay in London for a day or so and then journey across the channel. I believe Miss Cole has been in her ladyship's service for getting on for eleven or twelve years. What shocking ingratitude to leave so precipitately, particularly as her ladyship's personal maid – well,' Lily spoke in a suitably hushed voice and glanced rather theatrically round the room with a shiver, 'we all know what happened to her, do we not? This means that poor Lady Granville is left without a familiar attendant.'

Charlotte made sympathetic noises and returned to her cup of tea, wondering what it could all mean. No explanation sprang to mind however, apart from the ludicrous fancies that had occupied her earlier, so she made her apologies. With a mischievous nod to Barnard, she whisked the last piece of Christmas cake from under his nose and put it on her plate to take it up to her room on the pretext of resting before the proposed birthday festivities.

She still had some silver tissue paper left over from wrapping her Christmas presents so she made a neat parcel of the pocket knife for Oz. Tying an elegant bow in the half-yard of blue silk ribbon from her sewing box, she placed the birthday present on a small table, beside her gloves. She added the small kid reticule that contained a lace handkerchief, her embroidery scissors, needle-case, and some sewing silk, along with some pins for use in emergency repairs, so that there was no possibility of forgetting it, then she curled up in the fireside chair with her present from Barnard open on her lap.

'It's the latest edition of Bradshaw,' Barnard had told her, laughing at her puzzled expression as she surveyed the book she had just unwrapped. 'Railway timetables, Char, so you can plan your journeys when you feel the need to run away from us now and then!'

Dear Barnard, she smiled as she flicked through the printed pages. I could never hurt his feelings by running away; he knows that's not going to happen, even though…. She bit her lip and her eyes darkened at the knowledge of the undoubted sorrow that waited just around the corner. When Elaine Knightley finally took her leave of her beloved husband and home, Charlotte would not be the only friend to feel bereft; Elaine, quiet and gentle as she was, held a special place in the hearts of gentry and villagers alike.

'I can't bear to think…' Charlotte was unaware that she spoke aloud but a timid tapping at the door brought a welcome interruption to her darkling thoughts. Sibella Armstrong, dressed in readiness for the impending jollification, hovered there, poised for flight.

'Sibella?' Charlotte brushed a hand across her tear-stained cheeks, and stood aside to let her visitor enter. 'Do come in, you're just in time to distract me from some unhappy thoughts.'

Another tap at the door heralded a maid with a tray of tea. 'Mr Hoxton had Cook prepare this for you, Miss Char. He said it was a bitter cold day and he thought a young lady from foreign parts, where the weather's always hot, might feel a chill.' She set the tray down on the table beside Charlotte's gloves and Oz's present, and looked up at the two girls. 'I've brought tea for Miss Armstrong too,' she said, with a nod to the second teapot and cup on the tray. 'I saw you come in here, miss; will you take tea together?' The small flurry – thanking the maid, settling Sibella in a comfortable chair, pouring the tea – broke the ice and they both drank eagerly, warming their hands on the delicate, flower-patterned china of Lily's second-best tea set. Charlotte dismissed her visitor's polite concern regarding those miserable thoughts and the accompanying tears, and waited in a comfortable silence, wondering what had brought Sibella to her room once more.

'I am in a quandary, Mrs... er, Charlotte,' began the other. 'You have been so kind, I thought you might help me decide what to do.'

At Charlotte's eager assurance, Sibella continued. 'My brother-in-law, Dr Chant, suggests I accompany him to London when he leaves Hampshire in a day or two. He has numerous acquaintances in the capital and he tells me he is confident of securing a suitable post for me.'

'And?' prompted Charlotte. 'Forgive me, Sibella, but I've formed the distinct impression that you hold no warm regard for Dr Chant, nor he for you. Do you really wish to be beholden to him?'

'Ah, you do understand.' Sibella turned eagerly to her hostess, 'and you are quite correct, I've never liked him and I know he has decided views on the subject of poor relations, so I can't understand why he has come forward with this offer.'

'I can guess,' Charlotte gave a slight smile. 'I spotted the doctor closeted with my brother-in-law and knowing Barnard as I do, I can imagine that he said something rather fierce about family obligations. I don't mean,' she added hastily, 'that Barnard and Lily want you to go. By no means, in fact I'm persuaded Lily would like you to remain at the manor until her little Algy is old enough to require a governess!' She smiled. 'That being rather impractical however, I know that they really want you to stay here for as long as you wish and certainly until you have somewhere comfortable to go, among congenial people.'

Sibella started to protest but Charlotte interrupted, 'It would be a kindness to them,' she said soberly. 'I know they both feel it dreadfully that Mrs Chant was taken ill after her visit to this house, and yes – they realize that no possible fault can be laid at their door – but they feel it nonetheless. That being the case, may I join with them in entreating you to prolong your visit? It must be preferable than having to be forced to express gratitude to a man you cannot like.' She hesitated for a moment, then rushed on, 'I ... it is a trifle premature to mention this,' she said, glancing at the other girl. 'I don't know if you recall what I said at breakfast? That Miss

Nightingale has offered me a post in connection with her proposed new nursing order? Well, as I told Barnard and Lily, I have no intention of accepting her offer but I've not yet had the opportunity to reply and I wondered how you would look upon the idea of allowing me to put your name forward for the position? No,' she interrupted Sibella's exclamation, 'hear me out before you dismiss it out of hand. The position does not involve any nursing; it is an administrative post, which requires a clear head, a practical turn of mind, and a good deal of common sense. All three of these qualities are surely yours, after years as a governess.'

She picked up her cup and hesitated. 'Suppose you give the notion due consideration? I shan't press you for an answer and Miss Nightingale will surely not be offended if I delay my answer until tomorrow morning, but you must be aware of the advantages inherent in the scheme. For instance, there has been no mention of the kind of remuneration that the position incurs but it must be more generous than that of a governess, and accommodation would be included. You would live at Miss Nightingale's headquarters, which would surely be more agreeable than being shut away in a governess's forlorn attic.'

She smiled at Sibella, who was looking stunned. 'For now though, won't you take a holiday from care? My brother and sister are so anxious that you should have a real rest and an opportunity to recover from your ordeal.'

'You – and they – are too kind,' Sibella answered in a whisper. 'I should indeed like to stay here for a short time. I shall decline Dr Chant's offer, with great relief.' She finished her tea and nibbled absently on a piece of Cook's celebrated shortbread, then she looked at Charlotte.

'I should like to speak freely, if I may?' At Charlotte's nod, and assurance that any confidences would go no further, Sibella went on, 'You must have noticed that although I am shocked at my sister's untimely death, I am not stricken with grief. This must have made you wonder about us, about our relationship. I explained that we had not been intimate for many years and in fact we have met only a handful of times since – since our brother's disgrace.

'Verena was brought up to be as shallow and self-centred as her godmother who thought only of turning my little sister into a society belle and making a brilliant marriage, so, sad to say, I found her completely heartless. We met for the first time in years at her wedding and discovered that we had nothing in common. The invitation caught up with me when I was visiting London with one of my pupils and my employer was gracious enough to allow me to attend the celebrations.'

She frowned at her hands. 'Dr Chant and I did not take to each other on the occasion of our introduction, and our subsequent encounters, few as they have been, have confirmed us in our mutual dislike. I find him to be pompous and shallow, while he believed me to be waiting only for an opportunity to demand financial support from him, through my sister. I should like to make it clear to you, Charlotte, that I have never done so.'

Charlotte nodded; she could understand now why she had been attracted to Sibella from the first. They were both stiff-necked and proud, determined to make their own way in the world. I wonder whether she would have used the same methods, Charlotte mused, picturing her perilous flight across India during the late Mutiny, when she had snatched at whatever means of survival that came to hand, including theft and deception. Sneaking a look at the other young woman's firmly closed mouth and determined chin, as well as her steady blue eyes, Charlotte formed the opinion that Sibella was another of the same ilk, although her upbringing in a northern vicarage might possibly have been a hindrance when it came to theft and deception.

'On the few occasions when I chanced to be in London,' Sibella continued, 'I took care to send word to my sister. We were all that was left of the family now, since Edward was known to have died in Australia, and I thought we should remain in touch. It never answered though. Verena was always busy about some society ball or dinner and I was never easy at such affairs and Dr Chant continued to view me with suspicion, which was most uncomfortable.'

'What made you and your sister decide to visit Winchester for a holiday?' Charlotte thought it was time to turn the conversation towards recent events. 'I believe you said you had never been here before?'

'No,' came the low-voiced reply. 'I arrived in London last month with my latest pupil, a very sickly child, on our way to take the waters at Tunbridge Wells, when sadly the child took a turn for the worse and died very suddenly. Mercifully, his parents were at his side, but although he had not been expected to live for many years, it was still distressing. My employers paid me generously and left town but I was soon ill myself, with a feverish complaint. I had already notified Verena of my whereabouts so when she discovered my predicament she kindly said that as soon as I was well enough to travel, she would whisk me away for a few days' convalescence. She told me Winchester sprang to mind because some chance acquaintance of hers had mentioned a recent visit and recommended the excellent lodgings.'

The low, pretty voice faltered as Sibella shivered. 'My sister was actually very kind, sitting with me, holding my hand and tending to my wants, as well as paying generously for my medical care. What I did not at first appreciate was that I had been delirious for a night or so and that in that condition, I let slip a secret – a family secret.'

She buried her face in her hands then carried on, 'Verena made no mention of this until we were safely ensconced in the guesthouse in Winchester and I was fully recovered, although still a little languid. Then one evening, a day or so before Mrs Richmond invited us to the christening, she laughed and told me what she had learned. She said that it was all very delicious and that she had never imagined the staid Armstrongs might harbour such secrets.'

'Good God,' Charlotte jumped up out of her chair. 'What a bitch!' At Sibella's shocked gasp, Charlotte clapped a hand to her mouth. 'I'm sorry, Sibella, but that's what she was. Now....' she looked at the little clock on the mantelpiece. 'Heavens, I must dress for the tea party. You will excuse me, won't you? Carry on telling me about your sister while I change. You can help me, if you please.'

The last command was slightly muffled as she wriggled out of her dress, but after a startled glance, Sibella went on with her story.

'There isn't very much more to tell,' she whispered. 'Verena insisted that the – the family secret would remain just that, a secret and that she had no intention of telling anyone. What good would it do her, she demanded. It could only damage her own reputation, but she kept chuckling whenever she recalled it.'

'Was she like that with other people, do you imagine?' Charlotte was intrigued as a sudden notion had occurred to her. If Verena Chant had a liking for mysteries, had she chuckled over other people's dark secrets? Chuckled, perhaps, once too loudly?

'Oh no,' Sibella dispelled the unspoken suggestion. 'In public she was always circumspect, even in her flirtations.' She looked up to see Charlotte's speculative gaze. 'Yes, she was a flirt, I'm afraid, but it meant nothing to her. She was cold, you see, but no, she wasn't a gossip and I'm quite certain she would never have spoken so to anyone else. It was because of the family, you see, that was what amused her so much. I remember her saying once, "brought up in the odour of sanctity, as we were, and now look at the honour of the Armstrongs". She had no such fond memories of our parents as I had, as I have still.'

Charlotte emerged, slightly dishevelled, from the depths of the large walnut wardrobe and, with Sibella's assistance, arrayed herself in yesterday's elegant silk evening dress in her favourite dark emerald green. She and Lily had conferred together regarding the correct garments for a tea party to celebrate the birthday of an eleven year old boy, and had come to the conclusion that it would be far better to be over-dressed than otherwise. 'For,' had said Lily, her eyes wide with horror, 'It would never do to annoy Lady Granville by being too informal. I'm sure she would regard it as an insult.'

Charlotte could only agree, her brief acquaintance with the lady indicated that she would stand on ceremony and expect no less of her guests. Feeling foolish at dressing so sumptuously for a child's birthday tea, she added a creamy lace fichu to her modestly cut bodice, and pinned it with the emerald brooch that was Elaine's Christmas present. She slipped on her other present, the emerald bracelets and frowned at her reflection in the looking-glass. Lady Granville could not find cause to be slighted by this finery, she decided. After all, it had the double skirt and tiny puffed sleeves that Lily informed her were the very latest thing. And much I care for that, she added with a scornful shrug.

It struck her that the lofty stone pillars of Brambrook Abbey would prove chilly and she had little faith that the *sortie de bal* in cream cashmere, that Lily had insisted all the Richmond ladies must have, would keep her warm. Certainly it was an elegant evening cloak and at least it had a hood, but she put out her new shawl too, ready for when Lily should call her family to attention.

As she brushed her hair and rapidly re-plaited it, Charlotte was frowning. Did Sibella's disclosures about her sister have some bearing on the whole matter, she asked herself, but she felt quite certain she should tread warily. A false step would alarm Sibella and make her retreat, and that wouldn't do, Charlotte reflected. If I am to lay aside my wild conjectures and feel comfortable again, I need to know the whole story.

'You said your sister was cold? Did that apply to her relations with her husband?' The doctor's words, abruptly broken off, came back to Charlotte, 'we were not hap….' As she pinned a demure froth of lace on her hair, she waited intently for the reply.

'I'm afraid so,' agreed Sibella. 'I had very little opportunity, you must understand, to observe them together as husband and wife, but it seemed to me that she felt nothing for him. Or,' she added, 'that he felt a shred of affection for her either, though I think he was very jealous of her. He was certainly furious when he discovered she and I were in Winchester. He followed her down here and obtained an invitation to the christening too. Verena laughed and told me he liked to glare at her in disapproval.'

She rose and smoothed down her skirt. 'Thank you, Charlotte, for allowing me to talk to you so intimately. It is a lonely life, that of a governess, and I have had little opportunity for friendship.'

'I have felt something very similar,' admitted Charlotte, also rising. 'But before you go to your room, might I ask you one more question? Thank you. It is this: your sister implied at the christening that she was with child, and it has generally been accepted that this was somehow the cause of her untimely death. Do you have anything further to say about that situation?'

'How did you…' Sibella's colour rose and she looked startled but as Charlotte simply gave a noncommittal shrug, she frowned and chose her words carefully. 'She did give that impression, I know, but I'm afraid it was purely a mischievous impulse to torment Dr Chant. She – it was determined not long after her marriage, I am afraid, that she would not be able to – to bear a child; some physical malformation, I believe. She professed to be relieved, and I truly believe that she was not distressed by the intelligence, but her husband clearly felt cheated.'

'You mean he had married a beautiful young woman with a view to embellishing his status by the addition of a clutch of equally beautiful children?' Charlotte raised an eyebrow. 'I can well believe such a man as the doctor might feel he had made a poor bargain, particularly if there was no affection to bind them together, but what did he think, do you suppose, when she made that extraordinary statement at the party? Could he have wondered if, perhaps, that original diagnosis might have been wrong?'

'I understood that there could be no question of that, but if he did indeed entertain any such unlikely suspicion,' was Sibella's dry answer, 'he would be under no illusion that the child was his; my sister was quite frank with me on that subject. I don't believe, however,' she hesitated then shook her head, looking doubtful,'I would not have thought she would actually betray him. Her flirtations were usually conducted with older men, retired rakes, that kind of gentleman, but I'm sure she allowed no liberties beyond a dinner here, or a theatre box there, with perhaps a discreet kiss. Oh yes,' she turned back at the door of Charlotte's room. 'She had no scruples about accepting the occasional diamond bracelet, but I doubt there were any intimate moments. My sister was a cold woman.'

She smiled faintly as she left the room. 'Forgive me, Charlotte, I must take up no more of your time. I believe there is another hour until we leave for Brambrook Abbey, so I think I must go to my own room, to compose myself.'

Once the door was safely closed Charlotte gave a soft whistle. Heavens above, I had previously seen no resemblance to her sister or anyone else, but that was surely the smile that young Oz is wont to give. What in the world can it mean? Is there some connection between the Armstrongs and the Granvilles?

She sat down again in her easy chair and tried to assemble the facts and make sense of them. There had been that moment at the christening when she spotted an astonishing likeness between Oz Granville and Verena Chant; what am I to make of that, she wondered. But later I was told that Mrs Chant closely resembled her brother Edward Armstrong. Now Sibella also has a fleeting likeness to the boy. Can there be any significance in this, or is it nothing more than a singular coincidence?

She shook her head, frowning as she considered the question. What am I to think she asked herself, two vertical lines forming on her brow. The idea had, she knew, been lying just under the surface of her thoughts, kept there by her refusal to give credence to the notion that would not go away. She sighed deeply and held up her hand in order to count off the troubling questions: Edward Armstrong had been summarily dispatched to Australia upon the discovery of his deceit and wrongdoing, actions which had deeply distressed his employer, Lord Granville. This had occurred some eleven or twelve years earlier according to Sibella Armstrong.

Again Charlotte frowned, remembering with some trepidation, that today was Oz Granville's eleventh birthday. I really *am* romancing now she scolded herself, only to wonder anew. Can it be possible that there is some connection that links Edward Armstrong's disappearance from these shores with Lady Granville's treasured only child? She tested the theory and far-fetched as it seemed found herself believing that there could be a glimmer of possibility. So what am I saying, she murmured aloud. Am I – she found herself faltering – am I thinking then that Lady Granville, suffering years in a barren marriage, was minded to take herself a handsome young lover?

Charlotte was shocked because the whole idea seemed suddenly so plausible. A woman who had spent 20 years in a heart-breaking quest for a child might well have resorted to desperate measures. And what then? If this could possibly be true, she wondered, might not the story of Edward Armstrong's disgrace, be merely that: a story? What would Lord Granville's feelings have been? Delight and disbelief at the promise of the longed-for heir to his title and fortune? No doubt, but suppose the whole was revealed to him: the young lover, the success after so many empty years? Would his pride take over so that an heir by any means would be preferable to a devastating scandal?

It made sense, of a sort, Charlotte felt. At that time Lord Granville had been a member of the government, albeit in a minor position. In such a public role it would have been mortifying to say the least, to deny the child and send his wife abroad to a shameful exile. How much simpler to banish instead the handsome young man who had cuckolded him, and to put it about that the young man had committed some nameless treachery. If that were indeed the case, his lordship would certainly have required some promise, probably in writing, of continued silence together with continued absence from England, in exchange for some handsome form of payment. She had encountered plenty of remittance men in Australia, after all, some of them living hand to mouth between their quarterly allowances.

Charlotte jumped up and paced about the room, dashing a hand across her eyes. It looked possible, it could have happened that way; but even if that were the truth what possible bearing could it have had upon the sudden and untimely death of young Mrs Chant?

Chapter 12

PUZZLED AND DISTURBED, Charlotte paced the room again and finally sat down in her comfortable armchair, setting her mind to the question. But what is it to do with me, she asked herself with an anxious frown. A young woman dies too young, and too suddenly, a sad occurrence indeed, but young women die only too frequently, always too young, and often too suddenly. Why do I find this particular young woman's death so distressing?

Her fingers laced themselves together as her thoughts tumbled around in her head. Can it be simply because I had met her, however briefly? Charlotte shook her head; no, it was not only that, she was not one to leap to hasty conclusions. She was suddenly pierced by a memory of Elaine Knightley saying, with an affectionate smile:

'If I did not know you to be an exceedingly sensible young woman, Char, and thus not in the least given to flights of fancy, I should think you to be planning to write a Gothick romance!'

A sob rose in Charlotte's throat and she dashed a hand across her eyes where tears were welling. How was Elaine this afternoon? The memory of Kit's haggard face haunted her. For the first time in their acquaintance there had been no trace of humour, no twinkle, in his very blue eyes. Kit Knightley was breaking his heart and there was no comfort that she could offer him. She could only send up a constant stream of prayer that Elaine might soon fall gently into a pain-free sleep from which she would not wake.

Her thoughts were too painful to bear, so Charlotte rose and made her way across the room, her steps dragging. A difference in the quality of the light made her pause and look out of the window. There had been a fresh fall of snow but all was quiet outside, and the pale winter sun was breaking through the clouds, adding a sparkle to the landscape. There was a tap at the door and the maid thrust her head into the room to announce that the carriages were at the door and the master and mistress were attempting to assemble their party ready for departure.

Charlotte settled the hood of her evening cloak over her hair and picking up her shawl as insurance against the lordly chill of her hosts' home, caught up her reticule and the tissue-wrapped parcel, and hastened downstairs.

Earlier, Lily had been exercised on how to keep her warring guests at arms' length on the short journey to and from Brambrook Abbey. Between them, she and Charlotte came to the conclusion that, as the stable cat had now removed her family, it would be politic to bring out the brougham once more. Accordingly, Charlotte, Sibella, and Lady Frampton were tucked in to it, while the groom solicitously spread fur rugs across their knees against the biting cold. As with yesterday's expedition to church, Lily and Barnard took pride of place in the landau, which Lily hated as having been her mother-in-law's choice and too new and expensive to replace, though she had to admit that it permitted her to spread her crinoline skirts in comfort. She and Barnard sat facing the horses while Captain and Mrs Penbury, with the doctor squeezed between them, sat less comfortably opposite.

Within a very few minutes, Lady Frampton resumed her after-noon doze, while Sibella lapsed into abstracted silence, leaving Charlotte at the mercy of her jangled thoughts. Increasingly at the back of her mind was the untimely death of the younger sister, but now the idea that had occurred to her – namely that Edward Armstrong's disgrace might be somehow allied to the opportune arrival of the longed-for heir to the Granvilles – refused to go away, no matter how often she told herself that it was surely nonsense. The horrible death of Dunster the maid was still unresolved and now there was the mysterious and utterly unexpected departure of Lady Granville's hitherto devoted slave. Charlotte pictured Miss Cole, with her looped plaits and fiddly little side-curls, her plump pink cheeks and her permanently aggrieved pout, as well as her irritating habit of flapping a handkerchief as though beating time when she spoke. Had she been fond of her mistress Charlotte wondered, or had she merely suffered that lady's indifference – which at times had amounted to rudeness in public – for the sake of what appeared to be a comfortable position of many years' duration? If that were the case, no wonder she had jumped ship at the chance of a change of employment, though the timing and manner of her departure might almost be construed as a slap in the face for Lady Granville. Then again, what woman of straitened means would leave a comfortable situation on Christmas evening? Surely she would have waited until the festivities were over? Or had Miss Cole, so conveniently placed to startle the pony, also had a hand in old Maria Dunster's death? Certainly, by Oz Granville's account, the companion's behaviour had been peculiar on that occasion.

At this point in her deliberations Charlotte realized that Lady Frampton was awake and watching her, intelligence sparkling in her shrewd, protuberant, brown eyes.

'It's to be 'oped we don't get served with anything like that punch we 'ad at young Algy's christening,' she remarked. 'I certainly came to no 'arm,' she continued, 'but I doubt 'er ladyship will risk it, tasty though it was. What did you think of the wassail brew, Char?'

'I, er, it was a trifle too spicy for me,' Charlotte replied, feeling a little bewildered. Was there something on Gran's mind?

'I didn't drink it.' Sibella had clearly roused herself from her introspection. 'I don't care for the taste of cinnamon,' she explained. 'I had no wish to offend Mr Richmond as he was so pleased with his mixture, so I was happy to relinquish it to my sister.'

Could this be important? Charlotte struggled to place this snippet of information into the jumbled story that occupied her anxious thoughts. 'Do you mean, I beg your pardon, Sibella, but are you saying that Barnard himself served you with a glass of punch?'

'Oh no,' Sibella's expression was mildly puzzled as she turned to Charlotte. 'I merely mentioned Mr Richmond because of his kindness. I really have no idea who it was who handed me a drink. Why do you ask?'

Charlotte managed a laugh. 'No reason at all,' she shrugged, 'I was just picturing the scene at the christening party and realized that I have no idea exactly who was grouped around the wassail bowl as we drank a toast to dear little Algy.' She shrugged, and took care to wander away from the point that interested her so greatly, realising that such intensity might strike others as slightly odd. 'Lily was wondering.'

To her relief, Sibella lost interest and stared out of the window at the snow-covered hedge they were passing. Charlotte, however, was lost in thought; what made me say that, she wondered. And why did Gran suddenly think of that?

The horses' hooves clattered as the carriage left the lane and turned into the clean-swept drive to Brambrook Abbey. All speculation must, Charlotte realized, await a more suitable occasion. For now, her duty was to make sure that Gran enjoyed herself, which meant the old lady must be well supplied with delicacies for her tea. She must also look after Sibella Armstrong who was, after all, a stranger in their midst.

There was a flurry of greeting as Charlotte and her party entered the Great Hall. The lord and lady of the great gothic pile surged towards the Richmonds and their guests, his Lordship beaming all over his hospitable ruddy face, his hands held out in greeting.

'Well, well, well,' he cried. 'This is a delight upon my word. Welcome, welcome one and all upon this auspicious day. We are glad to have so many friends joining us, are we not, Hélène, my dear, as we celebrate the birthday of our dear young lad.' He shook hands, manfully surviving the sadly clammy fingers offered by Melicent Penbury and won Charlotte's approval by maintaining an air of apparent interest in the face of the captain's booming monologue upon the weather.

This was the first opportunity Charlotte had been given of observing the Granvilles' manner with their former young friend. Sibella's tale of her brother's disgrace and exile had wrung sympathy from Charlotte's soft heart and a glance at the other girl showed that she too was apprehensive about her reception. It was with relief, therefore, that Charlotte could see nothing more than a slight hesitation, natural enough in the circumstances, as Sibella managed a polite murmur and dropped a curtsy.

Charlotte, observing the meeting carefully, thought Lord Granville certainly displayed a shock of recognition on meeting his erstwhile acquaintance, but beyond a slight paling of his usual high colour, he took his cue from her and his wife, and made no comment, apart from a general mumble of greeting.

Lady Granville struck Charlotte as somewhat distracted, which was unusual in one so habitually composed, but no doubt her companion's desertion had upset her. The lady's dark eyes burned with an intensity that illuminated her haggard, dark, beauty and once again Charlotte was reminded of Lady Macbeth. It was impossible to discern whether her ladyship felt any greater emotion upon nodding to Sibella Armstrong, than for any other of her guests. However, her eyes lit up and her mouth ceased to droop when her son rushed to greet his friends.

'Mrs Richmond! This is capital, I'm so glad to see you.' He stammered a little in excitement and, reminded by a nudge from his mother, he turned to greet the rest of the party from Finchbourne Manor. 'Sir,' he whispered to Barnard. 'My father wants to talk to you privately, *very* privately,' he glanced apprehensively in his mother's direction. 'He has fixed upon the day after tomorrow for our own rat hunt and I do hope you can come?'

He bowed a little awkwardly to the other ladies, reserving a particular smile for Lady Frampton who greeted him in high good humour and Charlotte was amused to see the boy's eyes widen as they shook hands. Knowing Gran, it was not difficult to deduce that a sovereign had passed from one to the other, a suspicion that was confirmed by a wink from Lady Frampton.

A servant led them to a side room where the ladies could shed their outer wrappings, but Charlotte was grateful for the impulse that had made her pick up her new cashmere shawl. Good manners demanded that she lay aside her evening cloak when indoors but as she had anticipated, she was thankful for Lily's Christmas present as the stone walls did not improve the overall cold. Even on so short a journey her lace cap had become slightly flattened under her hood so she fluffed it up in the looking glass thoughtfully placed for such titivation and ventured out into the party. It was a relief to see several friends and acquaintances clustering around the huge fireplaces at either end of the Great Hall. Charlotte had harboured an apprehension that the party from the manor might be the only people invited to the birthday tea and, considering the mourning state of two of the guests, she worried that conversation might be difficult.

She shook hands with Dr and Mrs Perry who were good friends and anxious to know how she was enjoying her first taste of an English winter.

'I'm enchanted by the snow,' she assured the doctor, adding, 'particularly so when I'm looking at it through the window of a warm, comfortable room!'

'You're looking very smart, my dear,' said Mrs Perry, admiring the green silk gown. 'It must have been quite a feat for Lily to pull off a visit of this nature when she has two guests in such very immediate mourning, but I gather nobody has seen fit to put on their blacks?'

'It did give Lily some moments of mental struggle,' admitted Charlotte. 'She was torn, but as neither the poor young lady's husband or sister appears transported with grief and, in the husband's case, actually expressed an interest in attending the party, Lily concluded that the rest of us could turn up with a clear conscience.' She grinned and gestured towards her sister-in-law, 'At least Lily's chosen a decently sober gown for once and not her latest cerise satin.'

Lily was wearing a sumptuous purple dress, flounced and frilled and arranged over what was by far the widest hoop in the room. She had reluctantly agreed with Charlotte's suggestion that her new diamond necklace, a present from Barnard to celebrate the birth of little Algy, would not be suitable for a tea party. Instead she wore a more discreet *parure* of amethysts: necklace, earrings, brooch, and an amethyst star in her hair.

Sibella Armstrong had borrowed a half-veil from Lily and was demure in dark blue over a modest hoop, and with a high neck and long sleeves, topped by a soft grey shawl, while Lady Frampton was monumental in black brocade, hung about with strings of jet beads. As she wondered whether she should act as sheepdog to the bereaved governess, Charlotte was relieved to see her other sister-in-law Agnes, the vicar's wife, surge forward to greet Sibella, ready tears of sympathy falling freely as she did so.

Dear Agnes, Charlotte smiled and turned away, disinclined for conversation at present. She went back to looking at the fashions on display. Most of the neighbours were elderly, the ladies in black, or grey, or sometimes a daring dark red, rarely with any regard to fashion. Agnes, at five months pregnant, was swathed in shawls but looked so happy, and was so much loved, that everyone overlooked her usual dowdiness anyway.

Strolling round the hall, nodding and smiling as she was hailed by neighbours, Charlotte gratefully seized a glass of wine from a silver tray offered by an obliging footman. Perhaps it would alleviate the chill. She was about to return to circling the room when she was waylaid by her host, looking conspiratorial.

'My dear Charlotte,' he said, glancing round to make sure his lady was not in earshot, 'I believe you did say I might call you that?' She nodded cordially and he continued, 'I merely wished to say that, as I believe Oz has already told you, our own Brambrook rat hunt is arranged for the day after tomorrow. It would give him great pleasure, and me too, my dear young lady, if you would attend the event?' When she exclaimed in surprise, he hushed her, looking even more furtive. 'I realize it's an unusual invitation for a lady, but Oz is so sure that you would enjoy it. He's been telling me that you once shot a crocodile, so ratting will not faze you in anyway. But I have to keep it a little under wraps as my dear wife would not approve. And in any case,' his eye lit upon Melicent Penbury, at that moment languishing unattended in a draughty corner,'I doubt that the older ladies would enjoy it, so it is to be a secret.'

Charlotte hid a sigh. Ratting held no attraction for her these days but not for the world would she hurt young Oz's feelings, so she smiled and agreed to the engagement. His lordship peered round and she wondered if he could be looking for Sibella. What if my speculation is correct, she mused. Suppose I'm right about Edward Armstrong's part in all this, might Lord Granville have some inkling? If he has, he might hope to waylay Sibella, to question her.

He showed no sign of doing so, however, and she remembered

Miss Nightingale's comment about his sanguine nature. Perhaps he did suspect something but was content to let sleeping dogs lie, after all.

By some fluke of fortune, Charlotte had turned away and was talking to the vicar when Lady Granville's stately progress around the room brought her up to Charlotte's side. It was clear from her warm greeting that the lady had not observed her husband in close conversation with a young woman or the dark brows would have met across the noble beak of a nose.

'How kind of you, Mrs Richmond, to give Osbert such a valuable gift. Ah, here he is, to thank you himself.'

'It's capital, Mrs Richmond,' he told her, opening up each attachment so that she could admire them. 'I've always wanted a knife like this but Mama said I was too young.'

Oh dear, Charlotte's hand flew to her mouth to conceal a guilty grin but Lady Granville seemed unperturbed. 'I hope you will prove worthy of Mrs Richmond's trust, dear Osbert,' was all she said. 'Your papa and I rely on you not to damage yourself or anyone else.' She turned, with a gracious smile, to greet a newcomer. 'Ah, Mr Knightley, how kind of you to come, how do you do? May I enquire after Mrs Knightley's health?'

Kit nodded briefly in Charlotte's direction while bowing over his hostess's outstretched hand. 'Thank you,' he said. 'She is resting today.'

'What's that? Your wife unwell, sir?' It was Doctor Chant, who bustled up and shook Kit's unwilling hand. 'Perhaps I might have the pleasure of prescribing for her?' He glanced round and lowered his tone to a conspiratorial whisper. 'Dr Perry is an excellent enough man, for a country physician, but I fancy he is a trifle behind the times when it comes to the latest methods. Has Mrs Knightley tried hot and cold water treatments? I can promise you miraculous results, if you will place the lady in my hands. Why, only last month, His Royal Highness, the Prince….'

'My wife is dying,' Kit snapped, and Charlotte, in response to a concerned glance from Lady Granville, took his arm and marched him unceremoniously out of the doctor's reach.

'Come and sit by Gran,' was all she said, as the gong sounded and the assembled guests were ushered towards the lofty dining-room. 'She won't allow anyone to harry you.' He bit his lip and nodded, clearly unable to speak, and Charlotte continued, 'I'll go and see Elaine tomorrow morning. She'll like to hear about the party, if – if she's well enough.'

Charlotte saw him safely under Lady Frampton's wing and moved away, to find her hostess smiling approvingly.

'Thank you, my dear,' was all she said, then she nodded compla-cently at the guests who were finding seats. 'It seemed sensible to have tea in the dining-room today,' she pronounced. 'So much cosier than in the Great Hall and of course there are too many of us to fit comfortably round the tea-table in the drawing-room.'

Cosy? The room was vast and Charlotte stared round-eyed at the table that looked at least half a mile long.

'Charlotte?' It was Dr Perry, a frowning concentration visible on his brow. 'A word, if I may?'

'Of course.' Charlotte looked anxious. 'Is it about Mrs Knightley?'

'What's that?' He shook his head. 'Oh no, poor soul, that will come at any time; you'll feel it sadly, poor child. No, this is another matter entirely.' The furrows in his forehead deepened as he chose his words with care. 'Char, this is in confidence but I know you can be trusted. Have you heard of anyone else being indisposed after that party at the manor? No?' He shook his head. 'Nor I and that surprises me. That healthy young woman had no symptoms other than some kind of food poisoning, but her sister insists that they ate the same food. I know this because the Winchester doctor who attended her in her last hours is a great friend of mine, and he is both perplexed and mortified at her death.'

Charlotte stared at Dr Perry in dismay, his sentiments chimed so familiarly with her own. It was one thing, she discovered, to conjure up nightmares, but quite another to have not one, but two sensible, experienced medical practitioners suffering from the same uncertainty.

'What are you going to do?' she breathed, and could not decide whether to be relieved or even more anxious when he replied:

'I have no idea.'

At that moment, the guests were called to the table and the slight delay caused by her encounter with Dr Perry meant that the only available seat was beside Captain Penbury who was delighted to see her.

'How are you feeling today, Captain?' she enquired with a smile. In spite of her reservations about his wife, Charlotte was quite fond of the bluff sailor and felt genuine concern for his health after the fright at the christening. 'No trouble amidships with the musket ball?'

'Not a suspicion of it, Mrs Richmond – well then, Charlotte, if you wish, that's very civil of you.' He patted her hand, a smile of genuine pleasure brightening his large red face. 'No, as I was saying, Charlotte, I'm happy to say I find myself hale and hearty at present. In fact I gather there is talk of skating on the local gravel pit tomorrow if the ice holds, and as I consider myself proficient in the art, I shall enjoy myself a good deal.' He glanced across at her other neighbour, Dr Chant and addressed him, with a gesture of apology to Charlotte. 'I say there, Doctor. Have you ever come across a case like mine? Hey? I carry a musket ball around, d'ye hear? A relic of the battle when our gallant navy captured the Chesapeake from the Americans in the year '13.' He smiled reminiscently, as he went on, 'Of course, I was only a midshipman at the time, a mere lad, but here we are still to tell the tale, that Yankee musket-ball and I.'

Charlotte relaxed for the moment. At least Kit was safe from Dr Chant and Melicent was enjoying herself exchanging ailments with one of the neighbouring wives.

'You know, Captain,' Dr Chant had been frowning and now suddenly leaned across Charlotte with a perfunctory apology, 'with a delicate digestion like yours, you should be on gruel and water, not stuffing yourself with such rich delicacies as we are served here.'

Oh dear, not again. Charlotte leaned back and let battle commence as the captain started up in indignation.

'What's that you say, sir? Hey? I go to Bath to take the waters when I'm feeling out of sorts but otherwise I'm as fit as many men half my age, sir; aye, and fitter than many, despite always carrying round a musket-ball. I live by the words of some famous man of old – La Rochefoucauld, I believe it was – who said: *"Preserving the health by too strict a regimen is a wearisome malady."* As for exercise, why I propose to march back to the manor, when this delightful occasion is at an end. I defy you, sir,' he gobbled, his large face flushed and furious, with an ominous vein throbbing at his temple. 'Yes, I defy you, to tell me I am not a fit man for my age.'

Clearly unimpressed by this assertion, Dr Chant retorted with an aphorism or two of his own. 'Indeed, sir? Let me remind you of some other old sayings, *"Diet cures more than the lancet"* and *"Better lose a supper than gain a hundred physicians"*, and I tell you...' with a shrug, he clinched the argument, 'no violent exercise should be taken immediately after a heavy meal, Captain, I beg of you. Do you not recall the famous experiment in the last century, by Mr Hunter of Edinburgh, who fed identical meals to two dogs, then left one sleeping by the fire and took the other out hunting? When he examined their stomach contents an hour later, he discovered....'

'How in the world did he do that?' Charlotte interrupted. 'You mean he *killed* the poor beasts and dissected them?' Her horror was mirrored in several faces so that Dr Chant was forced to subside with an irritable mutter into his beard. Charlotte's indignation was tempered by the realisation that Kit Knightley had overheard and was actually smiling as he relayed the story to Lady Frampton, so in gratitude for that moment of respite for her friend, she devoted the rest of the meal to allowing the egregious doctor to tell her how wonderful he was.

Mercifully the meal did not in fact last for hours, it only appeared to do so, and just as Charlotte was becoming terminally bored and reduced to counting the carved Tudor roses that embellished the frieze round the room, Lord Granville stood up.

'My thanks to one and all, good friends and neighbours, for joining us,' he announced, his ruddy face beaming with pleasure. 'Please be upstanding to drink a toast to the hero of the hour, my dear son, Osbert, on this auspicious day.'

Glasses were raised, cheers threatened to lift the monumental roof, Lady Granville nodded to her guests, a gracious smile on her handsome face and Oz bowed with awkward but sincere thanks. There was a distinct easing of waistbands and the guests were encouraged to withdraw to the Great Hall once more or, for the ladies, to retire to the more genteel surroundings of the drawing-room while some of the gentlemen vanished in search of the library or the smoking-room.

Despite eating sparingly, the meal sat heavily, and Charlotte felt out of sorts as a result, so she eluded friends and acquaintances while she wandered round the enormous rooms, admiring and recoiling in equal measure from the handsome but enormous and uncomfortable stone benches and tables in what Lady Granville had proudly described earlier, as Norman in design. There were monstrous lamps too, rearing up at least twelve feet high, and ornately carved to resemble sea creatures – though Charlotte had her doubts as to their connection with the Normans – each hydra head supporting a glass bowl, the whole lit by gas.

At least Kit was looking less drained. Charlotte smiled as she watched him speak kindly to Sibella Armstrong before leaning forward to admire some of Oz's birthday presents which were arrayed on a side table. Sibella slipped away to stay close beside Gran when Lord Granville approached the table and Charlotte guessed that Kit might also be invited to the ratting party. The two men and the boy were clearly amused, even Kit managing a smile, while Lord Granville's face lit up.

What Charlotte saw then demolished her carefully constructed theories about Verena Chant's untimely death. Wild as the notion seemed, she had gradually come to believe that Lady Granville had somehow found herself with child by the elder brother of the two sisters from Northumberland and that as a result the Granvilles had paid off the brother and severed all ties with the family in an attempt to hide their secret. But now… from a discreet vantage point behind a pillar, Charlotte stared at the group by the table. She saw Lord Granville address the boy and young Oz turn to answer him; and she observed, without a doubt, that the slightly-built boy's flickering smile, combined as it was with a swift sidelong glance to see if his mother might be nearby, was identical to that of the older man.

In her agitation, Charlotte set out once more on her perambulation round the ground floor, all the time puzzling over what she had observed. I see other resemblances too, she told herself, now that the idea had planted itself. Oz laughs like Lord Granville, I've seen Lady Granville wince when they both forget themselves in a belly laugh, and he has the same quizzical lift to his left eyebrow.

Did I not notice these likenesses before, she wondered, or was I so enamoured of my theory that I wouldn't admit what is now so clear? The boy's blue eyes were set at an identical angle to her host's, also blue, and the tilt of his flaxen head mirrored the older grey bushy one.

But what did this mean? If the Armstrong brother was not, after all, the boy's father, how did it come about that he bore resemblances – unmistakeable, now that she had made the connection – not only to Lord Granville, but to Verena Chant? And none at all to the lady of the house. A solution to this puzzle dropped into her mind, so audacious as to make her gasp out loud, and causing the vicar to give her an inquiring look. She shook her head, masking her impatience, and slid back to her shelter behind the pillar. The group by the table had now broken up, but it made no difference.

In spite of Sibella's belief that her sister was unable to bear a child, had Verena Chant been Oz's real mother? Could that have some bearing on her sudden, shocking death?

Chapter 13

UNABLE TO MARSHAL her whirling thoughts, Charlotte sought solitude and making her way to the other side of the hall, found the passage that led to the mediaeval garden. It's astonishing how I can be chilled to the bone by all this stonework, she thought, yet I'm hot and stuffy at the same time. It was the work of a moment to slip out into the crisp night air. There was a full moon silvering the yew hedge with the ruined tower silhouetted against the light.

She stood, irresolute, on the wide path until the cold brought her to her senses. Fool that I am, she scolded herself, to go outside without even my shawl. At that moment the door to the garden opened and her hostess emerged. In a startled voice, Lady Granville exclaimed, 'Mrs Richmond? You imprudent girl! How can you be so venturesome as to brave the night air? Come indoors at once, I must insist.'

Even had she wished to, Charlotte dared not disobey the peremptory note in the older woman's voice. Lady Granville sounded both displeased and disturbed, so Charlotte hurried to apologise.

'I'm so sorry, ma'am,' she said, her evident sincerity clearly making an impression as her hostess's face relaxed its frowning disapproval. 'I forgot that the door is kept locked. It's just that I couldn't resist the chance to admire your garden once more, the moonlight is so enticing. It makes me long for the summer to come. It must be a wonderful sight then, in full leaf and the garden awash with flowers. The vine tunnel must look just like a passage way that leads to fairyland.'

She felt slightly ashamed of her gushing, though she knew Will would have egged her on. '*Ladle it on thick, young Char,*' he used to say. '*You can never be too flattering. Why, it was my earnest supposition that so great a sailor must have been subordinate only to Nelson that made me the pet of a prison guard who'd once been a seaman. I spread the butter thicker every day so that I was able to hoodwink him into letting me go off to market on my own.*' Will had grinned, with no sign of remorse. '*Poor old fellow, he must have been sadly disappointed when I didn't come back. I hope he wasn't flogged over that.*'

That memory also shamed her, so she felt impelled to make further small talk, even though Lady Granville's thoughts now seemed elsewhere.

'I'm intrigued by such an original premise,' she plodded on, although the cold was beginning to seep into her bones. 'To conceive the idea of recreating a mediaeval garden is so unusual and so – so *clever*, if you don't mind my saying so, that I'm finding it truly overwhelming.'

The real warmth of the older woman's expression was unmistakeable and she took Charlotte's arm.

'Ah, no,' she halted abruptly, an unfathomable expression on her face as she stared out at the moonlight. She shook her head and nodded to her guest, with a reluctant half-smile. 'It is by far too cold tonight, Mrs Richmond, in spite of the moonlight, but I am glad to know that you approve of my garden. So few of my visitors appreciate what I am trying to create,' she told her guest, a passionate note creeping into her voice. 'But history is of the utmost importance, do you not feel? It teaches us lessons from the past.'

Charlotte nodded and as they turned in to the house, Lady Granville continued, obviously encouraged by the intelligence in her guest's face. 'Yes,' she said, the brooding expression Charlotte had noticed earlier transforming her to momentary animation, 'history can show us many things; old problems repeat themselves and if we know how to read our history, old solutions can prove as satisfactory now as in past centuries.'

Charlotte took a puzzled but smiling leave of her hostess and walked back to the Great Hall to pick up her shawl and snuggle into it while she made sure that Lady Frampton was comfortable and enjoying herself. Enthroned in a massive oak chair beside the huge open fire, with Sibella safely beside her, the old lady was holding court and clearly delighted with her situation. As though aware of Charlotte's affectionate gaze, Lady Frampton suddenly lifted her eyes and nodded a greeting, to which Charlotte responded with a fond wave as she turned away.

The other objects of her concern also seemed happily occupied. Oz and his father were engaged in an animated discussion with Barnard Richmond and Kit Knightley who was, Charlotte noticed, shooting frequent glances at the grandfather clock in the corner. Yes, she sighed, Kit would be anxious to return to Elaine's bedside. Only his wife's strongest representations had made him agree to put in an appearance at this afternoon's party and Charlotte knew he would be slipping away as soon as he could do so politely. He caught her eye as she strolled past and for a moment the sad severity of his expression was lightened by a grin. He cocked an eyebrow towards his companions and she overheard Lord Granville exclaim,

'What's that you say, m'boy? Twenty or more rats? That's a grand haul indeed. We must see what we can do ourselves, hey?' His cheerful laugh rumbled out as he clapped his son on the shoulder. 'The honour of Brambrook is at stake, hey, Richmond? I swear we'll beat you at our return match the day after tomorrow, d'ye hear me?' He looked guiltily round, his shoulders sagging with relief when he realized that his wife was nowhere in the vicinity.

Charlotte returned Kit's smile and passed on towards the small group under a gloomy painting that depicted a forbidding female, alleged to be Lord Granville's great-grandmother.

'Char?' It was Kit Knightley who addressed her. Deep in thought, her circuit of the enormous room had brought her all unknowing to the entrance to the outer hall. Kit was now wearing his coat, his hat held in his hand.

'You – you're not leaving?' For a moment Charlotte felt something like panic, but she forced it down and gripped his hand tightly. 'Give my dear, dear love to Elaine,' she told him. 'I'll call tomorrow morning and hope to find her well enough to see me.'

'Is something wrong, Char?' Kit brushed aside her polite, though heartfelt, words as he retained her hand in his. 'You look, oh I don't know – you look somehow almost frightened, that's not like you. Has someone alarmed you, Charlotte?'

'Nonsense.' She had herself well in hand now and gave him a little push. 'I'm just very full of food, that's all, and it's making me feel slow and heavy! Off you go to Elaine and don't dawdle.'

He nodded, still frowning, but slipped out towards the front door, attended by the immaculate butler, who directed a disapproving frown at a gentleman who had shrugged on his own coat and retrieved his own hat. Charlotte stared after Kit, and wondered how Elaine fared tonight, as she turned back to the party.

Sibella Armstrong was tucked safely into a group composed of Captain Penbury, booming away on the iniquities of the Admiralty, along with his drooping wife who was smirking in a convenient mirror as she turned this way and that to admire the sheen on her new puce silk gown. Lily Richmond was there, queening it a little, and playing the lady of the manor to her heart's content until Lady Granville joined the conversation and naturally took precedence, apparently unaffected by the defection of her faithful handmaiden. Miss Cole's absence seemed to be regretted by no-one and all the guests appeared to be enjoying themselves.

Thank God for that, Charlotte breathed a sigh of relief. They're all happily entertained so perhaps I can escape for ten minutes or thereabouts? The noise of determined revelry in the Great Hall was deafening and Charlotte's head was beginning to throb painfully. A swift glance round showed that nobody was looking in her direction so she slipped quietly through the massively-carved oak doors to find a temporary refuge in the small room where Lady Granville had entertained her on that first visit to the Abbey. Sinking gratefully on to one of the cushioned settles she pondered on the notion that had struck her; Lord Granville was rumoured to be a 'one' for the young ladies. Exactly how young did he like them? And just how young had Verena been, twelve years ago? Could she have given birth secretly to Lord Granville's child? And was that child passed off by him and his lady as the legitimate heir?

Bessie Railton, experienced midwife though she was, could

have been wrong about Verena's situation at her death. There was that woman in Adelaide, Charlotte mused. Will had been called in to christen the twins that had unexpectedly arrived one stormy night. *'Poor soul,'* he had told Charlotte and her mother. *'She'd been told by every doctor under the sun that she had no chance of bearing a child, so there she was, 48 years old and thinking she had a belly-ache from some pork that had gone past its best.'* His laughter rang down through the dozen or so years as Charlotte remembered. *'They lived in a little house tucked in between the pub on one side and the little Catholic mission on the other, and by God! One of the babies was the spitting image of the publican – a fine figure of a man who must have been near seven foot tall, and the other the duplicate of the priest next door, ugly as sin and red hair like a bush. So there she was with one baby with his head covered in a red fuzz, and the other the longest new-born baby I'd ever seen, and her man pleased as punch at his prowess in fathering the pair.'*

She sighed. Yes, it was just possible that Bessie had been wrong about Verena. Or could the malformation referred to by Sibella rather have been damage caused by giving birth at too young an age? And if so, had her husband, a medical man himself, drawn his own conclusions about secrets kept from him? That could account for the coldness between them. She drew in a sharp breath. Yes, and it could have given him a motive to dispose of a barren wife now that his star was rising.

She dashed a hand across her eyes. It was equally possible that Lady Granville had indeed borne a longed-for child by her own husband and that the resemblance to the Armstrong brother and sisters was purely a coincidence. I'm being nonsensical she told herself firmly and cast about for something to distract her mind. Beside her on the settle lay an ancient-looking book, which had evidently been laid aside for the moment by its reader.

'A True History of the Queens of England' she read, tracing the gothic lettering with difficulty, much of the gilt having been rubbed off. As she idly scanned the pages an idea sprang to mind and she turned to the chapter about Queen Eleanor of Provence, who had provided the inspiration for Lady Granville's mediaeval garden. Or, as the lady's husband had irritably described it, 'A damned

depressing monument, if you ask me. Fancy making such a palaver about a dead queen's garden!'

Oh well, perhaps I should see what there is about the 'dead queen' to offer such inspiration and refreshment to Lady Granville, Charlotte decided, wrinkling her nose as she flicked through the florid prose. So, the gist of it was this: Queen Eleanor, a dark-haired beauty with fine dark eyes to match, had come from her warm, sun-drenched home in the south of France to marry Henry III in 1236.

Charlotte paused. Was this where Lady Granville began to see parallels between herself and the queen? Herself a noted dark-eyed beauty, also born in southern climes and brought to England for her marriage, her ancient lineage in return for her husband's money? It had been politics not money that drove that long ago royal lady's alliance. Charlotte read on, interested now. Hmm, the parallels ended almost immediately; Queen Eleanor had borne five children and lived to help bring up her grandchildren, whereas Lady Granville must have suffered agonies during those decades of barren misery, seared by her husband's infidelities until the miracle had occurred.

At the thought of that miracle child, Charlotte gave an involuntary smile. Oz Granville as an angel sent from heaven was a hard image to swallow but miracle he was, and as such was adored by both his elderly parents. A frown creased her brow for a moment, but once more she firmly pushed aside her doubts. No good could come of asking questions, she told herself sternly, and her conjectures as to the Granville family must remain in her head alone. Besides, it was probably all moonshine, she admitted. Oz must indeed be what he purported to be: the astonishing gift when hope had almost vanished.

It came to her suddenly that Lord Granville had addressed his wife as Hélène, the first time Charlotte had heard her given name which, surely, was the French version of Eleanor? It struck her as heartbreakingly poignant that the unhappy, barren Hélène of modern times should identify herself so closely with her fecund royal namesake as to create a garden in her honour.

She sighed and returned to the ancient book but however

venerable, it had to be admitted that the style was a mere chronicle of dry facts. Lady Granville might preach the benefits of reading the lessons shown by history but Charlotte was finding nothing pertinent in her skimming of these pages. As she went to put the book back where she had found it, she noticed that the pages yawned open a little, as if at a chapter that had been read over and over again. She slid her forefinger curiously into the gap and opened it once more.

She was unprepared for the shock as the name on the page jumped out at her, and she drew in a sharp breath. Was this it? Could that be the story, there all the time? She frowned, drawing a hand across eyes suddenly grown weary: a story familiar from her childhood, one of the tales from history beloved of Lady Meg who had regaled her young goddaughter with them on their frequent journeyings across Australia.

She could remember the bare bones of the tale but she glanced down at the printed page to refresh her memory. Oh my God, she thought, closing the book once more and setting it firmly down on the cushion beside her. I think I see it now, I see it all. I cannot be right, but I fear that I may be.

An earlier Queen of England born and bred in France, another Eleanor; was she the one known as the She-Wolf of France? Charlotte thought not, but though she racked her brains to try and recall Meg's tales, nothing sprang to mind – except the story of that other Queen Eleanor – and the crime that supposedly made her infamous. Here, she thought, might be Lady Granville's lesson from history.

She pressed her hands to her temples, trying to rub away the headache, trying to banish the suspicion from her mind. If I am right, she fretted; if my wild imaginings are cold, hard truth, what then? What do I propose to do with such knowledge? Her thoughts flew to the man who had so recently left the party. I cannot go to anyone in authority, Kit Knightley, for instance, as he is a Justice of the Peace, and say to him, I believe Verena Chant was murdered. Nor can I possibly say to him, yes she was murdered and this person, I believe, is the murderer. I have no proof, merely suspicions borne of glimpses of character, comments referring to past events, circumstances that could mean it to be so.

She caught her breath; still less can I say that the reason I believe this to be true is because of a murder that a long ago Queen Eleanor of England is said to have committed.

She was still safely alone in Lady Granville's room, had been there for fifteen minutes or more, but the thoughts jangled to and fro in her brain and gave her no rest, so she picked up her new paisley shawl and went quietly to the door.

I cannot go back to the Great Hall just yet, she told herself, it must be only too clear that I am disturbed and what explanation can I give? The passageway was empty for the moment so she wrapped herself warmly in the cashmere folds and made her way towards the outside door. It was the work of a moment to turn the handle and she slipped silently out to the gravelled walk, this time unchallenged.

Fresh air was what she craved, but the icy chill struck her at once and she shivered, clutching the shawl more closely to her throat, but as she faltered there, she saw that Lady Granville must have left the door to the garden ajar. She hesitated, glanced around, and saw nobody, so she pushed the heavy door and entered the mediaeval garden undeterred and unobserved. I need to think, she told herself as she set off at a brisk pace down the path at the side of the stream, wishing ruefully that she had worn stouter shoes; her glacé kid slippers were woefully inadequate for the task.

What *am* I to do?

Her anxiety made her careless and she frowned in dismay as she stumbled awkwardly off the path and onto the snow-covered earth. How fortunate, she thought briefly, that Lady Granville has had these fearsome-looking torches set high on the wall at either side of the entrance to the house. His lordship might laugh at his lady's obsession with antiquity, but on a night like this, in spite of the brightly shining moon, Charlotte was only too glad of the flaring pitch. In the silent garden she could still hear the crackle and hiss of the flames and it gave her an illusion of safety, made her feel less entirely alone.

There were no torches at the far end of the garden but still something attracted her attention in the moonlight. The snow had drifted in the hollow at the corner of the two adjoining walls where, in warmer weather, the little stream flowed through a stone arch; though today the splash of water was silent and frozen.

'What on earth is that?' Charlotte spoke aloud in the still air as she stared at something black just visible on the piled drift of snow. 'It looks like...' she gave a shocked gasp and regardless of her thin slippers, she scrambled across to take a closer look. It looked like the heel of a shoe. A shabby, black shoe, the kind of shoe worn by a woman of slender means. The kind of shoe, in fact, worn by....

'Miss Cole? Oh no, no....' Charlotte hardly dared breathe the name as she bent down and, with a sudden futile urgency, scraped away the snow to reveal a stout leg, attired in a black woollen stocking. And another, both protruding from under a sodden black dress.

Charlotte backed away in horror until she found herself on solid ground, her hand to her mouth. What did this mean? Her instinct, all her training from childhood, was always to run away from trouble. To run and run and keep on running, so that nobody could associate her with whatever had gone wrong. That was the way she had been brought up, but common sense prevailed and halted her urge to flee. This had nothing to do with her, she reflected, as her breathing settled to a more regular rhythm, and she began to feel calmer.

I must get help....

She summoned her distracted thoughts and turned back towards the garden door.

I need say nothing of my worries, my suspicions about that – other matter. All I need to do is tell the truth, that I found the door unlocked and felt like a last stroll round the garden by moonlight and – and found her. Because it *must* be an accident, mustn't it?

As she hastened back to the house, Charlotte puzzled over this shocking discovery. Could it be that Miss Cole had not, after all, abandoned her mistress in so cavalier a fashion? It had snowed heavily yesterday afternoon, Charlotte recalled, so perhaps the poor woman simply strayed into the garden where she slipped and somehow died. Drowned in the stream perhaps?

But there was a note....

Charlotte stopped in her tracks. Miss Cole had left a note of explanation and farewell to her employer.

Hadn't she?

A shocking thought came into her mind. Had Miss Cole, the woman who had been so conveniently on the spot on so many occasions – the death of the maid, Dunster; the wassail cup that might or might not have been tampered with; the bolting pony – had she in truth been responsible for all these occurrences? And could the note to Lady Granville have been a ruse? Could the woman, in fact, have slipped into the garden to do away with herself?

Shivering, and not only from the cold, Charlotte slipped thankfully into the house, leaving the garden door as she had found it, slightly ajar. Fortunately there was no other occupant of the small room set aside for the ladies, so she was able to effect what repairs she could to the damage caused by the cold and damp. Towels and soap lay ready for the guests to use, so she removed the worst of the moisture from her skirt while a brisk rub warmed her hands and feet when she removed her slippers. A wipe with the cloth made these presentable enough. What a fortunate circumstance, she thought, that they are black kid; it would be impossible to disguise any soiling on satin shoes.

She tidied her hair at the looking glass and made her way back to the Great Hall, slipping over to warm herself at the fireside. Lady Frampton waved again, and Lord Granville was still holding forth in his jovial way to Lily and Barnard, while Oz stood proudly at his side. But where was the boy's doting mama? There was no sign of Lady Granville nor, Charlotte realized as she tried to stare discreetly round the assembled guests, was Sibella Armstrong to be seen. Captain Penbury was still booming away to anyone who had the misfortune to stray into his grasp, but Miss Armstrong was no longer seated beside him. Besides, though this troubled Charlotte far less, the captain's lady, Melicent, was nowhere to be seen.

Chapter 14

OH, WHY DID I let Kit go home? I could have confessed my anxieties to him and let him laugh me out of this ridiculous state of panic. If that still did not suffice to allay my fears, I could at least have inveigled him into coming out to the garden to support me while I found someone to bring that poor woman's body indoors. But how am I to do that without ruining Oz's party?

She glanced round the hall again. Barnard was a steady creature, but how could she extricate him from the clutches of Lily and their host without raising a hullaballoo? Dr Perry was another obvious candidate but he was at the far end of the room in a group of local gentlemen who were clearly enjoying Lord Granville's best brandy. No, the doctor could not help her – and under no circumstances did she feel any urge to confide in the other physician present: Dr Chant's assistance would not be welcome.

A passing footman paused to offer another glass of wine and she hesitantly asked whether he knew of his mistress's whereabouts.

'I believe her ladyship is showing her tower to one of the ladies,' he told her. She thanked him and he turned to go on his way when she called him back.

'If you have the opportunity,' she faltered. 'I should be glad if you would tell Mr Richmond that I'm going to admire the garden. Pray, do not interrupt his conversation with Lord Granville, but it is – rather important so, when he is at liberty, please ask him to come out to me. I may join the ladies in the tower.' There, that was the best she could do without making a fuss. She wrapped the shawl more tightly round her shoulders, took a deep breath, and slipped out through the glass door once more.

They must have gone outside while I was drying myself in the ladies' room, she frowned; ah, thank goodness the wooden door was ajar still. The dead queen's garden shone silver and black as she slipped inside, the shadows sharply defined and now, to her heightened senses, looking sinister so that when something skittered across the path in front of her, she was only just able to repress a scream.

'Oh, you dreadful creature,' she held a hand to her heart as a scrawny ginger cat halted in its progress and came to see if she had anything interesting about her. 'I almost had a heart attack, puss.' The cat rubbed its head against her skirt, uttering loud yowls of either pleasure or hunger, probably both. She pushed it firmly, shooing it away from her. 'Be off with you now, I've nothing for you.'

Ignoring its persistent miaowing seemed to do the trick. The cat disappeared in search of more rewarding company and Charlotte hastened her steps along the central path between the flower-beds. There was no sign of Lady Granville or Sibella and when she reached the crossway she could see no further tracks in the snow to where Miss Cole lay undisturbed. There were certainly footprints leading to the ivy-clad tower at the end of the garden, however.

As she hesitated, Charlotte stared at a flicker of light up on the battlements; there was someone up there, someone carrying a candle. She took a deep breath, and another, to try to calm her fears, then gritted her teeth and headed for the narrow archway at the base of the tower.

If I am completely wrong about all of this, she told herself, if there is no mystery and Oz the belated blessing he is said to be, while Lady Granville is merely being polite to an old acquaintance – even so I must still catch up with her and tell her what I have found. It's her garden and her companion, she is the lady of the house and she must be told first. Somehow, the possession of a legitimate errand gave her courage and strengthened her resolve. Never mind her almost hysterical romancing, here was a real task ahead of her.

The door to Lady Granville's garden-room, in the thickness of the wall, was shut and barred. The mock-mediaeval torches on the stairs were unlit and no comforting spit and crackle of flames warmed her, but she could hear distant voices away up at the top of the turret. Her heart in her mouth, she began to tiptoe upwards, wondering what on earth she could say when she reached the top; then, when she was halfway up and approaching the niche within the walls, allegedly for an archer to stand guard by the arrow slit, she tripped over something hard and fell heavily to her hands and knees.

Her stifled cry was echoed by a gasp from someone else, very close by.

'Who – who is it?' she whispered, shakily feeling about her to see what had caused her fall. To her astonishment she saw that Melicent Penbury, just visible in a glimmer of moonlight, her eyes wide and terrified, was lying in an awkward huddle in the archer's bay, her false leg – which Charlotte had tripped on – lying at an unnatural angle across the step. Charlotte bit off the startled questions that sprang to mind and crawled over to the captain's lady, who was clearly scared out of her wits and in considerable pain besides.

'What on earth has happened?' she hissed. 'Let me help you to sit up, Melicent. Here….' She thrust an arm round the older woman and helped pull her into a more comfortable position, fishing a handkerchief out of her pocket as Melicent burst into tears of relief. 'Hush, now, hush, it's all right, don't fret.' Her brave words rang hollow to herself but Melicent seemed reassured. 'Quickly, tell me what you're doing here? Are you hurt? Did you fall?'

It seemed to Charlotte that it was more urgent to attend to Melicent than to creep up the last turn of the stairs; besides she was ruefully aware that emerging at the top of the turret was at this moment the last thing on earth that she wanted to do. She patted the other woman's hand and bent to listen to the anguished whisper.

'I heard Lady Granville press Miss Armstrong to see the ruins,' Melicent stammered. 'And I was rather affronted that she didn't ask me too.' She started to bridle at the memory but Charlotte hushed her again, so she continued, 'I thought it was impolite but I decided that if I simply followed them and came up to them, in a casual sort of way, it could not signify and they would be bound to invite me to join them.'

Charlotte sighed. Poor Melicent, always left out, always resentful, never understanding why she annoyed people so.

'Go on,' she murmured. 'So you followed them into the garden and into the ruins, what happened then? Did you fall?'

'I slipped in the dark,' said Melicent. 'I don't know how I did it but I twisted somehow and in falling, I felt the strap on my harness break.' She shuddered and dabbed her eyes again. 'The harness on my – my leg, you see.'

'Oh goodness, you poor soul.' Charlotte's ready sympathy rose up and instantly banished her uncharitable thoughts. 'I'll go for help in a minute, and don't worry, I'll be very discreet. Nobody will know a thing about it, other than that you felt unwell and had to be taken home. Just let me go up and see if – if Lady Granville is at liberty so that I can tell her.'

Melicent shrank back and Charlotte understood. 'I won't betray your confidence, never fear. I'll make up some story about you dragging yourself in here to shelter.'

It sounded unlikely in the highest degree that a woman in such a case could have reached the halfway point of the staircase but it was the best Charlotte could do on the spur of the moment and it seemed to satisfy Melicent, which was all that mattered just now. As for tackling Lady Granville, Charlotte admitted to herself that she was quite terrified. She strained and could still hear a murmur up aloft, so she crept up the stairs and hid at the top.

'Why do you not answer me? You do not speak. Tell me, why did you come here, to Winchester?' The voice had to be Lady Granville's because it was so much deeper than Sibella's, but otherwise, Charlotte would not have recognised those anguished tones. 'I could not believe my ears when Cole told me she had seen you and your sister in the Cathedral that day. She knew you at once, she said, and hurried home to tell me that you were to attend the Richmond child's christening.'

'I didn't know, I thought you would be in town. I assure you I didn't know you were in the country, Lady Granville.' That was Sibella's voice, ragged and breathless. 'My sister suggested a short visit to Winchester and I had been so ill that I went where she took me. I would not have come here for the world, had I known you were here. You must believe me, you must.'

'All these years,' the other woman said, a sob rising in her throat. 'All these years and I was safe. My maid…' The harsh voice ceased for a moment and Charlotte shuddered anew. 'But she – died and only Cole remained. And then, there *you* were, the pair of you, your sister simpering and smirking and you, never saying boo to a goose.'

Charlotte held her breath. What on earth should I do, she agonized. Dare I run for help? How can I leave Melicent here in this state? Tension had her nails running into the palms of her hands as she wavered, meanwhile Lady Granville was speaking again. What was Sibella doing, she wondered. Was she cowering away from the passionate anger in the older woman's voice? And am I right about what this means, she wondered, ashamed that curiosity should be uppermost in her mind at such a time.

'Dunster had become senile and she talked too much so … oh well. Then, when Cole told me,' the voice sounded calmer now, almost reflective, as though the speaker were reminiscing, 'I was beside myself at first but I realized that I could take steps to remove yet another threat to my son's happiness. What?'

Charlotte felt a shiver run down her spine as Lady Granville actually laughed, albeit mirthlessly.

'Allow my darling to be disowned, cast out as a bastard? I think not. It was simple enough in the end, to decide on a solution. I had only to spend time working in my garden, always a place of solace, and as always I found peace here.'

'What – what do you mean?' Sibella sounded farther away. Had she moved to the other side of the tower? Charlotte wondered. She found herself nodding in approval; that's right, she thought, keep her talking. It was only too clear now that whatever the truth of the matter Lady Granville was definitely sounding dangerous, even more so as she responded to the timid question.

'You did not drink the punch,' she said in a cold, level voice. 'Everyone knew that Barnard Richmond was brewing up some kind of wassail at the behest of his vulgar little wife, so it was easy enough for a garden-lover to think of a remedy. "If thine eye offend thee, pluck it out," she declaimed suddenly, her voice rising, "Pluck it out."'

As Charlotte digested this remark, Lady Granville snapped at Sibella. 'Why did you not drink the punch?' she demanded, 'I made sure you took the glass. I have been experimenting for years, drying seeds, trying new varieties of plants, and last year I dried some seeds from Queen Eleanor's yew, though I had no real thought of using them, knowing how deadly they can be. When Cole told me you were to be at the manor I made up a tiny packet of seeds, and tucked it into my pocket. There was a gossiping crowd at the table and nobody paid the slightest attention to me so it was the work of a moment to whisk out the packet and sprinkle the seeds into a glass for you. I did have a fancy to suit my potion to the season and indeed, had intended to add a handful of berries to the wassail, holly and mistletoe and the last berries of the yew. They would have looked handsome floating on top of the brew but I decided it was too dangerous. You took the glass, but why did your sister drink it, and not you?'

There it was; Charlotte heaved a shaky sigh. She had been right all along. Right about Verena's death being suspicious, and right about the reason. But wrong about the real mother of the child. *Sibella!* It was Sibella who had given up her baby to Lady Granville, and it was Sibella who should have died.

What in the world am I to do now? Charlotte was racked by indecision. Lady Granville had stopped talking in that chilly, rational tone and from the sound of it she was pacing round the roof of the turret. Was there time to go for help? Charlotte thought not.

I've heard enough, she concluded. Enough to warrant going up there and trying to rescue Sibella, but how am I to do that? It would be foolish to assume Lady Granville is unarmed but I daren't leave the ruins to look for some kind of weapon. If only her ladyship's love of historical accuracy ran to halberds and pikes hung on the walls of her ruined castle.

Suddenly a solution sprang to mind. Something so ludicrous that an hysterical giggle almost escaped her lips in spite of the gravity of the situation, but rack her brains as she might, nothing else offered, not even a stone to throw. She crept back down to Melicent and bent beside her.

'Lady Granville is – is very angry about something,' she whispered, ignoring the other woman's gasp of disbelief. 'I know, but it's true and I'm afraid she is beside herself and means to harm Miss Armstrong. I, er, I believe she's having some kind of seizure, or a fit of mania or something and moreover, I'm afraid she might harm the pair of us if she stumbles over us, as she may well do at any moment. I need something to use as a weapon, in case she attacks us and – listen, Melicent, and whatever you do, don't scream – the only thing I can think of, is your false leg.'

Foresight made her clap her hand across Melicent's mouth to stifle the outcry, and she went on in a rapid whisper. 'I know it's dreadful, but I assure you, I've thought and thought and I can't see any other solution. I daren't leave you here unprotected....' She smiled in involuntarily sympathy as she felt Melicent's heartfelt shiver of agreement, and pressed home her argument. 'Just shut your eyes and I'll fish under your crinoline and try to extricate your leg. If the harness is broken it shouldn't be too difficult and – goodness, I had no idea I was still carrying my reticule, what in heaven's name was I thinking.' She sighed with relief. 'My embroidery scissors are in it. They were my godmother's, the only memento of her that I have.' (And wouldn't Lady Meg have hooted with delight had she been privy to the use her goddaughter was making of her keepsake?)

Mercifully the gravity of their situation seemed to have penetrated Melicent's muddled consciousness so that she made no demur when Charlotte reached under the puce skirts and fiddled with the harness. A few moments as she sawed at the leather, and the leg was free. As she tugged it out from under Melicent's crinoline, Char surprised them both by giving her a quick kiss on the cheek.

'Bless you, Melicent,' she whispered, in a warmer, more affectionate voice than she had ever used to the former governess, words she had never thought to hear herself say. 'You're being very brave; let's hope we can save the day between us.'

There was no time for further exchanges and armed with her

makeshift weapon, Charlotte sped back up the spiral staircase, only to hear her own name spoken.

Lady Granville still sounded rational as she confided to her reluctant audience, 'In case some mischance led the finger of suspicion to point in my direction, I made sure that young Mrs Richmond could testify that I was distraught at the thought that there had been at least three attempts on my son's life. That being so, there could naturally be no question of my involvement in any other incident.'

The voice tailed off into a murmur and Charlotte took a deep breath. It's now or never, she told herself, devoutly praying that it could be never, but knowing she had passed the point where she had a choice.

'You foolish creature,' Lady Granville sounded calm again, but there was still that distinct menace in her voice. 'You'll fall, of course, and I shall be distraught. Oh heavens,' she affected a sob. 'I shall weep and say the young lady was so insistent when she heard about the ruins, that I could not disappoint her, but somehow she tripped – just there; yes, by the break in the battlements, so tragic – and before I could reach out to her, she fell. Such a sad, unfortunate accident....'

'I don't think so,' Charlotte stood at the top of the stair, the artificial leg concealed in the folds of her skirt. 'Lady Granville, I think you should allow Miss Armstrong to go down, if you please. By the stairs, that is,' she added. 'Not by the means you have just suggested.'

The moon came out from behind a cloud and shone down on the two women on the tower; shock and anger on the elder's face, dawning hope in the younger. For a moment all three stood in frozen silence then Charlotte swallowed. 'I think you should be aware that I've just found Miss Cole's body,' she said, and watched with fearful interest to see how Lady Granville reacted.

'Do you think to alarm me by telling me that?' She shook her head. 'The woman clearly had a sentimental impulse to wander round the garden one last time before deserting her post and I suppose she tripped, or had a heart attack, or something similar. I found her last night just before the snow, but I had other matters on my mind, so it seemed sensible to leave her there.'

She turned to Charlotte and, although she had shown no apparent interest in the fate of her erstwhile companion, there was now real pain in her expression. 'And now Mrs Richmond, you tiresome girl, you will have to fall too. It will be clear that you made a valiant but vain attempt to pull Miss Armstrong back from the brink.' She shook her head, in genuine regret. 'I thought I had put you off the scent, you know, by masking my intention. I made an outcry at the church, and when that foolish old man was felled by indigestion.'

'But you didn't even know me,' protested Charlotte. 'That time in the church, we had barely spoken, apart from when Lily introduced us. Why should you wish to deceive *me*?'

'You – your sister-in-law – anyone at all. It made no difference to me, as long as I was able to instil some suspicion in case my plan went wrong. Indeed I wish it had *not* been you, I liked you so much, Mrs Richmond. We could have been friends, for I have seldom met with such intelligent understanding when it came to my garden, but now....'

Lady Granville's attention was held for the moment by Charlotte, who noticed out of the corner of her eye that Sibella was edging her way towards the spiral stair, her back up against the parapet. Charlotte dared not make a sound, or any movement herself, but she approved wholeheartedly of what Sibella was up to. Only a few more feet and the enraged older woman would be between Sibella and Charlotte. Surely there must be some way to deflect her maddened strength?

Sibella stumbled and for a moment Charlotte thought her heart would stop. She hastily broke the silence, to draw Lady Granville's attention to her.

'It's what you told me about history, isn't it?' Charlotte stammered a little, but Lady Granville stared at her, a glint of interest lighting her face. 'You said history teaches us how to solve problems. You felt you were like Eleanor of Aquitaine, wife of Henry II, didn't you? The Queen of England who is said to have poisoned her husband's mistress, Rosamond of Woodstock.'

Her diversion seemed to be working, as the older woman nodded almost in approval, so Charlotte ventured another question as Sibella resumed her stealthy progress. Only a little further....

'Does Lord Granville know about all this?' she asked, trying to keep her voice even, 'about Oz and Sibella?'

'What?' Lady Granville stared at her in patent astonishment. 'Are you mad, girl? Of course he does not. We led separate lives, in many ways. He held a position in the government and I devoted myself to my garden and my tours of famous abbeys and shrines.

'My maid discovered this wretched young woman's secret, though not the name of the child's father. That was left to me to deduce, knowing as I did my husband's taste in young women. I had noticed his increasingly admiring glances in her direction so it was not difficult. The only other people who were privy to the business were my late maid and Cole.' She broke off for a moment and clicked her tongue. 'Dunster was nearly 80 and senile so I couldn't trust her loose tongue. I was up here one day last week and spotted her limping up the drive. She stopped for a rest immediately below me so I dropped one of these small ornamental cannonballs on her head.' Lady Granville sounded indifferent as she continued, 'I'm a good shot with a ball but either way, killed or maimed, Dunster would be a threat no longer. Cole was here in the garden so I sent her out to bring the ball back here, but she turned out to be a fool and a dangerous fool at that, so I had to silence her too. She was proud of herself, like a dog bringing me a bone, as she told me yesterday how she stuck a hatpin into that pony's flank at the church. She hoped to make it bolt and get rid of you that way.' She cast a darkling glance at Sibella who shuddered. Lady Granville heaved a dramatic sigh as she went on,

'When I found out that there was to be a child fathered by my husband it seemed the answer to my prayers. I knew my husband could have no suspicion as I had never refused his occasional demands, so there was no danger that he would question what I told him.'

Her voice rose and she turned back to Sibella. 'I watched you tonight.' Her voice grated, harsh with emotion. 'Vile, ungrateful creature, you were making overtures to Osbert, talking to him, making him like you. *My* son. You were going to turn him against me, but I can't allow that. I'll kill you first.'

Taking Charlotte off her guard, Lady Granville sprang towards Sibella, hands reaching out for the younger woman. 'He is mine. Mine alone.'

As Sibella, gasping denials, recoiled and fought to pull aside the hands that were clawing at her throat, Charlotte recollected Melicent's artificial leg. She grasped the foot and swung the makeshift weapon like a bat, seized by the memory of her conversation about sports with Oz, and with her stepfather's laughing injunction in her ear, '*Hit her for six, young Char!*'

Sibella's harsh gasping filled the air as she was forced to the stone floor, so Charlotte raised her makeshift weapon and smashed it down with all her force on to Lady Granville's arm. At the same moment a familiar yowling reached her ears and the unkempt ginger cat leaped up, dancing on its hind legs, to bat at the leather strap dangling from the harness on Melicent's leg.

Sibella managed to struggle back to her feet, pale and terrified, and she and Charlotte faced up to Lady Granville, who, sobbing with pain and cradling her right arm, began to stumble backwards. The cat abandoned its chase of the exciting flapping thing and advanced towards the maddened woman, as it renewed its plaintive cries for food, for love, for attention.

Out of the corner of her eye, Charlotte saw light spilling out from the glass door to the garden and, with a sob of thankfulness, heard a familiar, much loved voice calling her.

'Char? Are you still out here in the cold? Bless the girl, what folly is this?'

Barnard, dear Barnard, had come to find her. She did not dare call out to him, but she turned to her erstwhile hostess.

'Please, Lady Granville,' she implored. 'The squire is heading this way. Come down from the tower, this can all be forgotten. Sibella and I will swear never to speak of this again.' She hesitated and, seeing her stalwart brother-in-law, clearly visible as he looked irritably around him, she whispered, 'Please, Lady Granville, for Oz's sake?'

The older woman glanced down into her garden and towards

201

the house, then the cat, emboldened by the sudden silence up on the tower, began to rub its head against her skirt.

As she shrank away, she turned her ravaged face towards Charlotte, tears glistening in her dark, tortured eyes. 'My son,' she whispered. 'My little, little son.'

And then she jumped.

Chapter 15

In the aftermath of St Stephen's Day and all it had brought, Charlotte found herself fully occupied, first and foremost with comforting Oz Granville, bereft of the only mother he had ever known. His father too, asked constantly for her opinion on this course of action and that. How to word the announcement of Lady Granville's death? What order of service should be chosen? Did Charlotte think this hymn or that one would be appropriate? And which day did Charlotte consider would be most suitable for the funeral.

To her dying day, Charlotte was to recall her relief that Barnard had obeyed the summons passed on to him by the footman. When the air was rent by Charlotte's cry of distress, along with a tremulous scream from Sibella, as they lunged in vain to try to halt Lady Granville's leap, Barnard broke into a run, followed by Dr Perry who had accompanied him to the door, saying he too would enjoy some fresh air.

Almost gibbering from shock, she reached for Sibella, both of them desperate for human comfort, and Charlotte, even though her teeth were chattering, managed to impress upon Sibella that they must say Lady Granville had tripped over the cat and fallen through the broken part of the battlement.

'We must never, ever tell anyone what really happened,' she whispered, shivering as she did so. 'I'll get hold of Melicent too and swear her to secrecy, though I don't think she can have heard anything that was said.'

There was no time for more. Barnard was leaping up the stairs two at a time, exclaiming as he encountered his sister's former governess. 'What the devil? Wait there, Melicent,' he barked, as though the poor creature had a choice, Charlotte shivered. 'Char?' In two strides Barnard crossed the icy roof and folded her in his arms. 'What in God's name has happened here?' He gave her a little shake. 'I couldn't see what happened exactly but when I saw a woman tumbling from the roof, for one ghastly moment, Char, I thought it was you.'

Charlotte found it impossible to stop shaking but she managed to summon enough presence of mind to stammer out some kind of explanation.

'Lady G – Granville, she fell. Oh, Barnard, she went over the edge, by the broken wall.' He held her tightly in his left arm and, in a gesture that spoke volumes of his kind heart, reached out his other hand to pull Sibella Armstrong into his warm, safe embrace. 'It's so icy and then the cat, the cat must have been curious and come up to see what we were doing, but she didn't like cats. She told me so the other day so she just kept going backwards....'

At this point Charlotte burst into a storm of sobs, broken only by a sudden cry. 'Oh, Barnard, you mustn't let Oz see her, it's too dreadful. Make them keep him indoors, he mustn't come out.'

He barked an order to the bewildered pair of servants at the foot of the keep and turned back to the two women. 'You must come down now, Char, and you too, Miss Armstrong. You'll catch your death....' He coughed and continued briskly, 'Yes, yes, don't worry, Char. They'll keep the boy indoors, but Lord Granville has been called for. And don't fret about Melicent, poor soul, we'll get her carried indoors and Dr Perry can take a look at her.'

Charlotte barely comprehended her journey from the top of the tower to the warm sitting room she had left only half an hour before, but when she was laid on a sofa and wrapped in shawls and blankets, she sat up with a startled cry.

'Oh, Dr Perry,' she was glad to see him in the doorway. 'How could I have forgotten? You must send some men out to the far corner of the garden. I found Miss Cole's body there, she's by the stream.' She began to stammer, then Lady Granville's voice rang in her ears and she knew what she had to say. 'I think she must have packed her trunk, and written her note, then decided on a last look round the garden before leaving. It's the only explanation. She must have slipped and the heavy snow covered her.'

'Good God.' The doctor frowned fiercely at her and hastened to the outer door where she heard him issuing abrupt orders. He returned and came to feel her pulse. 'Aye, well, you'll do, Char, with a night's sleep, but what a mare's nest it all is.' He stared down at her, pursing his lips. 'So that's what you're telling me, is it? Her ladyship fell when she backed away from the cat, and Miss Cole either had some kind of seizure or she fell and knocked herself silly, then froze to death?'

She looked him straight in the eye. 'Yes, Dr Perry. There can be no other explanation.'

As a widow, albeit a young one, Charlotte was permitted to make long visits to the Abbey unchaperoned and untrammelled by the proprieties. After the first dreadful hours, which she had spent on the sofa in Oz's bedroom, Charlotte deemed the stricken household able to cope with her absence and she stepped thankfully into the Brambrook carriage which was turned out for her next morning.

First there was Gran to be comforted. 'Oh my dear child,' Lady Frampton kept repeating the words over and over, unable to say any more as tears ran down her round red face. 'You could have been killed, dearie,' she managed in the end. 'Thank God it wasn't you what tumbled off the tower, that's all I can say.'

After a few further broken words of thanks to Barnard and a surprisingly warm and tearful embrace from Lily, Charlotte made her way upstairs to see Sibella who had been packed off to bed the night before, but now professed herself quite fit and ready to go downstairs later.

Their greeting was warm but subdued. The moments of utter terror that they had shared formed a bond between them and Charlotte was aware of a sense of friendship, something to explore when all this was behind them. She was conscious also that Sibella already seemed less bowed down now by her situation and the reason was soon forthcoming.

'Only to you, dear Charlotte,' she whispered, clasping the other girl's hand. 'Only to you can I admit to this feeling of relief, even though I feel guilty at the thought. I'd made a life for myself and managed well until Verena discovered my secret. Since then the burden has been intolerable, but I know now there is no chance of Lord Granville and – and Osbert, discovering the truth, for I can trust you with my life.'

They drank the tea Lily had thoughtfully sent up and agreed, almost without a word spoken, that the events of the previous evening should never be mentioned to another living soul; Charlotte kissed her new friend and went to her own room.

Refreshed by a few hours' sleep, and after some discussion with Lily and Barnard, Charlotte returned briefly to Brambrook where she sought out Lord Granville.

'Barnard wishes me to give you this note,' she told him. 'He asks, most pressingly, that you and Oz should come back with me to Finchbourne Manor for a few days. He and Lily feel it would spare him the initial strangeness and sadness of his home and that you and he might find it more comfortable to be with friends.'

Lord Granville fell upon this idea, a wistful look on his usually rubicund face, but he could only accept on his son's behalf, and not his own. With robust good sense he roused himself and nodded agreement to all her stratagems, saying:

'Well, poor lad, that's a good plan, let him be free of all this for now. I thank your brother for his kindness, indeed I do, most generous of him and his lady, but I'll be better seeing to it all here. But aye, keep the sadness right away from the lad, d'ye see? You'll bring him here for the funeral, of course? That's good, that's right and after that, I think I might take him up to London for a spell, get him away from these sad associations, what?' He frowned as a sudden thought struck him. 'Trouble is, my dear, that tutor of his has taken it upon himself to go and get married, so I'll have no-one to keep an eye on the boy. Take some thinking about, hey?'

Charlotte was inspired. 'I wonder, Lord Granville,' she suggested with a diffident smile. 'I wonder if it might be better for Oz to have a governess for a while? I'm sure your housekeeper would prove a splendid chaperone and it would just be a temporary arrangement, of course. A woman's company might help to soften the blow, and I think a puppy would be a comfort too.'

He turned to her in astonishment. 'Is there no end to your useful-ness, my dear Charlotte, hey?' He chuckled, then remembered hastily that levity was out of place, and took her hand in his own. 'What a capital notion, why that's just the thing, a pup and the woman's touch, hey? But where are we to find such a lady at this short notice? Dare I hope that you would do it my dear?'

'I'm afraid Barnard wouldn't allow that,' Charlotte shook her head, gently withdrawing her hand. 'There is someone on our very doorstep, however. Miss Armstrong is without a situation at present, which is why she was at liberty to come to Winchester with her late sister. I am sure she would be happy to consent to help. She and Oz are already acquainted and having had a brother of her own, Miss Armstrong is well able to manage a boy and enter into his interests and pursuits. I'm sure they would deal delightfully.'

'I have acted as *deus ex machina*, Elaine,' Charlotte said airily. 'I have delivered the mother to be companion and I hope, trusted friend, to the son. Lord Granville's eyes nearly popped out of his head but I was all innocence and explained that Sibella is now alone in the world and urgently in need of employment. He took a turn or two around the room as he harrumphed a little and peered at me from under his brows, and then he agreed with my suggestion without a murmur. I believe Miss Nightingale has it right and his disposition is sanguine enough to dismiss the old story and march on with the new. Sibella is willing, so who knows? Propinquity, combined with the former affection, may do its work and as soon as it is decent, Oz may have a stepmother who is more closely related to him than he or his father will ever know.' A thought struck her. 'Speaking of Miss Nightingale, I must write to decline her flattering offer once and for all, and I shan't now be recommending Sibella to her.'

'How *do* you do it, Char?' Elaine Knightley had received her friend in her room, too frail to undergo the ordeal of being dressed and carried downstairs after the illness of the past few days. Her voice was weak but she was bearing up surprisingly well.

'You seem to be a magnet, attracting desperate characters and untimely accidents; only recollect our visit to Bath last summer. No,' she smiled slightly. 'I absolve you this time, you could not help becoming embroiled in Lady Granville's drastic attempts to maintain her secret, and I am only too thankful to know you and the young boy are safe. As for your prediction, I'm sure you're right. His lordship is by nature a cheerful man who likes his comforts and I suspect Miss Armstrong will keep him from straying, so they will settle down to a happy family life.

'It seems beyond belief that he knew nothing of Sibella's pregnancy or his wife's lack of one,' she smiled with a flash of her old impishness. 'But my experience of men is that they are the most unobservant of creatures, to which we may add that the Granvilles met infrequently in those days, though as you say, her ladyship, poor woman, seems to have been certain that they had encountered each other at least once somewhere near the appropriate date.'

She glanced at Charlotte's pale, drawn face and settled herself comfortably to distracting her visitor, her own needs typically set aside. 'Are you at liberty to give me any details, Char? You know I will be as silent as the grave.'

At Charlotte's gasp, Elaine gave the ghost of her mischievous grin. 'Oh my dear, I beg your pardon, but you must allow me a few moments of amusement, however inappropriate. Don't be afraid, I'll compose myself now and indulge in no further shocking behaviour.' She held out a hand. 'There now, am I forgiven? Then tell me all the details that must otherwise be concealed for ever, beginning with why in the world Lady Granville and Miss Armstrong were up on the tower on such a winter's night?'

Charlotte squeezed her hand and laughed. 'You're incorrigible,' she said, and they both ignored the sob in her voice as she continued, 'I managed to have a private conversation this morning with Sibella and we routed out all the secrets and, as you say, agreed that the subject must never again be mentioned.'

'I told you, did I not, that the Granvilles were very kind to us all?' Sibella had begun, as they took refuge in Charlotte's room at the manor, knowing that Oz was recovering sufficiently from his shock and grief to go for a ride with Barnard.

'My brother was received almost as a son, so great was their affection and trust in him, which was what made his behaviour such a betrayal.' She bit her lip. 'What I did not mention earlier was that Lord Granville paid me particular attentions. I was lonely and his kindness made my misery less dreary, so that gradually we slipped into an affair that would have grieved my parents, though I did feel a sincere affection for his lordship and, I believe, his feeling for me was similarly warm.'

She bowed her head for a moment and Charlotte silently refilled her glass. 'I had no idea that I was with child until the day after my brother's treachery was discovered, when I called on Lady Granville to see whether she knew of Edward's whereabouts. All I knew was that he had left town in a great hurry, leaving no forwarding address and not even a note of explanation to me.

'Lady Granville received me very angrily and regaled me with the whole history of Edward's perfidy, and I was so shocked by the discovery that I fainted. Her maid was summoned and finding me in a sad state, made some very personal enquiries. In the end Lady Granville came to me and told me that they believed I was with child and that, from her own observations, the father of the child was none other than her own husband.'

She raised tear-drenched blue eyes to Charlotte, who took her hand in a warm, companionable clasp. 'You can imagine my sentiments. I was mortified and frightened and so ashamed but Lady Granville, having left me to recover for an hour or so, became brisk and informed me that if I consented to do exactly as she ordered, nobody would ever know of my shame. Situated as I was, I had no option but to obey so shortly afterwards I was sent down to Bournemouth, to a small house she had taken. In my ignorance I was already well into my fifth month, so Lady Granville told her husband that she was once again with child and had concealed the news until she felt that this time she had some confidence of reaching term. In due course she arrived to take up residence in Bournemouth.

'When I was confined I was allowed a month to recover then I was taken to France by Miss Cole who had lately joined the household. I was placed in an impoverished but noble household, to teach English to the children, while improving my own French. I believe Miss Cole was empowered by her employer, to whom she was distantly related, to pay my way for six months, after which time I found further employment in France.'

'So Miss Cole actually knew you?' Charlotte was intrigued. 'But there, Lady Granville said as much up there on – on the battlements. It was Miss Cole who recognised you and heard that you were to attend little Algy's christening, that she told Lady Granville, who then decided to make away with you. It's the most fantastic tale.'

'I know,' Sibella looked brighter, clearly relieved by her confession and in finding only sympathy and friendship from Charlotte. 'But we both heard her say it, didn't we – that she knew the centrepiece of the party was to be the Finchbourne wassail brew. And that gave her the idea that it might prove the way to – to dispose of me. Her plans were thwarted when my sister drank the cup that was intended for me.'

'So there you are, dearest Elaine.' Charlotte sat back with a sigh of relief. 'I believe Lady Granville succumbed to a moment's temptation when she pushed at Sibella in the church doorway, though she cannot have hoped it would end with more than a broken leg, but she recovered quickly and pulled the wool over everyone's eyes.'

'And this morning was that other poor young woman's funeral?'

Charlotte nodded. 'Verena? Yes, it was simpler to bury her in the churchyard here in Finchbourne and her husband made no difficulty. In fact, I think he was quite touched. It was very quiet, of course, but Percy conducted the service beautifully and Sibella was glad to be amongst friends.' She shook her head. 'Oh, I didn't tell you, did I? Melicent, poor soul, was carried home that night in a shocking state, suffering from severe chills and after a day of high fever has no recollection whatsoever of how she came to be found half way up the ruined tower.' She shrugged. 'I told everyone that she'd been invited to join Lady Granville and Sibella but had slipped on the stairs. It was easy enough to persuade Melicent herself of this, as it chimed so well with what she wanted to believe. As for the dreadful accident, I told the truth: that Lady Granville was afraid of the cat and backed away from it, obviously forgetting that there was a break in the battlements just there.'

She gave a wry smile, slightly shamefaced. 'Sibella is proving kind as well as sensible and made no difficulty about putting out this version of the proceedings so Melicent is able to feel herself something of a heroine, though I did have a few awkward moments when she asked how her leg had become detached from its harness.'

'I'm glad,' was all Elaine said, then she reached out a frail and languid hand to the small table at her side. 'I must not forget, my dear, here is your birthday present. I want you to take it now, rather than wait until Saturday. I might not be here to give it to you then.'

Charlotte's gasp rang out in the sudden stillness of the room and she put out her hand in an involuntary gesture of protest. 'No, no....' The cry was bitten off abruptly and she raised her head to look her dearest friend in the eye.

Elaine took the younger girl's shaking hand and cradled it in her own slender, wasted ones. 'Thank you, dearest Char,' she whispered and when Charlotte looked up again, a question in the hazel eyes that were swimming with tears, Elaine nodded. 'Why thanks? For letting me be honest with you,' she answered. 'For allowing me, just this once, to share the knowledge with you that I *am* truly dying. Kit cannot bear to speak of it or even to think of it and for his sake, even now, I go along with his wishes. But you have been so much my friend – my sister, my child – all of these things, and I'm glad that it should be you who shares with me this last gift. The gift of honesty.'

With a slight shake of her head, Elaine changed the subject and urged Charlotte to open the parcel she indicated on the side table. 'Come along, Char, let me see how you like it.'

With fingers that shook, Charlotte untied the silver ribbon and unwrapped the complete works of Miss Jane Austen. The books were not new and inside each cover was the inscription: '*To my dearest Elaine on her 17th birthday, from her loving Mother.*' Below this, Elaine had written her own message: '*For my dear Charlotte, with love and gratitude for friendship so generously given.*'

'Yes,' Elaine would brook no argument. 'Take them, Char. My mother gave the books to me because she had loved them so and I've loved them dearly in my turn. It gives me great happiness to know that they are safe in your hands and that you will cherish them too.'

New Year's Eve, 1858.

The afternoon

CHARLOTTE AND Lady Frampton had been back at Rowan Lodge for a day when the summons to Knightley Hall came in the middle of Friday afternoon. She could barely speak in acknowledgment of the butler's tearful greeting, so sore was her distress and the effort to maintain her composure. With a nod she followed him up the wide Jacobean staircase and along the oak-panelled landing to where Jackson, Elaine's maid, was in urgent conversation with one of the other servants.

'You bring up the Madeira this instant,' Jackson was sternly issuing orders. 'And plenty of glasses. Madam....' Her voice cracked for an instant but a ferocious scowl helped her resume command of herself. 'Madam frets that the master won't leave her bedside and the doctor is expected to call soon, so to make sure she'll rest easy I want you bring up wine and cakes and tea, as well. Bring it every hour, on the hour, come what may. I won't have her upset for a single moment....' She turned at Charlotte's trembling approach.

'Ah, Miss Char, Mrs Richmond I should say.' An imperious wave dismissed the waiting servant, whose face was blubbered with tears as she hastened to do Jackson's bidding. 'Come right in at once, Miss Char, she's that anxious to see you.' The woman bit back a sob and added, in a whisper, 'The doctor has been giving her morphia for the pain, my dear, so she keeps drifting off to sleep. Best thing for her, and I know you'll sit quietly with her.'

Elaine's bedroom was painted in delicate pastel shades and filled with flowers sent in by sympathetic neighbours. Charlotte's face quivered at the sight. Elaine was so passionately fond of flowers so Charlotte had tied ribbon round some of the stalks of lavender she had dried in the summer and kept in a vase in her own room. A fire burned brightly in the grate and the room was warm and welcoming, with no hint of the desolation that hovered at hand.

Kit Knightley sat in a chair close beside the bed, his wife's hand lying in his own and his head bent. He looked defeated, more than ten years older, and Charlotte felt her courage fail. If Kit could despair so, all must indeed be lost. At Charlotte's quiet approach, urged thereto by Jackson, Elaine's beloved old nurse and now her personal maid, the frail woman in the bed turned her head very slightly and summoned up the ghost of a smile.

'Char?' It was a whisper, no more. Charlotte could tell only too clearly how great was any effort at speech and she knelt beside her friend, holding back the anguished tears that smarted behind her eyelids. Kit Knightley raised a ravaged, grieving face but it was plain that he could not trust himself to speak.

'Dearest Elaine.' Charlotte took the thin, beautiful fingers in her own warm, sturdy clasp then she laid her head for just a moment on the pillow beside that of her friend. 'Don't try to talk, just let me stay here with you for a while, quite quietly.'

'Need to tell you....' Elaine ignored the younger girl's whispered words and struggled to speak, gasping on every breath and frowning at Kit and her nurse as they tried to intervene. She lay back against her pillows but with the desperate courage that was such a feature of her character, she continued, 'Dearest Char, so much love....' Charlotte's tears were falling now, unheeded and unchecked, as she laid the tiny spray of lavender, the scent still discernible, in Elaine's hand and bent to kiss her delicate cheek. The dying woman gave a faint, loving smile in acknowledgement. 'Your birthday tomorrow, dearest.... Be happy. You shall have my most precious gift by and by....'

The whisper tailed into silence and she fell into a light doze so Kit rose to help Charlotte to her feet. Still not able to speak he jerked his head at Jackson who obediently poured Charlotte a glass of wine and stood over her, and Kit likewise, while they both forced down food that tasted of sawdust and ashes.

There was a fluttering sigh and Elaine's grey eyes sought the younger girl once more. Charlotte bent close enough to hear the thread of a voice. 'I trust you, Char,' she breathed on a sigh. 'With my dearest treasure....'

New Year's Eve 1858

Late evening

'DOCTOR PERRY?' Charlotte jumped up, her anxious face brightening in delighted welcome, casting her sewing aside. 'Come in, do come in. How very pleasant to see you, just when I was feeling the need for company. Is there....'

'No, there is nothing from the Hall.' The doctor eyed her with sympathy as she dabbed a handkerchief at her eyes. 'Can't settle to anything, eh?' He clapped a hand on her shoulder before sitting down beside the drawing-room fire, with a nod of thanks to the little maid who was bobbing at his side with the decanter.

'Ah, that's better. It's a cold night out there, Char. Now,' he looked round the room and raised his eyebrows at her. 'Where's the old lady then? Not gone out at this time of night, surely?'

'No indeed,' Charlotte gave him a faint smile as she sipped at her own glass of brandy, and avoided the thoughts of Elaine that had weighed so heavily upon her all day. 'Her bosom friend from down in the village has been here for dinner and is to stay the night so they have removed themselves to Gran's room across the hall where, I presume, they loosen their stays and indulge in scurrilous gossip, away from my inconveniently sharp young ears.'

'Ah well, gossip is why I've called in to see you so late, my dear,' confessed the doctor with a slightly furtive expression on his weather-beaten face. 'And although I know I can trust your own discretion, I can't deny I'm glad not to have the old ladies present. What I have to tell you is between the two of us only, if you will be so good.'

'I'm all agog,' she told him frankly, topping up his glass and her own. 'And of course you have my word that nothing you say shall be repeated.' For a moment she looked very grave. 'In all conscience I have enough secrets locked of my own in my heart, and that's where they'll stay.'

He cast a speculative glance in her direction but clearly thought better of pursuing the topic. They made an unlikely pair, the doctor in his fifties and the young widow, but they were firm friends. Dr Perry was aware though that Charlotte's nature was reticent in the extreme, particularly about her past history.

'I mentioned that a friend of mine had attended young Mrs Chant, did I not? Well, I've been dining with him and with the coroner,' he launched into his story. 'They're both very old friends of mine, we were at school together and we have few secrets left between us after all these years. They had a couple of interesting items of news to tell, all in the deepest of confidence, you understand, but I shall tell you, in spite of that.'

She contained her curiosity while Dr Perry nibbled thoughtfully at a ratafia biscuit and took another sip at his drink. No use trying to hasten his narrative, she knew him only too well by now, so she folded her hands in her lap and let him take his time. She knew too, that while on occasion he was not above a spot of gossip, he mostly kept his lips very tightly closed, so she felt honoured by his confidence in her.

'You're a peaceful creature,' he said suddenly, reaching forward to give her an avuncular pat on the arm. 'Most women drive a man to distraction with their questions and frettings, but I've never known you act like that. It's a rare gift.' He smiled at her as he continued his story.

'I am very well aware, you know, and so is my friend the coroner, that we'll never get to the bottom of the events of the other night. Oh no,' he laughed at her as she made a slight gesture of denial. 'It's of no use for you to tell me that nothing happened, other than that remarkably plain tale you told when it was all over. You think I don't know there was some mischief afoot? And no, you can rest easy. I shan't press you for details for I know you would never divulge them anyway.

'No, the inquest will let you have it your way. Lady Granville, carried away by her much trumpeted passion for her garden, took it upon herself to show you and the other two ladies her wonderful ruins by the light of the full moon. Very spectacular it must have been too, I judge, by the way that first one lady seems to have slipped on the stairs, presumably overcome by the grandeur of her surroundings and not minding her footsteps in spite of her infirmity, and then her ladyship herself took that fatal tumble off the top of her home-made ramparts.'

He shook his head in mock wonder. 'Surprising, I'd have thought, considering her lord told us she was in the habit of walking those battlements in all weathers and at all times of the day and night. But there, it was a frosty night and I daresay her ladyship was carried away by the excitement of it all; the feasting, the boy's birthday, and all.'

'I'm sure you must be right,' Charlotte's voice was meek and submissive but she met her visitor's eye with the faintest of twinkles in her own. 'It was indeed a very cold night and there was ice on the steps. I slipped once or twice myself.'

'Indeed you did,' he rejoined. 'I examined you myself, if you recollect? Mind you, it's a very strange thing to reflect that slipping on the ice gave Miss Sibella Armstrong considerable bruising round the throat. A very singular circumstance, but we won't go into that again. No, what I have to tell you, is something much more interesting, to a couple of students of human nature such as ourselves, my dear.'

Maddeningly, he took another sip of brandy before coming to the point.

'What my coroner friend told us, his two old friends and colleagues, in confidence,' he said gravely, 'was that when he examined the body of the late Lady Granville, he found that, contrary to popular belief, (and contrary, I should say, to her own husband's belief), the lady had quite clearly never borne a child.'

He sat back to watch her reaction and nodded complacently at the suddenly arrested expression on her mobile features.

'Yes,' he said. 'I see that doesn't surprise you in the least, does it, you surprising young woman. Would you care to share with me your speculations as to who might be the unacknowledged mother of his lordship's allegedly *legitimate* son and heir?'

'No, Dr Perry,' she told him, in a polite but decided tone. 'It's my belief that we should cease all speculation from this time forward. I am truly grateful for your confidence but the lady is dead and the child has to mourn the only mother he has ever known. Let us not even breathe aloud any hint that there could possibly be another side to the story.'

She said no more and he smiled. 'The other piece of news is also shocking but again, we – my fellow medical man, the coroner and myself – have taken it upon ourselves to suppress it. It will be given out, as indeed you yourself suggested might be the case, that the unfortunate companion, Miss Cole, seems to have ventured upon a last sentimental visit to her ladyship's beloved garden, and there suffered some kind of spasm that resulted in heart failure.'

He grinned mischievously. 'Such a convenient diagnosis, is it not? Heart failure? After all, all hearts cease to beat when death arrives.' He took a sip of brandy and looked directly at her. 'Ever come across taxine, Char?'

'Taxine?'

'It is a poison derived from the seeds of the yew tree,' he told her soberly. 'As to why I raise the subject, I heard tonight that the examination of the young woman who died so tragically after the christening at the manor, showed that she was suffering from taxine poisoning.'

Charlotte drew a shocked breath and gazed at him in mute supplication.

'I told you, did I not, that the doctor called to her bedside was also a friend of mine? His particular interest is in determining why hitherto healthy young people so often die of what appear to be trivial illnesses. In furtherance of his studies, he reserved some of the unfortunate Mrs Chant's vomit, and caused it to be analysed.'

Charlotte turned pale and he gave her an encouraging nod.

'However, Miss Cole seems to have died quite peacefully, which would scarcely have been the case after taxine poisoning, witness the other poor young lady's travails, so let us agree that she died, as I said earlier, of heart failure and no more questions asked.

'As I said,' he went on, 'With the death of Lady Granville, my friends and I decided that there had been enough grief for Lord Granville and his son, so you need have no fear. There will be no further revelations.'

She reached out to press his hand in gratitude, but paused as he leaned towards her with a mischievous twinkle.

'Ah, you don't escape so easily, my dear,' he smiled. 'Fair exchange is no robbery and if I learn nothing else, I should like to know how it came about that Lady Granville broke her arm? It will be given out that it happened during the fall, but I was there and she was cradling her arm just before she tumbled down. Relieve my curiosity on this point, Char. What happened?'

She tensed for a moment, then relaxed with a faint smile. 'She was throttling Sibella so I hit her with Melicent's artificial leg,' she confided.

He let out a bark of astonished laughter. 'You broke her arm with Melicent Penbury's leg?' he gasped. 'By God, Char, you'll be the death of me yet. I'll die laughing about that, you'll see, and never be able to tell my dear wife why!'

He patted her hand, still chuckling, and then cocked his head to one side. 'And her ladyship's maid, eh? What of her?'

'But Doctor Perry,' Charlotte was wide-eyed and innocent. 'The coroner himself said she was done to death by person or persons unknown.'

'Ha!' He gave a great snort of laughter. 'Person unknown? To be sure, to be sure, that's the best verdict all round, I'd say.'

They both rose abruptly as an urgent knocking was heard at the front door. Betty hastened into the drawing-room, wide-eyed with anxiety.

'If you please, Miss Char,' she gasped, with a brief curtsy to her mistress. 'There's word come from the Hall, from Mr Knightley. The doctor's wanted there at once. The groom saw the horse at the door. "The utmost urgency," he said.'

'Oh God,' Charlotte's hand flew to her mouth and the colour drained from her face. 'Is it time?'

Dr Perry shrugged himself into the coat Betty was holding out for him and paused only to take both of Charlotte's hands in his own.

'Courage, my child,' he said harshly. 'I'll send word if she's able to see you, even for a moment.'

Mutely she nodded and gave him a little push, and then he was gone.

New Year's Day, 1859

SEVERAL HOURS AFTER midnight, Charlotte rose from her bed where she had been lying awake. I won't wear black, she told her reflection fiercely as she dressed in her warmest and most serviceable dress, her shawl at hand on the bedrail; I won't let myself believe she can have died, not Elaine, not when she is so beloved by all. I will not tempt providence. She's rallied so many times, every time she's seemed on the brink of death, and every time she has recovered once more. It will be no different this time. I'll pretend it's so, for as long as I may.

She knew it was a delusion. At midnight she had opened her window and stood, unheeding, in the freezing cold, to hear the bells. The villagers, under the vicar's ineffectual supervision, rang out the old year and in with the new, and with it her twenty-fifth birthday. The tears fell then as she sobbed out her bitter grief, for no word had come from Dr Perry at the Hall, and she knew that meant her dear friend was beyond receiving even the most loving of visitors.

Charlotte tried to pray but the only line that came into her head seemed a mockery, 'And joy cometh in the morning.' With a sob she hoped that her friend was at peace at last, and all pain ceased; a sort of joy, she supposed.

Suddenly she heard a bell, tolling relentlessly. She counted all thirty-one strokes and fumbled for a handkerchief as she crossed again to the window, her limbs dragging with weary sorrow. For a moment her heart contracted, for there, casting a long shadow in the sparkling moonlight, was Dr Perry. Rarely had she seen him astride his serviceable long-legged roan unless he was trotting briskly about his business or ambling along in earnest conversation with an acquaintance; or galloping off to an emergency as he had the previous evening. This morning the doctor's shoulders were slumped in weary dejection as he rode out from the church and across the green.

As she stared down at him, fighting against the news she had learned from the tolling of the bell, and read in his bearing – denying it to the last – Dr Perry glanced upward to see her silhouetted in the window. He stared at her for a long, dreadful moment and then turned his horse towards Rowan Lodge.

Biting her lips, Charlotte caught up her shawl and made her way downstairs to let him in.